THE NORTH OF ENGLAND HOME SERVICE

GORDON BURN

The North of England Home Service

faber and faber

First published in 2003
by Faber and Faber Limited
3 Queen Square London WC1N 3AU

Typeset by Agnesi Text, Hadleigh
Printed in England by Clays Ltd, St Ives plc

The right of Gordon Burn to be identified as author of this work
has been asserted in accordance with Section 77
of the Copyright, Designs and Patents Act 1988

A CIP record for this book
is available from the British Library

ISBN 0–571–19545–8

2 4 6 8 10 9 7 5 3 1

for Carol Gorner

Ray Cruddas, a name half remembered by the older generations of listeners and viewers, went to the window and looked across at the trees. He had a battery shaver in one hand and a steaming cup of tea or something – today it was tea, although on other days it would be a clear dumpling soup maybe, or blood-red borscht with a little apple vinegar added to counter the natural sweetness of the beetroot, depending what Marzena, his wife, had prepared and left in a cylinder flask on his bedside tray – in the other.

This was his getting-up routine every day now, ever since he came back to live in the town after very many years away. He had grown up close to here in a house in one of the densely packed terraced streets that had been pulled down in his absence to make way for blocks of dirty lemon-yellow high-rise flats which in their turn had been flattened for an estate of fast-build boxy brick units which had quickly become known as a bad address and cropped up frequently in reports on the local news.

This recent history of the area was clearly traceable across the allotments that were visible from the window where he was standing, absently working the razor over what he regarded as his old man's grey beard. Heavy four-panelled wooden doors of the type he remembered from when he used to live in the back-to-backs round Turkey Street had been incorporated with fifties 'flushed' doors – the same old doors with new, modernizing sheets of hardboard pinned to them – fibreglass cottage beams, corrugated-iron sheeting and strips of carpet manufactured in tufted nylon to make the structures that together formed the whole rambling, ramshackle hutment. A number of sheds on the allotments were made entirely of doors – doors with raw gashes where letterboxes had once been and ghost numerals, erected shoulder to shoulder – and these tended to be the Georgian doors with built-in fanlights that had been the first sign of owner occupancy on the newly privatized council estates but which had recently clearly fallen out of favour.

The style around that way now was all for the white UPVC – white nylon-framed windows and fondant-white nylon doors, some with decorative glass panels in the singing, chemical blues and yellows of alco-pops and TV-advertised detergents. The ubiquitous white doors never failed to remind Ray (three times married) of wedding-cake mouldings or (he had been trying to think of a way of working this into the act without it being interpreted as a kick in the eye by his audience) slabs of sculpted lard.

Ray's own house was part of a Grade-II-listed terrace of clear classical lines and much touted classical proportions that ran the whole length of the north side of Allotment Field. The ceilings were high, the windows elegant, the courses repointed, the fault lines pinioned, the view across the Field (always known as 'the Moor') to the Park a couple of hundred yards away unimpeded. When new bricks had been stitched in, they had been chosen from old stocks to match the existing ones and created the illusion of a seamless web.

The allotments themselves were away to the right and acted as a baffle against the noise of traffic on a busy main road. Even though it was very close to the centre of the town, dairy cows were brought to graze on the Moor as a result of some centuries-old by-law or ordinance. And this too helped to preserve Moor Edge's timeless period aspect. It had been a common failing among the terrace's succeeding generations of residents to imagine that they were eighteenth-century landed gentry, looking out on an open vista disposed and ordered at their pleasure. All hell had broken loose when the plans to hand over some of the southern acreage of the Moor for a People's Park had first been made public more than a century earlier. A slanging match had ensued between the elected representatives of the people who opposed the provision of amenities for the contaminating rabble and the progressives who pushed the social and hygienic benefits of having a place of outdoor recreation so close to the homes of the poor. Now the poor had other things to amuse them than afternoon boating and quoits. The bowl of the lake was cracked and leaking; the block stone of the Victorian enclosing wall was soot-blackened and perpetually sodden; every plinth inside the Park was topped off with a spiky tuft of reinforcing cable instead of the original stone alderman or whiskered city merchant.

And now that the dairy and the brewery and the dry-cleaning plant where several of Ray Cruddas's female relatives had worked as Hoffman-pressers while he was growing up were all gone, the number of people crossing the Moor to and from work every day was probably in the dozens rather than the hundreds. The Moor had become the terrain of dog-walkers and joggers and the small herd of watchful, indolent, ear-tagged, inner-city cows. Daffodils appeared in bright patches every early April. There were bluebells in May. Ray Cruddas, not previously known for his calmness or equanimity, had certainly slowed down a lot since he moved there.

Like today. He was late, as he was always late, but he was unhurried. Using the fingers of his free hand to guide the razor to the usual holdouts of irritating stubble, he was content to go on watching the day move past his window: the heavily rouged old woman with the pack family of Yorkie dogs trailing their leads around the perimeter path of Allotment Field; the old man in the boilersuit with 'NORTH EAST GAS BOARD' in faded letters on the back having his daily conversation with the cows, quite possibly his only conversation of the day. Daisy, Flossie, Bessy, Dolly – there were more, perhaps a couple of dozen in all, but Ray quickly ran out of suitable cow-sounding names – moved their big Neanderthal carcasses towards their friend in lowing, lumbering recognition.

Very soon, Ray felt sure, a Sumo-like Labrador–Rhodesian Ridgeback cross called Fleet would appear, towing on the end of a long washing-line lead a permanently exasperated Filipina screaming 'Fleet! Fleet!' at the top of her lungs. Moses was a lurcher; Annie was a Jack Russell with anal-gland problems constantly dragging her bottom against the ground; Beetle was an albino boxer with a pink velvet muzzle and damp red vampiric eyes.

All these Ray had come to know, as he had come to recognize the ties of familiarity and affection that bound each animal to its owner and criss-crossed Allotment Field as plainly as the beaten tracks made by both humans and animals and the official paved paths with their occasional benches of perforated steel. The owners, on the other hand, he noticed hardly spoke to each other and often would step away from the path they had been taking if this meant they could avoid an awkward encounter with one of the other walkers on the Moor.

It was late February, already nearly spring, but spring tended to arrive late up there, a fact that, if he ever knew it, Ray Cruddas had forgotten. Brightness, he knew, was forecast for later. But now a sharp draught edged in where the windows were loose in their frames and raised the hairs on his skin.

There was a stand of trees on the Moor. By bending his knees slightly he was able to bring his face in line with the leafless but still distinct scribbled cloud shape of the trees and that way see himself clearly mirrored. One of the things he had learned in life was that things that grabbed him were always things he didn't understand. And it isn't a great exaggeration to say that he had spent a substantial part of his nearly seventy years being in some way haunted – even inhabited – by these trees which rose as the only vertical punctuation on the humpy flatness of the Moor. They lived in him as a shape which, both onstage and elsewhere, he would unexpectedly find himself imagining; as a mood – a secret atmosphere – which could momentarily overwhelm and debilitate him; as a place he would experience sudden inexplicable yearnings to be.

This is something he has revealed to nobody and always kept to himself. Although recently his hard-working Polish wife, Marzena Szymborzaly, had been moved to recite to him a folk lyric learned in childhood, and he had momentarily wavered.

> There was an old tree in the park
> Even stuck there when it was dark
> And it witnessed such acts
> Wrought by devilish pacts,
> And its tales held captive the lark.

Marzena spoke this in her still heavily accented English, and laughed the gay throaty laugh he had come to listen out for on the rare occasions when she was in an audience, and he almost came out with it then.

Too small to be called a wood, too cave-like to be regarded as unconditionally welcoming, this clump or copse or grove, whatever you chose to call it, had, for various reasons, stayed with him from being a child. But what could the reasons be?

He could have said it was its outlined shape he remembered from the wartime bombing, flashed up like a simple piece of marquetry pattern against the strafed and stirred-up night sky. Or the paler, less emphatic brain shape these trees made in the all-clear when they were sometimes wreathed in a red-tinged vapour drifting back from the coast. He could have said this, if the truth hadn't been that he had quicker memories of the times spent below ground in the barrel-vaulted tunnel that ran under the Moor and then all the way under the town – the Bus Station, the Infirmary, the Grand Assembly Rooms, the Dreamland Ballroom De Luxe – to the river.

The tunnel had been built by colliery owners in the previous century as a way of getting loaded wagons down to the quayside under the force of their own weight and had been drained and re-opened for use as an air-raid shelter in the war. And it was there, as has been often told, that as a schoolboy Ray Cruddas learned how to handle audiences paying more attention to the drone of bombers overhead than to his quips and songs, and that his career as an entertainer began.

Apart from the dramatic, rather dream-like glimpses he caught of it while the sirens were wailing, and again when the emergencies were over, he could think of only one other instance of the little grove on the Moor making any direct contact with his life.

This had happened even further back, before the war, when his mother and father were still together and apparently on the up and happy in a way that many of the people who met them in those days even commented on. The three of them had been on their way back from a small shopping errand down the town and were walking across the Moor towards home when there was a sudden downpour that none of them had seen coming. His mother was the first to make a break for it off the path, skipping across the springy turf towards the cover of the trees. She was wearing a pretty summer dress that Ray was always particularly pleased to see her in and flat orthopaedic sandals and shrieking like a girl as the rain falling from the black skies slicked her hair and Ray ran behind his mother, still holding tightly on to her hand.

His father laughed at the two of them. 'Only sheds love being under sycamores,' he said, flinging his head back to throw a rope of water off his heavily greased hair. They stood in the green light, just a few feet under the thick canopy of the trees, and soon felt the chill that was at the heart of the little grove moving on their backs. In the winter the mud floor had been churned up and it had dried into those shapes. The plate-sized feet of the cows were imprinted in the ground, and away from the cool centre, in the spaces between the hoofprints, grew complicated, saw-edged ferns and other plants that favoured shade.

Small clumps of grey and sandy-coloured hair had become attached to the trunks of the trees from the cows' big swelled bodies chafing against them. The rain came down around them like a curtain through which a shaft of sunlight could soon be seen falling on the allotments which were no distance away at the other end of the Moor from where they were standing. The sensation was of standing in one room, looking through to another where lights were on and life was happening.

Raymond's father, who was called Tommy, was wearing broad canvas braces over an open-necked shirt. The shape of his vest was visible where the shirt stuck to his body. Although he was standing in front of his parents, Raymond was aware of them holding hands, and this embarrassed him. He imagined they must look like the mannequin models of a mother, father and small boy that that winter had appeared in the window of their neighbourhood draper's, exciting much local comment. The shop had been taken over by a new man – a Londoner (although in fact he was from the Isle of Sheppey in Kent). And the display he had put in place to demonstrate the unparalleled waterproof qualities of the new season's stock – the family group of three dummies in mackintoshes and rain hats with water from a sprinkler device washing down over them – was regarded as being both showy and wasteful of water.

In an area where most families still shared an outhouse in a communal yard and paid ninepence to bathe in a cubicle at the municipal baths it was seen as being typical of bright but bogus southern ideas. The southerner soon afterwards packed up and left (headed for the cheap fur trade in a growing, good-class neighbourhood, it was rumoured). But to Raymond the window display was hypnotic, and he had found himself being drawn again and again to watch the indoor rain drizzling over the finely cracked hands with the painted-on nails and the feet with the painted-on dull black shoes.

It was a classic tableau of the happy family, and it was easy to imagine them frozen into these postures for all eternity, just as it was easy for Ray, standing under the dripping trees on an early August afternoon all those years ago, to believe that it was always going to be this way, him and his mam and his dad, the three of them easy-going and happy together, for ever. (In fact, his father would walk out on them both just over a year later; his mother was now dead.)

The sound of his mother's handbag snapping shut made Ray jump. Turning from the still steady downpour, he saw her handing his father a plain brown-paper bag. She did it in the slightly furtive way she always slipped him a handkerchief when his nose was running in a public place. But Raymond knew what the paper bag contained.

In many ways the Cruddases were typical of their neighbours – the people who stayed in their own neighbourhood, loving it, enjoying the closeness, the friendliness, the familiarity, and trying to save enough money to move out. In this last respect, Tommy Cruddas was doing better than most. He worked as a costing clerk at the ABLE machine shop just across the road from their house – ALWAYS BETTER LASTING EQUIPMENT; it ran along the side of the building in fiery red letters.

But he had a part-time evening job as leader of a seven-piece dance band and played Hawaiian guitar. The main point of their trip into the town that day had been to buy a piece of sheet music from the big lavender-polish-smelling music place in the arcade which Ray always liked visiting because he was allowed to play with the latest, inner-illuminated mahogany-cabinet radios that stood in the window.

The piece of music that his father bought that day, and that he cast his eye over as they waited out of the rain under the trees, had a peach-tinted photographic cover of a dark-skinned young woman with hibiscus in her hair and what Ray now knew to be plumeria leis covering her breasts because he spent his second honeymoon at the Royal Hawaiian Hotel in Honolulu, dining alfresco with his new wife Charmian amid date palms hung with Chinese lanterns on Kuhio Beach, serenaded by guitars and ukeleles.

(Following his father's death, a woman he had been living with at the end sent Ray a hula-skirt-clad figure sixteen inches tall which, when you turned the key in her back, went through the movements of the hula dance and the shimmy. As a PS to her brief, badly written accompanying note she said it was worth a considerable amount in the sale rooms, but he left it behind where he was appearing, in a hotel or a car or a dressing-room somewhere.)

But in his memory none of the bad things had yet happened. He was Raymond Cruddas. He was three and a half. His father was Tommy Cruddas, twenty-four; his mother was Eliza Cruddas, twenty-two, known as 'Betty'. They lived together in the thick of the little black-brick terraces that some people regarded as monuments of mean ugliness and beastly, but that they regarded as secure and home. It was summer. It was 1936. They had not been beaten down by the Depression; money was coming into their pockets; they loved one another.

As his father hummed the simple melody off the page, the sun started to spread from the allotments where it had been lighting up the cracked glass of the huddled buildings with a furious glowing, and swept across the Moor to where they were standing like an empty spotlight.

When he was that age, Raymond thought the movement of the branches of trees caused the wind.

*

9

Now Ray did two laps of the trees on Allotment Field every day. Much to his surprise, he was a jogger. During his decades away, the trees had been like a dream he kept having in which nothing occurred. Now he mostly saw them through a scrim of sweat with the sound of his own heart hammering between his ears.

It was part of his routine. He rose late and ate whatever Marzena had left for him to have. Then he did two circuits of the Moor and waited at the tea van outside the main gate of the Park for his old oppo Jackie Mabe to collect him and take him to Bobby's, the club they ran, where he spent the whole of the rest of the very long day. It would be the early hours and sometimes later before Jackie delivered him back home again.

The jogging had started after a health scare, of course: furred-up arteries, high cholesterol, just what you would expect for a man of his age. What he hadn't at all expected was that you could enjoy it. He hadn't yet experienced what they called a runner's high: the ecstasy-inducing rush of endorphins to the brain. But he wasn't one of the sad cases with the dowager's humps and Walkmen that he saw dragging their poor arteriosclerotic carcasses across the Moor. He was quite quick. He could be at any rate. He still experienced the novice's pleasure from propelling himself on big metallic, light-trapping trainers, with the advanced shock-absorbers and the fluorescent flashes and panels. ('Bigged up', along with 'respeck' and 'well wicked', were some of the phrases he'd recently picked up from the kitchen porters and young waiting staff at work. He liked to stay abreast: 'The Thief of Bad Gags', as he used to be known – 'He was laughing so hard he dropped his pencil,' one of Ray's local rivals used to regularly joke about him in those days – hadn't lost his habit of vigilant earwigging for up-to-date and potentially useful material.)

Ray's 'dress-hair' was waiting to be fitted at the club. The hair of his own that he had left was a deep chestnut brown, and a small patch of hair of a similar colour had been stitched into the

'D' at the back of his baseball hat where a half-moon of white scalp would otherwise have been framed. It was one of the demands of the job, as he saw it, to stay trim and presentable. He had weights and a tanning bed in his dressing-room.

But he had a recent history of letting himself go. This had happened when the TV work had eventually dried up and the phone stopped ringing and he slipped into the show-business shadows, just doing the odd after-dinner appearance and Rotary Round Table and living in a ranch-style house backing on to a golf course in Devon. His second wife had taken up with a man who made a decent living wearing a wetsuit and flippers to retrieve golf balls from the course's ponds and water hazards, the biggest of which was near the end of their garden, and had moved in with him.

He'd given in to lassitude, gloom and resignation then. Let the grey come through in his hair. Piled the weight on. Eating the same food sitting at the same window table in the My Blue Heaven village Italian six nights a week while Tony and Aldo and Giuseppe smoked and fingered their watches and watched ear-splitting football on the television. Seafood linguine and escalope of veal every night for he didn't want to remember how long. Bottle of the house red. Glass of limoncello with the sharp-as-hell almond biscuit things that shredded his gums.

It was the first time for years that he hadn't had Jackie there to deflect attention and at least simulate conversation. At that time, for the first time in all the years they had been together, Jackie was having to earn his own living. He opened a caravan park for short-stay vans. He built the lavatory block and put down the soil pipe himself; but they kept disappearing without paying, even when he padlocked the main gate overnight. That had cleaned him out. Next he'd gone on the road, peddling bar sundries and colour-coded boning knives and the new regulation anti-bacterial chopping boards to pubs and restaurants, with second-hand books at car-boot sales as a sideline. He would come round to

Ray's and sit at the kitchen table over a beer, stacking his takings in columns.

This is not something that would have happened if Charmian had still been there. Charmian had never got on with Jackie. She never saw the point of him; Charmian had always refused to be able to see what Jackie was *for*. And as she found her place in the gin-and-Jaguar hierarchy slipping as Ray's face faded from the television and the invitations to high-profile occasions trickled to a halt, things came to a head.

Ray had built up a reputation for being a big tipper. 'When you've got nothing, act like you've got loads' had been his motto when he set out, and it was what he still believed now that, after a lifetime of free spending, he was having to pull his horns in. It had always been their arrangement that Jackie carried a substantial float of cash to tip the maître d', tip the waiter, tip the cloakroom girl, tip the taxi driver. Tip, tip, tip, with Charmian, when she was there, scowling blackly in the background at all times.

Ray was always telling Jackie to pick up theatre tickets for this one, send a bottle of Jack to that one, collect one of the cars from the garage, send flowers to somebody else. And then Charmian grabbed her moment when she saw Jackie taking a note from a stack of several notes wedged under a framed photograph in their bedroom and accused him of stealing from the house. Pointless to say he was only doing what Ray had told him to do (which Ray confirmed). Equally pointless, when Charmian demanded to know why he hadn't come and asked her, to remind her that she questioned every purchase and every expense, wanting to know why it was bought, where, for how much, and for whom.

But Charmian, it turned out, was already having secret moonlight meetings in the bunkers with Gavin, her flippered golf-ball retriever, by then. So Jackie was soon back round, letting himself in with his key, counting his coins at the kitchen table like a back-street busker; while Ray, greying, balding and surplus to requirements, slumped disconsolately inside his neon tan. Not so much Don Juan and Sancho Panza, more Bob and Terry (or Terry and June, as Jackie liked to say). Coram and Jennie, a knife-throwing act they used to tour with. (He ended up winging her with a tomahawk one night at the Palace of Varieties, Leicester, after too much to drink at the end of the first house.) Mutt and Jeff. Both of them running on the rims.

It was soon after this, with nowhere left to go, that Ray had come home.

His route took him up to the end of his terrace, then sharp left through a heavy sprung gate whose banging sometimes kept him awake, on to the Moor. To his right, over towards the allotments, the old man continued to discuss the price of corned beef with the cows. The light was still flat and grey, but the weather was lifting. It would soon be lunchtime, and the day had been aired, as his mother used to like to say.

''S'goin', boss?' Danny the soft lad said from his bench as Ray jogged past. Approaching, Ray had caught the glint of light through the ribbon of lager as it travelled the four inches from the lip of the tin through clean air straight to the back of Danny's throat.

'You're here to sell it, not sup it,' the bar manager at Bobby's was always telling his staff, and it's a rule that Ray often wished he could apply to himself. Many of the old theatre managers he'd known had felt very strongly that performers should stay on their side of the curtain and kept the pass door between the auditorium and backstage locked for that reason. If you wanted a drink you sent out for one and had it brought to the dressing-room. But in a club it didn't work like that. The locals' deeply rooted devotion to drink meant they took it as a personal insult if you refused one. 'Aye, twist me arm, I think I can manage a pint.' How many times a night did Ray hear himself saying that? And last night, which hadn't been in any way an uproarious one, he had got on to 'binoculars' – two tall hundred-gram glasses of vodka, downed in one. Another night recently the trick drink at Bobby's had been a Depth-charger, which involved letting go a heavy-bottomed glass of vodka into a pint glass of lager and drinking them off together. The customer who had treated Ray to the first of these had assured him that part of the attraction was the possibility of the shot glass gathering speed inside the pint glass and smashing your teeth.

The difficulty of saying no, and saying it in time, was why Ray had taken to wearing a black bin-liner next to his body, under the satiny tracksuit top: to help sweat it out.

A large-headed mongrel dog he had never seen before came yapping at his ankles as he pounded along a path that cut through tall weeds and brought him close to the stand of trees. The dog then veered away again as suddenly as it had arrived. The silence held by the trees amplified the echo of his footfalls on the compacted wet ground and the catch of his breathing. Then something in his peripheral vision, or maybe a sound, made him turn in time to see two boys setting fire to one of the benches on the Moor.

He recognized them by their baggy jeans concertinaed around their ankles and their big baggy oversized shirts as the two boys who had called out something pissy-sounding to him when he had overtaken them a few minutes earlier. (He was pretty sure he'd heard the word 'grandad'.) As he continued to jog backwards, he saw a brief blast of pure red flame as the plastic laminate covering the metal of the bench caught, followed by a dirty flowering of sooty black smoke. The two munchkins were already halfway across the Moor, body-charging each other and whooping and heading in the direction of the allotments, by the time he turned around and righted himself (nothing he could do) and started running in the direction of his own house once again.

The roofs of the terrace were steeply pitched with dormer windows peeping out of them. Some houses were colour-washed in pale pinks and greens, but most of them had been stripped of their rendering in the past few years and brought back to the original brick. In the case of Ray's house this had been done with a rather heavy hand: the grit-blasting had turned the façade an unnatural, too-bright nursery red he didn't imagine it had ever been. The pointing had also come up too white and synthetic-looking, and the general effect was of a jealously protected but never-played-with doll's house.

He didn't know any of his neighbours to speak to, but from their appearance and the hours they kept he supposed they worked in solid professions such as accountancy, insurance, local government, computers, the university of course. The bright, open aspect of their houses, their tacked-up children's paintings and honeyed pine, was in marked contrast to the houses of the few remaining elderly residents whose dim interiors hid behind once dark and heavy, now faded and thin, chenille curtains and dust-laden window plants. Only one house in Moor Edge Terrace bore the signs of multi-occupation: batik-pattern and Indian bed-spreads at all the windows; overturned black plastic dustbins with the flat numbers daubed in white paint rolling around the garden. It was the people in this house who Ray believed were responsible for the night-time slamming of the Moor access gate.

The terrace had been erected at around the same time as the football ground. For most of their history a kind of parity had existed, but now Moor Edge was dwarfed and dominated by its closest neighbour. A hundred years earlier Ray could have stood in one of his back bedrooms, thirty feet above the heads of the spectators standing on an earth embankment raised at the south end of the ground, behind the goal, and watched teams of terrier-like, mostly pitmen players in heavy dubbined leather boots and baggy drawers ploughing up the mud. Many of them would have taken the motor bus and then the electric tram in from the outlying villages where they lived, crush-loaded with other miners who were coming to see them play. Even as late as the 1950s the top-floor bedrooms still commanded a view over the concrete terracing straight into what was already being referred to, sentimentally but not misleadingly, as the Theatre of Dreams.

Now from the same window you could almost reach out and take hold of the scaffolding ribs of the recently erected skeleton structure which supported a cantilevered roof roughly equal in area to the pitch. This was a landmark visible from every part of the city. It was separated from Ray's house by the length of a narrow garden, and a cobbled alley, designed originally for horse traffic, which the ribby white superstructure of the Ned Corvan Stand overhung like a cataract of snow about to slide off a roof.

On match days, the physical sensation of noise leaped the gap between the great metal skeleton of the stadium and the houses of the terrace, adrenalizing them from basement to roof joists, like a current: windows shook in their frames; bottles hummed in unison in bathroom cabinets; cups would rattle in their saucers.

Although the ground itself had gradually, and then very quickly, mutated, the football club's role had never changed: it gave people a way of identifying with the city that was their home. It was the kind of identifying Ray had never experienced during his first distant life there, and that he thought he could make up for now.

When he had lurched past his house to begin his second lap of the Moor, he had wondered if he only imagined that he could hear a phone ringing inside. Twenty minutes earlier, just as he had been about to open the front door, he had heard the phone and had gone back in to take a call that turned out to be about one of the thousand niggling details connected with Bobby's that dogged his existence. Did he know that hand-drier in the Gents that turned itself on every time somebody walked past it? (Did he!) Well, they had had an engineer looking at it all morning and it still kept happening; it was a persistent fault that seemed to resist fixing. What to do?

The administrative chores involved in running a business, and the constant stream of decisions he was called on to make, the petty arithmetic, tightened Ray's skull. Most of the previous three days had been taken up investigating the matter of some cheques that had been stolen – three cheques clipped out of the middle of a new cheque book sitting in a drawer in his dressing-room/office, stubs included. This only a matter of days after picking up the phone to hear a young woman telling him that his platinum card had been what he believed she called 'skimmed', and just ten minutes before had been used in a transaction involving the purchase of cigarettes and petrol on the forecourt of a garage in somewhere called Semdinli on the border between Turkey and Iran. Could he also confirm (he heard the spongey click of practised fingers on a computer keyboard) that neither he nor his wife had earlier that week been staying in the Hotel Resort Ariston in Tirebolu on the Black Sea coast, paying for the hire of a car with driver, and running up a room-service bill to the total of £878.00?

This was his life. He was having lessons twice a week to try to familiarize him with e-mail and the Internet. There was the bitter struggle to get on top of the new spreadsheet software. His first appointment of the day he knew was with a former player for United who now worked as a traveller for the brewery and was coming in to discuss income from the club's pool tables (further implications of sticky fingers) and to update target figures for 'wet sales'. (Alan Harries was an outside left whose dislike for blatant physical confrontation had earned him the unfortunate nickname of 'Gladys' and the regular taunt from the terraces: 'Where's your handbag?') There were the inevitable, on-going sagas of personnel in-fighting and staffing problems lying in wait. Carpet tiles to look at. A new rota shift system to throw in his two penn'orth on. Plans for an extension to the kitchen (chef, a rough-tongued Mackem, was threatening to leave unless he was given more space). What did it have to do with walking on, making people laugh for half an hour, and getting off again?

As the time approached for him to be collected by Jackie, he realized he was rushing towards an engagement with these responsibilities when all he really wanted was to turn round and start running in the opposite direction and keep going and running until the endorphins flooded his brain and he hit that high that was the highest high and from which he might never come down. Like everybody, he had always been wanting to blow the doors off his life.

A broad, downward-sloping path brought him off the Moor past the boundary fence of the allotment gardens to the main gate of the Park. But before he got there he reached under his clothing to tear at the bin-liner he had been wearing and, when he had succeeded in dragging it away from his skin, stuffed it in a bin which occasionally contained gory pornography, but not today. The act of disposing of the clammy black plastic was something he always did in a furtive, guilty-looking way, because of the risk of appearing to be involved in something indecent. The possibility was increased by the way he had to hold his chest away from his lower body in order to avoid getting his trousers and his trainers drenched in sweat.

He knew that Mighty would have his orange energy drink ready and waiting, and his anticipation was high: in his mind he could already taste it exploding on his tongue. It was as he began to allow the gradient and his earned exhaustion to carry him forward that he got his first sense of disturbance or perturbation – of something out of the ordinary happening that was exactly the opposite of the few minutes of nothing happening that he came here every day to enjoy.

Mighty's Scran Van had been parked in the same place outside the main Park gates for about as long as anybody could remember.

The gates themselves had long disappeared: rust stains on the square stone columns where the bolus hinges had once been fixed were the only sign they had ever been there. The broad slope that Ray had just run down had once been a carriage drive. The gateway to it was recessed from the road in a wide half-moon shape, and two slat-backed corporation benches, recently given a lick of emerald-green paint, squatted in the curves either side. The van itself was tucked in beside the bench to the left of the gate, gaudy with hand-written Day-Glo signs, plus a wipeboard with the day's specials on it. In addition to the benches, there were a few battered tin tables and some mismatched old chairs scattered around.

It was nowhere. It was nothing. It reminded Ray of a picket encampment outside a factory, or the navvies huddled around their overnight braziers that he recalled watching from his bedroom window when he was a boy. (It had seemed a romantic life, being a navvy, with a corrugated-iron shelter and pals to share confidences with and a billy-can, and his first ambition had been to be one.) And yet the Scran Van was one of those nothing places, hardly noticed by the hundreds who drove past it every day, that had become vital to the small community of regulars who washed up there to eat Mighty's home-made pies and drink Mighty's famous tea, but mostly just to have the light of Mighty's beneficence, a port in every storm, shine upon them.

The focus of the unusual amount of activity was the bench on the other side of the gate from the tea van. Two old boys with proud kettle-drum pot bellies and shot faces could usually be counted on to be sitting there at that time of day. But all Ray could see as he drew close were a number of milling figures, with Mighty at the centre of them wearing a wrap-around apron and carpet slippers and leaning forward in a way that made it clear she was trying to comfort somebody. He instinctively stopped running, and approached at what he hoped looked like a nonchalant stroll.

'Divven cry, lover,' Mighty was telling a tiny, bird-like Chinese woman. 'They're bastards. That's all they are, bloody bastards. Young'ins. If they were mine aa naa what aa'd do. Tan their arses till they were red raw. There yar, chicken,' she said, taking the small gill bottle of brandy that had been offered by a man Ray knew was called Stanley (never Stan) and tipping it into the hot drink that the woman was clutching on her knee. 'Steady the norves, hinny,' Stanley said as Mighty handed him the bottle back.

The woman was dressed all in black with inch-wide margins of grey either side of the parting in her otherwise raven hair. Somebody had brought one of the big puffed-out jackets and put it around her shoulders, but she was still shivering convulsively from the shock. There was a red weal around her neck where her necklace had cut her flesh before it snapped. Ray knew this without even having to ask. He quickly learned that a mobile phone had also been taken from the woman.

'Arreet, John.'

'Canny.'

'All right, John.'

'Canna grumble.'

Ray brought his drink from the Formica counter and found a place to sit. Only men who had known each other back to their schooldays – fifty and sixty years in some cases – called each other by their given names. Everybody else, to everybody else, was 'John'.

Ray hadn't lost the habit, instilled in him after years of dodging the attention of autograph-seekers and, in recent years, of the didn't-you-used-to-be-ers, of sitting where he was able to see without being seen. (Unless being seen was the point of being somewhere – a charity event, a restaurant – which was different.) He chose a table where he was shielded from the road and looked around on the ground for the wadded Marlboro packet that he knew was usually jammed under one of the legs of the chair he was sitting on to stop it rocking.

Mighty was down on her knees, dabbing at the Chinese woman's leg now with a paper napkin and Ray noticed that passengers on some of the buses, usually away with their own thoughts and oblivious to their existence, were craning their necks to see what was going on. He could see the woman had a bad gash on her right knee just above the flesh-toned half-stocking that Mighty was in the process of carefully rolling down. Under the bench, at her feet, was a pink nylon mesh bag with coloured flowers appliquéd to it which he hadn't spotted until then. The Heavenly Terrace, a Chinese supermarket, had recently opened on a piece of spare ground behind the Texaco garage, and that had almost certainly been her destination when she was attacked. (By, he was prepared to bet, the pair of troglodyte pyromaniacs he had encountered earlier on the Moor.)

This piece of speculation, though, was purely Ray's own. Nobody at the van was using the event as an excuse to stir up some small excitement or for gossip, or behaving in any way differently than they normally behaved. Only the two men who had given up their seats to the Chinese woman and had moved to a table where Ray had never seen them sitting before were giving any outward indication of being affected by the incident. Although they were trying not to be, they seemed resentful, and were braced for when they could reclaim their places, knee to knee on the bench. It was the displaced attitude of children who had arrived at school to find strangers sitting at their desk.

Most people, having weighed up the situation, had quickly gone back to doing what they were doing before it occurred: working out an accumulator or a ten-bob e/w on the 3.30 at Lingfield, or browsing in the paper, or trying to bring out a crossword. The habits of a lifetime are hard to break. But it wasn't out of disregard for the distress of the Chinese woman, or callousness,

21

but rather as a show of good manners and a determination not to make a bad situation worse by adding to the woman's disorientation and sense of shock at being set upon by foreign devils in a foreign city that they had made an effort to re-immerse themselves in the ordinary dull routine of an ordinary dull day.

Somebody had even turned the radio back on after a while. But it was low, and the banal songs and the cheap chatter were perfect for establishing a sense of nothing going on. (This, in fact, had been the Ray Cruddas show-business philosophy when he started out, before the times, and his personal circumstances, forced him to go blue: a few songs, a few laughs, an act that pays no attention to the facts of life but just goes down the road. It's only how things were. Nobody's idea of a good time then was to be scared witless or scarred for life when they went to the pictures or to see a concert party. In the British films of those times, the formula was tried and tested: simple tales, simply told, dealing in the main with nice people doing nice things.

It was first brought home to Ray how far the world had turned when the owner of the Villa Capri Casino Nightclub, Kettering, gave him the benefit of his showbiz credo one night in the early seventies: 'Give 'em a gamble, bare tits and a laugh and the buggers'll shit money all night.' This same man kept his money packed in a very large concrete safe with a mattress on top where his children slept.)

'Five letters. Begins with p and ends with p. Means clubby.' Conversation at the Scran Van rarely extended beyond that, and the occasional reaction to some phone-in comment ('Yi naa what you're supposed to call shoplifters these days, divven yiz? "Non-traditional shoppers"'), or speculation on who had the number-one hit in August 1958 with 'Carolina Moon', or which famous screen actor's real name was 'Frederick Austerlitz'. (A: Fred Astaire. Ray knew it but didn't pipe up.) Every Friday Big Alf went round depositing the monkey nuts and liquorice allsorts he carried in his pockets in little piles in front of people he knew. Now and again somebody might offer Ray a joke they'd heard and were happy to pass on. Big issues were never addressed, and big thoughts were never spoken: it would be regarded as breaking the code somehow to speak them. Anything likely to provoke argument, such as a live broadcast of the Budget speech, or a programme about the relevance of the monarchy to modern life, was discreetly turned off. Mighty's was no place for amateur priests, or preachers. The only issues to get debated were things like which has the most ache in it, a rum hangover or a gin hangover. The Scran Van was a place to go to briefly get away from life. A snug harbour.

Jackie Mabe had stood between Ray Cruddas and the world for more than thirty years. Jackie was Ray's eyes and ears; he was his butler, gofer, personal assistant and wife. Jackie was the reason Ray couldn't tell you the price of a newspaper or a pint of milk; why he didn't know how to boil an egg, and why he hadn't travelled on public transport (he liked to say) since Keir Hardie and the horse-drawn tram.

To be famous is, in many ways, to be an exile from life. Fame breeds a kind of contagion among the famous whose major symptom is a fear of going where other famous people don't go. For many years Ray had refused to believe this applied to him. And then one day Jackie asked him: When was the last time he'd been in an off-licence or picked up his own cleaning? Or walked in a park, or shopped for a present for a friend or his wife, or bought himself a tie? What was he scared of? (They both knew. A familiarity with ordinary dailiness by definition meant you couldn't be considered special, or consider yourself special, any more.) How did you rent a video, or put a bet on in a betting shop? When did he last walk in a room on his own without knowing in advance who everybody in it was going to be?

Easy question: what did a cinema ticket look like these days?

Ray, who still carried a mental image of a woman in her ticket cage dinging up narrow folding tickets through a metal slot while smoking a cigarette down to the end without taking it out of her mouth once, even while talking (she has a deep cigarette cough; she likes vigorous colours; her big breasts pointing through the thin vulgar summer dress; she does not mind being stared at; the big breasts and the blown charm – he remembered such a woman from the Brighton, and then later the Gem, which itself in time became the Beth Shan Tabernacle), had to confess he didn't know.

His solitary meals at the My Blue Heaven osteria in his village had been an ordeal without the wall of protection constituted by Jackie, but in the end it had been considerably less stressful than the alternative of shopping and cooking for himself. His daily run, and his recuperation period at the tea van at the gates of the Park, had marked his first real attempt at a re-engagement with life, and he had felt comfortable there among Mighty's regulars from day one.

It was a relief to Ray that nobody at the van wanted to test him by offering the friendliness that, for many years, as a face coming into their living rooms, a familiar voice drip-drip-dripping into their kitchens, he had appeared to invite. They were cordial and outgoing, but they left him to himself.

Some residue of resentment would have been understandable. Everything about the trajectory of his life and its reporting in the press could be interpreted as a repudiation of how they lived and behaved; even of the way they spoke and what they wore. The more he achieved by going away, the more dissatisfaction they could have reasonably felt by being left behind. For a long time for the men of his generation in that area he had been an index of their mean ambitions and low horizons; a standard against which to measure the featurelessness of – nobody might ever have said this to them, but the implication was always there – their 'sad little lives'. Unlike them, he had got on the bus before it passed him by and gone on to become, in the opinion of the disaffected, all suede shoes and Babycham.

But now he was back, and he was only an old bag of bones like themselves; flesh and old bones. The essence of life at the Scran Van was not judging other people and not expecting to be judged by them. If Mighty had had a motto, it would have been that. 'Judge not, that ye be not judged.' (That, or another favourite verse from Matthew: 'The foxes have holes, and the birds of the air have nests; but the Son of man hath not where to lay his head.')

Nevertheless, in the miserable months before he slunk home to the North East to live, Ray had believed that in one area of his life he was going to be particularly vulnerable to rejection and even vilification. Like Jimmy Tarbuck and Ted Rogers and others who had also grown up in the old industrial regions, his attachment to the Conservative Party in general, and to Mrs Thatcher in particular, had ensured that at one stage he was virtually court jester at Downing Street.

Ray had first met Margaret Thatcher soon after her election as leader of the party in 1975, and had entertained the delegates at the annual conference in Blackpool that year, a town he knew well. In 1979 he had appeared for her at a televised election rally, and had been rewarded with a gilt-framed grip-and-grin picture of the two of them together and an invitation to her first drinks party at Downing Street as Prime Minister.

Unlike Tarbie, who was squat and perspiring and still carried the authentic whiff of a working class she had made no secret that she regarded as idle, deceitful, inferior and bloody-minded, Ray was the cut of a man it became increasingly clear the Prime Minister liked. 'Perma-tanned' and 'smarmy' to his critics, who by then were many, and baying, she was clearly captivated by his tailoring (Duggie Millings of Soho for stage and television; Kilgour and French of Savile Row for civilian and formal), his tonsure (silvering, but still all his own), his attentiveness, his use-fulness as a social lubricant, and his charm.

His way in had been through Gordon Reece, her director of communications and producer of Ray's first showcase series for Associated Television in 1965. *Ray Cruddas Invites* . . . was dropped after six weeks because it failed to find large enough audiences. But the two of them had had other successes together (*Holiday Star Time*, with Esther Ofarim, Reg Varney and Acker Bilk; *Ray Cruddas's Monday Night Live*, with its popular 'Spot-the-Tune' interlude in which cash prizes could be won), and had remained firm friends. Their shared lack of interest in the substance of political issues also found favour with the Prime Minister, who turned to them increasingly for advice on how to project the most authoritative yet televisually engaging image of herself.

Reece had already demonstrated to her how the handling of the camera and lighting can aid the performer in his or her expressive task. Reece too could claim credit for getting her to sharpen her hairstyle and lower her voice. But she was constantly on the look-out for new phrases and pay-off lines, and this was where Ray was able to help. Ray it also was who pointed out that she was using her arms a little too predictably and a little too often, and assured her that the key word in television perfor-mance was nonchalance – 'carefully studied nonchalance'. (She made a careful note of this in a small, leather-bound notebook which she kept in the slip pocket of her handbag, when he had expected a laugh.) But perhaps his greatest contribution to her TV persona was the suggestion that she might like to try slightly whiter make-up on her upper eyelids to lighten up her eyes, and the colour stick he gave her that he had used himself since the coming of colour television to tone down the fleshy, other-worldly fluorescent pink of his tongue.

'Mr Ray Cruddas and Mrs Charmian Cruddas' were regular

guests of the Prime Minister's at official receptions at Westminster and in Whitehall, and eventually in the more intimate surroundings of Downing Street, where they were gratified to find they were able to hold their own with the members of Mrs Thatcher's 'kitchen cabinet' who included Alan Walters, her trusty guru; the old intriguer, Alf Sherman; Ralph 'Rolf' Harris, the founding father of the Institute of Economic Affairs; her Chelsea neighbour, Sir Laurens van der Post, the traveller and semi-mystic; and the self-made computer millionaire, John Hoskyns, who always seemed to back Charmian into a corner on these occasions and start banging on about Britain 'going down the tube'. The wife of the educationalist Sir John Vaizey, a canny American in a kaftan dress, once confided to Charmian that they had a cat at home that they called 'Lady Daisy Vaizey', and she dined out on that for years in the bungalows and light-drenched villas of the South Hams.

It was the passing of these times, following Mrs Thatcher's fall from power in November 1990, that Charmian had especially mourned: the after-hours washing-up at the sink in the little flat under the eaves of Number 10 with Margaret – who Charmian always addressed as 'Prime Minister' even when she was only asking whether she would prefer to wash or wipe – while the men shared a joke against a background of light-orchestral music over their single malts in the next room.

One of the first things Charmian packed when she gave up the ghost and went to live with Gavin, the flippered golf-ball retriever, was a letter that Mrs T. had written to Ray in the middle of a particularly bad spell when she knew he was struggling, and that Charmian had had framed and hung over the tallboy in their bedroom. It quoted four lines of an inspirational poem:

> Does the road wind up-hill all the way?
>   Yes, to the very end.

> Will the day's journey take the whole long day?
> From morn to night, my friend.

Charmian had gone out and found the book it had come from – it was a collection by Christina Rossetti – and the book from that day forward had become her solace and her constant companion.

Looking around him at Mighty's regulars, the lame ducks and lost causes who gathered round her daily at the tea van – men for the most part who had never owned a car or a passport, all of them products of the old industries – the heavy industries – that had created the character and culture of that part of the world, who didn't really own anything other than the clothes they stood in – Ray occasionally allowed himself to see it from Charmian's perspective, and inwardly grinned when he thought how his former wife, happening across him now, would feel vindicated in seeing what she had always said would happen come to pass: she had kept on telling him that (once a Geordie, always a Geordie) he was going to end up without a pot to piss in, living in the gutter.

Except that, in the matter of their appearance at least, the Scran Van regulars didn't conform to the street-corner-dole-wallah, flat-cap-and-rag-muffler stereotype of the old North East. They were a colourful bunch, kitted out in synthetic animal-pelt fleeces and comfortable sweatpants and the big padded training coats and replica team shirts with iridescent watermark patterns that strobed when they caught the light. It's something Ray had particularly noticed since he'd gone back there to live: that everybody dressed sportily younger than their years – or sportily older in the case of the nursery-age children in their cropped tops and bare midriffs and hip-hugging jeans. People of all ages and both sexes seemed to have decided that the best age was around seventeen. A disco dolly with glossy long hair and chiffon bell-bottom trousers could easily turn out, when she turned around, to be a grandmother of seventy. At Mighty's, steel toe-caps and heavy work boots had mostly been replaced by trainers with Velcro fastenings and reflectors, fat laces and fashionable signature logos. A group of four men who regularly used the table closest to the van's counter looked like a boy band persevering well into their sixties. Their shoes, and virtually everything else they were wearing, Ray knew had come from 'Magpie' Jeff who sold out of a suitcase from a wall screened from the road by bushes, just behind the van, and always knew where to get what you wanted if he wasn't carrying it himself. It's from Jeff that Ray had got his Kappa tracksuit and the fluorescent monsters he was wearing on his own feet.

A large part of the success of Bobby's, the nostalgia enterprise he had launched eighteen months earlier – its slogan was 'The kind of club that takes you back even if you were never there originally' – was due to the fact that people could go there wearing the clothes traditionally associated with the area – the proletarian 'Andy' caps and turban scarves, the unravelling 'ganzies' and massive 'pinnies' – and celebrate the fact that these things had been consigned to history. Another reason that business at Bobby's was booming was that people liked to go there to be reminded of simpler, less neurotic (and less dangerous) times.

'He's late the day, lad.' The regulars had got to know Ray's habits as well as he'd got to know theirs. And it's true that Jackie should have arrived to collect him by now. The man who had spoken had seen Ray irritatedly looking at his watch. 'Howay, here they come,' the same man said then, at the sound of a police siren coming closer. 'It's only tekken them half an hour. They must have stopped somewhere for a cuppa tea on the way.'

The Chinese woman was still sitting on the end of the bench where she had been sitting when Ray first saw her. She was holding a napkin as a pad against her knee. The wound around her throat had darkened but she had stopped shaking so violently. A few new customers had arrived at the van, and Mighty had

29

served them. People on the buses had stopped craning their necks to follow what was happening as they passed. The Red Lion opposite had opened. The day had slowed back into its own momentum. But now the police siren tore it open.

The police car slowed almost to a halt outside the Red Lion and then accelerated into a tight U-turn that halted the on-coming traffic and made the tyres squeal on the asphalt road surface. 'Fucken Fangio,' the man said, as all heads turned to watch the car and the young officers – one male, one female – who quickly emerged from it. They were wearing sleeveless, official-issue black quilted jackets over crisp white shirts, and as they moved away from the car they took their caps off and clamped them up in their armpits. Mighty came down the wooden steps pushed up against the door at the side of the van and assumed responsibility for relating what had happened.

The female officer knelt down on the right-hand side of the Chinese woman just as Mighty had earlier. Her colleague, mean-while, remained upright with his notebook in one hand and his pencil poised, scanning the faces on the benches and at the tables in a half-amused, knowing kind of fashion. 'It is my duty to warn you that anything you say may be taken down, totally fucken twisted and used to nail you,' the man near to Ray said in a carry-ing voice. When the male constable had first got out of the car Ray thought he'd noticed something unusual about him. Now that he had turned to face in their direction Ray could see that he had an ash mark thumbed on his forehead. Its shape was more distinct than the starter moustache he was growing. Mighty had a similar mark, although part dissolved in grease and perspiration and consequently much fainter, in the same place on her head. Ray had thought it was a smudge from the kitchen or to do with the commotion surrounding the woman, but now he remembered: Ash Wednesday. The day before, Mighty had had pancakes on the board and, seeing people tucking into jam pancakes, and pancakes served with lemon juice and sugar, he had seriously wavered.

Pancake Tuesday – Mardi Gras in other places: 'Fat Tuesday', a big carnival – was the day before Lent. It was the day to use up all the rich things – eggs, fats, cheese. Ash Wednesday was the first day of Lent, a forty-day period of self-denial; of retreat and austerity leading up to the death of Christ. In some cultures it was a period of scourging and self-flagellation. But in the First World it was increasingly just a convenient framework in which to try to get healthy or lose weight by giving up cigarettes or spirits or Chicken Whoppers.

'I always like to get Easter behind me,' Ray remembered Mighty saying yesterday as she broke eggs for the new batch of pancake mix she was making in a chipped blue enamel jug. 'I always have. I don't know why that should be. All those bright colours. It feels like a weight's lifted.'

It felt strange to Ray to imagine Mighty and the policeman getting up and going to church this morning, leaving their houses when it was still dark, only a few lights on in the street. And then he wondered whether, unknown to each other, they had both been kneeling before the same altar while the same priest in the purple intoned the same age-old liturgy as he pressed a thumb dusted in ashes against their heads. 'Remember man that thou art dust and unto dust thou shalt return.' It struck him suddenly as a very lonely thing to do.

Ray had grown up in the same street as Mighty. He had known her parents, Iris and George. George had had a fish barrow that he pushed around the back lanes selling kippers, soused herrings, freshly caught haddock and cod, and he had a good reputation: people used to look forward to him coming, and to hearing his familiar cry and the clatter of his bell. He used to allow the children to play with the bell, which was engraved brass with a polished wooden handle, and with the lead weights for his scales, while he wrapped their mothers' purchases up in newspapers.

Ray had been to school with Mighty's brother, Arthur, a good footballer who, after a protracted illness (it was cancer, a word never mentioned in those days), had died when he was still a very young man, shortly after the war.

Mighty's given name was 'Merle' after Merle Oberon, who her father had seen playing Anne Boleyn in *The Private Life of Henry VIII* on his first ever visit to the cinema. But although as a baby she was dark, Mighty had grown up petite and blonde. Now that she was older, she had sun-streaks applied to her hair, which she wore short, in an easily manageable style. She wore very little make-up. Apart from a wind-burned flush high across her cheeks, her skin had an opalescent sheen like the inside of a shell; bright days picked out the transparent blues and greens under her eyes. Mighty wore several swagged brass ear-rings around the rim of her right ear, and a broad wedding ring on a chain around her neck. The slender link chain she wore around one ankle, and her usually crimson orange toe-nails, added to her healthy, outdoors, Mediterranean appearance.

But the knuckles of her hands were starting to show the first signs of arthritis; they were inflamed and slightly swollen-looking and Ray noticed she was having to use two hands for many simple lifting tasks now where previously she used one. Under the laminate counter were a row of plastic bottles containing homeopathic remedies, plus ginkgo biloba for her memory ('Now where did I put them again?'), and DHEA, a hormone that 'fools the body into thinking you're only forty'.

Many years earlier a local photographer had spent some time taking a picture of Mighty in a characteristic pose at the serving window of the van. The photograph had later appeared at an exhibition and in the evening paper, and the piece of yellowed newsprint was still taped to the back wall adjacent to the hot-water geyser above the sink. Staring out of it, standing behind a row of squeezable dispensers filled with mustard, and brown and red sauce, was a fresh-faced girl with more than a passing resemblance to the girl in Manet's popular painting (a framed print of it had hung at the back of the classroom in Ray's last year at junior school) *A Bar at the Folies-Bergères*. The photographer obviously had the painting in mind when he made his composition, ironically substituting the carefully wiped-down sauce and malt-vinegar bottles for Manet's green absinthe and sweating bottles of champagne.

Mighty's customers brought her flowers off the allotments – daffodils and tulips and the russet pom-pom dahlias that they knew she particularly liked; and every year on her birthday she was snowed under with cards. People she might not have seen since the same day the previous year made the trip to see her especially, sometimes bringing forty cigarettes or a small box of chocolates as well as a card.

She had women friends who came and stood at the side door and enjoyed a cigarette with her, their loaded carrier bags propped against the steps, the uniforms of their jobs as supermarket shelf-fillers and nursing auxiliaries and cleaners showing at the necks and the hems of their coats. But there was only one woman regular among the men at the van. They called her 'Dolly' on account of her being 'a bit Dolly Dimple', meaning simple. But she had a cultivated speaking voice and wore tweed jackets and big groundsheet headscarves like the Queen's, knotted under her chin. She also wore wing glasses whose lenses, Ray had noticed, were clouded and scratched. Mighty always made her eggs the way she liked them, boiled and then mashed up with butter in a tea-cup, which she ate with 'soldiers' and a spoon. Dolly was sometimes there and sometimes she wasn't, with nothing to explain where she went when she went away.

The young policeman had spoken into his collar to summon an

ambulance, and the ambulance arrived with its roof light flashing and its siren whooping a blood-curdling two-note scream. It swung to a halt tight in behind the police vehicle, and the paramedics – another man–woman team – threw the back doors open and hauled out a stretcher on wheels. The siren had stopped slowly like a winding-down toy. With the siren silenced it was as if there had been a high wind which had dropped suddenly. The stretcher wheels juddered as they were pushed towards the Chinese woman who was still sitting with the borrowed coat around her shoulders on the bench and looking startled as the thing came towards her. She started shaking again inside the black silk cloth of her slacks.

Where he was sitting, Ray had an excellent view – better than he actually wanted – straight into the interior of the ambulance. Another lonely place to have to go. He could see a plastic leather bench (for easy wiping) and a number of draw-string bags and coiled black rubber and a black rubber oxygen mask on the wall. He felt profoundly happy not to be the person getting into it.

The Chinese woman was still resisting getting on to the stretcher and protesting that she was able to walk. Then, as if at a signal he hadn't noticed, the male stretcher attendant touched a lever that dropped it down to her level and the two uniformed women, each taking an arm, steered her firmly on to it. The female paramedic, a substantial woman in a green V-neck and pressed green trousers, bent down quickly and swung the woman's legs over so she was in a semi-prone position. There was a paper-covered pillow on the stretcher, and tough restraining straps hanging down, and a waffle-textured coverlet which they threw over the Chinese woman's thin trembling legs.

The stretcher trolley jolted as they negotiated the kerb, and at that the patient levered herself half up and commenced to do stiff little oriental bows from the waist all round, like an actress leaving the stage. The effort of doing this caused her jacket to come open and exposed a lurid, rubberized, tattoo design and the name of a rock band splashed across the front of her T-shirt.

It was another detail, though, that wrenched Ray as the woman glided past him on her way to who knew where. Her tiny feet were poking out of the blanket and he could see how, on either side of the round-toed black leather shoes she was wearing, a careful razor cut had been made. This brought back a rush of memories of his own poor old mother who, in order to relieve the terrible pressure on her bunions, would take a single-bladed carpentry razor and carefully mutilate each new pair of shoes that she bought.

The legs under the stretcher automatically lifted as it was guided into the ambulance and folded themselves away. The policewoman followed the stretcher in and the male attendant tipped the retracting steps in after her. Her silhouette was visible briefly behind the opaque white window and then it disappeared. The siren started as the ambulance claimed priority in the traffic and sped away.

The policeman gave them all the benefit of another knowing look as he walked round to the driver's side and got in the car. Ray saw that the two old boys who usually sat there had reclaimed the bench. One of them waved sarcastically and the police car toot-tooted in reply as it pulled away.

Ray checked his watch again. Jackie was now very late.

Mighty was back in the van, squirting some aerosol cleaner at a glass case with rolls and sandwiches and small pieces of green plastic parsley in it when Ray shouted over to ask if she would mind giving Jackie a call on her mobile. He didn't need to tell her the number.

'Tell him not to forget those shirts. And the videos for tonight,' Ray said. 'Oh and my new socks.'

'You two,' Mighty said, screwing up her eyes to look at the illuminated panel on the phone. 'The pair yiz. Warra yous like.'

2

Jackie had been in traffic snarl-ups all morning. The roads around Rusty Lane, the former mining village five miles north of the city, where he lived, usually deserted at that time of the year apart from the hourly 'hopper' buses and the occasional muck-encrusted farm vehicle, had been filled with activity connected to the out-break of foot-and-mouth disease. The first case had been reported not many miles away just six days earlier, and foot-and-mouth confirmed as a national emergency – an almost certain catastrophe, with millions upon millions of sheep and cattle facing slaughter – on the Monday of that week. Now it was Wednesday, and the countryside was awash with representatives of the many agencies who had been given the task of shutting it down.

Jackie had been prevented from taking his turning at Townfoot by a convoy of transporters bringing in temporary barrier fencing. Traffic on the coast road had been brought to a halt by a wagon carrying disinfectant footbaths and sprays that had spilled its load. The road was covered in a convex pearlescent green slick which turned into a scum of evil yellow bubbles where it drained off the ragged edge of the road surface, steaming into the ditches. Seagulls circling overhead were reflected in it, and the long stratus clouds in the sky. Road maps were open across the steering wheels of most of the backed-up traffic. Nobody seemed to know where they were going, or where they were.

The first indication Jackie had had that the day would call for a change of plan was when he walked the dogs down to the stile at Stantonfence which usually took him on to the Lonnings, the old opencast workings, and then down along Bassett Burn into the woods. There was a plastic-wrapped 'DO NOT ENTER' sign on the stile and a barrier made of wide black-and-yellow caution tape. The sign was dense with writing like a pamphlet about Jesus and antiquated-looking in its lack of design. And Jackie was reading the small print enumerating the reasons for the footpath's closure, the murderous transmittability of foot-and-mouth, and the serious consequences of ignoring the warning when Telfer the shepherd lifted his leg against the hawthorn hedge where they were standing and Jackie remembered too late to try and take a sample in the scoured-out margarine carton that he was rather self-consciously holding. The idea was to get it down in time to catch enough urine to transfer to the small plastic bottle he had in his pocket. The dog had anyway toppled over when his other leg failed to support him and ended up in a disconsolate, sorry-looking mess on the ground.

Telfer was one of two Belgian shepherds who were usually left to guard Bobby's overnight; Ellis was his working partner, and over time the two dogs had grown inseparable. At four years old, Telfer was the younger by two years. But a congenital condition had caused the tendons of his hind legs to contract, and as a result he sometimes had to half drag his legs behind him. He didn't seem to be in pain and it wasn't irreversible; with surgery the tendons could be cut and lengthened, and that had been due to happen in a fortnight. But then recently Telfer had started spotting blood. Jackie had noticed it on the floor of the yard at the club, and then he had seen blood beading blades of grass the dog hovered over on their walks. The vet had asked Jackie to bring a sample in, and he was intending to deliver it that morning before picking Ray up at the Park.

Jackie's own dog, who lived permanently at the house, was Stella, a small rough-haired terrier from a long working line bred originally for catching rabbits and ratting. 'As in the lager, not the song,' Jackie would tell anybody who asked him why he had given a girl's name to a boisterous, apparently normal young male dog. (By 'the song' Jackie meant 'Stella by Starlight', one from his own era that he used to slow dance to at Johnny Cooney's and the London in the old East End and, later, at the Café Anglais when Harry Roy's band was resident, and Jo Longman's Club du Cinq in Paris. In the end, somewhere deep, deep down – too deep to usefully fathom: a sweet unsignalled and unexpected piano run; a pretty smell; a never-known or long-forgotten association – the song was probably the real reason for Stella being called Stella anyway. It was a joke that he was stuck with.)

Jackie had been a boxer. He bore none of the obvious signs of being an old pug – some slight build-up of scar tissue around the eyes and the almost imperceptible drooping of one eyelid due to the dead nerve in the lid (this was more pronounced in pictures and when he had had a drink) was all he had to show for his career in the ring. But most people were able to guess without being told that that was what his background had been. Boxing as 'Nipper' Jackie Mabe, first as a featherweight and then latterly as a 'lightie' in the lightweight division, he was still only about half a stone heavier than his best fighting weight of nine to nine and a half stone. He gave the impression of compactness and solidity at the same time as being light and quick on his feet. Like many boxers, his hands were surprisingly small and, because of the years of being steamed in gauze and leather and sweat, unexpectedly soft. The letters 'WORK' were still just visible, tattooed on the knuckles of his right hand; 'PLAY' was tattooed across the knuckles of his left. His hair had faded to a pale nicotine yellow, but he still wore it combed back at the sides and nodding forward at the front in a cheerful cockateel quiff.

'You were on the floor so often you should have a cauliflower arse,' Ray used to joke Jackie. ('If bullshit was music, you'd be a brass band' was Jackie's habitual comeback to this. Either that, or:

'If your life was a fight they'd have stopped it by now.' The two things that people often remembered best about Jackie were the lack of deference he was prepared to show that star of stage, screen and the labour exchange, the great Ray Cruddas, and the strangulated high pitch of his voice.) But the truth was that Jackie was good. Gaining his licence at the age of fifteen in 1945, although claiming to be a year older to comply with British Boxing Board of Control rules, he had made a more than promising start. After 43 fights his record read: 37 wins (18 by KO), 5 losses, 1 draw. He had given boxing a try and had, as *Reynolds News* and the old *Mirror of Life and Sporting World* (Jackie's favourite literature) would have it, 'been caught in the fistic net'. And then in a split second it was (Jackie liked to say) Goodnight Vienna. 'Curtains. Boof! All over. Goodnight Vienna.' He was twenty-one.

Jackie had started walking back from Stantonfence in the direction of the village. Telfer and Ellis, used to spending their lives cooped up, and unpredictable in traffic, were on short leads; Stella was free and running on ahead, stopping every so often to throw his head back and bark at them with what seemed a mixture of jealousy and delirious impatience. The day was cool and grey, with the long grey clouds moving slowly against the grey sky. There was a chance of rain, with bright periods forecast for later.

All three dogs took it in turn to leave their mark (the younger shepherd just managing to remain upright this time) against the zinc dustbin that had been put outside the main gate at Nettle Hill Farm for the benefit of the postman (somebody had written 'POST' on the lid). A second notice had been fixed to the gate: 'PLEASE KEEP OUT. WE ARE NOT CONTAMINATED. WE WANT TO KEEP OUR ANIMALS.'

Stella was standing at the corner of Half Nichol Street with his tail whirlybirding nuttily in circles, waiting for the signal to tell him whether to continue straight on or turn right into what was known locally as the Settlement. Old Nichol Street, New Nichol Street and Half Nichol Street were narrow cinder alleys cutting between rows of miners' cottages. The Settlement was the oldest part of Rusty Lane. Jackie lived in the new part of the village along with most of the other 'blow-ins' in a modern development called Manor Grange (or 'New Kennels' to the locals, after a large sign with fluorescent arrows that had gone up on the trunk road pointing traffic in the direction of Jackie's estate. The developer's 'traditionalizing' elements at the New Kennels – cast-iron foot scrapes, decorative cobbles, 'Victorian' street lamps incorporating a make-believe flicker – had also been the target of considerable mockery.)

There had been two pits in Rusty Lane, but they had both been closed for over twenty years. The pit rows in the Settlement, once tithed to the colliery, were now occupied by retired miners and families with close mining connections. Without the renovations of recent years, the cottages would have been museum pieces. (Identical cottages from a nearby village had in fact been transported brick by brick to an open-air theme-park museum, where they formed part of a hands-on interactive display.) The cottages had had temporary-looking, semi-prefabricated structures added on front and rear: new kitchens and bathrooms at the back; glassed-in porches erected around the existing front doors. And, after the now nearly unimaginable privations of their predecessors, the people who lived there were proud at last to be able to consider themselves modern. The porches, which were sun-traps, were showcases for all styles of resort furniture – fatly padded recliners and loungers, and wrought-iron and bamboo occasional tables and sofas. Tinkling wind chimes were popular, as were tweeting budgerigars and lovebirds in domed cages. Many houses had vertical swivel blinds at the windows and most had a black, colander-like satellite dish probing the ether for sport and films round the clock.

What Jackie was always most struck by when he walked through the Settlement, though, was the way relics of the old industrial past had been reassigned a new use as hanging baskets and planters. All summer, French marigolds and nasturtiums and petunias frothed out of Davy lamps and pitmen's helmets. Love-in-a-mist and sweet william grew in the old rusting tubs that half-blind, bow-legged ponies had once pulled along the tunnels of a busy underground town. (The ponies would be tossed on top of the coal and hauled to the surface themselves when they had outlived their usefulness. Jackie had heard tales of them being shot *en masse* in the fields of Nettle Hill Farm after modern mining methods had made them redundant, and bulldozed into mass graves.) Strangest of all, pairs of pit boots that had once been put to warm against the kitchen fender in preparation for the beginning of a cold night shift were now home to busy lizzies and hardy annuals in a few of the Settlement gardens: it was as if the owner of the boots had been detonated out of them, like a scene in a Buster Keaton film, leaving a straggle of flowers instead of trouser tatters and trails of curling cartoon smoke.

The prettifying of industrial relics – turning miners' helmets and steel-toe-capped boots into garden ornaments – was only a domestic version of the glut of ambitious landscaping and reclamation projects that had been instigated in the countryside around Rusty Lane in recent years. In this process, the scars of the mining past had been flooded with ponds and lakes, and planted with meadows and saplings. The slag heaps from the twin collieries had been levelled off and grassed over (and in the case of the spoil heap at the Lee, turned into a dry ski slope); the railway line the coal wagons had trundled along was now a nature trail; the headgear for the main shaft was a picnic area complete with a flushing toilet and scribbled-on, but as yet relatively unvandalized, comprehensively illustrated information panels. (Herons and bitterns, little ringed plovers and reed warblers had come back to breed at the recently established deep sump lake.)

The countryside around Rusty Lane was blistered with man-made hills filled up with hundreds of tonnes of household rubbish and organic waste, where sheep and cattle grazed on the lower slopes. Vast tracts of disturbed land had been designated a Heritage Park. An unnerving silence lay over the area, whose new orderliness and cleanness, although representing a kind of progress, struck the people who had lived all their lives there as queer.

Before they reached the end of Half Nichol Street, Jackie called to Stella to come so he could put him on the lead. There were two horses on the scrap of spare ground at the end of the street, and the dog had yapped around worrying them in the past. Stella didn't want to come and thought about it for a minute, but then did, with his tail down and his haunches low in submission and his belly almost scraping the ground.

The horses were piebalds, and they were tethered by heavy clinking chains, morosely cropping the thin litter-strewn grass. Rusty Lane was situated on a high ridge in sight of the coast. Sea coal from the coal seams that rose in the sea-bed was washed ashore all along the coast there and the horses were used to collect this in little carts. Blue plastic sacks lined with coal dirt had been split and opened and tied over their backs. They followed Jackie and the dogs gravely through their milky eyes and their curled pale lashes as they passed.

Jackie kept all the dogs with him as he skirted behind some modern school buildings at the edge of a playing field. He faintly heard a chord struck on a piano, then children's voices singing, and the dogs in the nearby (canine) New Kennels baying for their morning feed; he tried to avoid starting the dogs off by not slamming his car door hard when he got home from Bobby's in the middle of the night. Two-thirds of the way down the field, behind the metalwork room, which was emitting the smell of a coke fire and melted solder, a hole had been torn in the wire mesh fence. It would have been easier to let the dogs off here, but there was a lane on the other side of the steep embankment that cars (driven by buzzed-up, showing-off ex-pupils) sometimes came tearing along too fast. Jackie put his foot through the fence on to a pile of cigarette ends and had to shoot a hand out to stop himself falling when the dogs started trying to scrabble all together to the top of the denuded muddy bank. When he was satisfied there was nothing coming he let them go, and followed them across the lane and over a stile on to a footpath which, as he suspected, the men from the Ministry hadn't been able to get to to rule out of bounds yet.

Jackie still had the margarine carton inside his jacket. And when Telfer, who had quickly lost ground to the others, tentatively lifted his leg against one of several dozen blue plastic tree tubes that this part of the field was bristling with, he grabbed his chance. He transferred the unhealthily sluggish sample to the plastic bottle and buried the carton in nearby bushes while Telfer hobbled away in pursuit of Ellis and Stella, who had hared off in the direction of a perfectly bone-shaped pond, developed from a settling pond used to trap silt from rainwater run off during open-casting and newly colonized by dragonflies (an illustrated board explained all this). Telfer's rich sable tail was tucked miserably into his blond hindquarters and he was moving in a way that couldn't help but remind Jackie of himself.

There was an old saying among the fraternity of punchateers: First your legs go, and then your money, and then your friends. Jackie's legs had gone and his career had hit the buffers in another age, on another planet, more than half a century earlier, on the night of 11 December 1951.

It was in a British lightweight title eliminator at the Empress Hall, Earls Court. He was on the undercard of Arthur Danahar vs. Omar Kouidri. His opponent was Alby Ash, a Hackney plumber who boxed under the name 'Kid Bostock'. Jackie knew he wasn't fit at the time of the fight, but he was boracic, as everybody seemed to be in those days, and needed to be earning. Six weeks earlier he had been doing some sparring with the European and Empire featherweight champion, Al Phillips, who was known as 'The Aldgate Tiger', at Jack Solomons' gym in Soho, his home from home, when Jackie had felt his knee go. He felt it pop. But he had kept on going and afterwards the Tiger had taken him downstairs to the billiard hall, where there was a coffee bar, and bought him a cup of tea, a cheese roll and five Woodbines. The next day Jackie had been back for more punishment, and a couple of weeks later had even sparred for two rounds and eight pounds with Sandy Saddler, the featherweight champion of the world. In the run-up to the eliminator with Alby Ash, instead of resting the knee, he had punished it by running up and down the terraces at West Ham's ground at Upton Park, where one of his hundreds of cousins from the Fens had signed papers as a junior. He spent hours alone on the terraces, high-stepping up and down, punishing himself; up and down.

On the night, he began by giving Alby Ash a boxing lesson and was ending by handing him a large-size hiding when, about a minute into the fourth round, he threw a left hook at the hapless Hackney plumber. Jackie's foot got caught on something loose in the canvas. His body went with the punch but his leg didn't move. His knee made a terrible pop, and split like it had been sawn in half. He got up and kept hopping on one knee, throwing punches. And then he blacked out. They took him off on a stretcher. The cruciate ligament was torn and repair proved to be out of the question. The hospital operated on the medial as well as the cruciate ligament, and his leg was set in plaster from the ankle to the groin, with the knee in a bent position. That's the way it had to be for three months. But at the end of that time Jackie knew it was over for him, even if other people didn't. He remembered

44

telling Mr Solomons, who was his manager, of his belief that it was all over. Mr Solomons was rotating a cigar between his lips to light it evenly. Jackie heard the *sip sip* of his pull on the cigar and watched the flame flare up on Mr Solomons', the very powerful operator's, cheeks and brow. Naturally Jackie was tearful. It was a difficult moment. But Mr Solomons stood and walked over to the fan-backed green-leather club chair where Jackie was sitting and kissed him lightly first on one cheek, and then on the other. Jackie felt the yellow tea-rose Mr Solomons habitually wore in the buttonhole of his jacket touching his face. When Mr Solomons had kissed him on both cheeks he also kissed him lightly on the top of the head. Jackie understood this to be a kind of anointing, and so it proved.

Jackie's duties from then on might have involved only gym-bum duties and general dogsbodying, acting as bucket-and-sponge man on fight nights, seeing to it that Mrs Solomons and her party had everything they needed before and after fights (Mrs Solomons was a champion eater and always required three hot-dogs, one before and two after, with a triple serving of onions with each dog), but Jackie was *mishpochah. Kosher*. Jackie was family, and into the bargain a well-respected, fondly regarded lifetime member of the fraternity of the thick ear.

(A strange postscript to this affair was that, although his immediate family was allowed in to visit Jackie at the hospital, Tina, his wife at the time, didn't appear. Tina was a vivacious bubble [bubble-and-squeak = Greek] who waitressed for her father in his café in what Soho *habitués* knew as Frying Pan Alley. They had been married for only a few months at the time of the accident, but whenever Jackie asked about his 'child bride' [Tina was seventeen], they changed the subject. Eventually she arrived after about four, maybe five, days, and her normally dark skin was drained of all colour. Jackie attempted a joke about her looking paler than the sheet that was draped over him. But she floored him with something he'd never expected to hear: 'I'm afraid I've had a miscarriage.' He hadn't even been aware she was pregnant. 'Well,' Jackie would say when he related the story in later years, 'you didn't ask at that time.')

Jackie hated everything about getting old. The twinge in his knee was something he had come to be more conscious of, and his limp, although still only slight, had become more noticeable now than when he was a younger man. When he breasted the hill, he saw Telfer limping towards the lake and he could see Ellis was in the lake making contrails on the otherwise still surface with Stella tearing up and down the foreshore but staying well clear of the water. There was a wood beyond the lake with a dry stream-bed path leading uphill to Back Church Lane and the village.

This was land that had been repeatedly mined, cultivated, stripped bare and restored for three centuries. There had been an aerial ropeway bringing coal from Spylaw Colliery to the screens at Rusty Lane 2, a distance of over three miles – 32 tonnes of coal an hour, 23 hours a day. Its high pylons had marched across this field, but there was no sign of them now. Now the blades of a row of tall white wind turbines turned in unison in the distance, churning the wind. The lake here had originally been formed by subsidence. Then it broke through into old mine workings and, after an interval of many years, the lake had been relined with red clay and refilled. When the clay had been laid it was pressed into place with the revival of a tradition dating back to the first Industrial Revolution. This involved driving a herd of cows up and down and around the lake basin until, like the case for a muslin-wrapped suet pudding, it was judged watertight and uniformly thick. There had been a carnival-like atmosphere on the day the cows had been brought to do a job at the lake, pounding down footprints like fish scales that might still be there, and people had travelled from miles around to see it.

The interpenetratedness of the life that had been lived under

46

ground for generations and the modern lives currently being lived above ground was something that was constantly making itself felt. The previous summer large numbers of homes in Rusty Lane had had to be evacuated when polluted mine water from the old mines flooded the main street, slicking it ferrous orange. More recently a pensioner had died from inhaling stythe – mine gas pushed to the surface and expelled by the rising rank water. Jackie was always aware that wherever he walked there were complex networks of roadways and tunnels below him where day after day for a hundred years men had gone to work in the closed body of the earth.

Much in the way that Ray, in his new commitment to being more outward as a person, had fallen right in with the regulars at the Scran Van, so Jackie, blow-in as he was, felt a strong affinity with the former coal-hewers and tub-menders he was obliged to rub along with at this latest (quite possibly the last) staging post in his life. Just as he had been marked up by his job, so they carried the marks of theirs in the form of missing fingers and eyes and coal dust worked into worm shapes and spirals and blackly fused with the contours of old accident scars under the skin.

One day, flicking the pages of a Spanish-language pin-up magazine already hundreds of customers old while he waited his turn at Barnet Fair, the barber's over the pork shop in West Allen, Jackie had fallen into conversation with a retired pitman, one of the old school who liked to be shaved with a freshly stropped cut-throat razor and expected to have the stiff hog hairs on the meat of his ears and at the base of his neck burned off with a wax taper. 'If I was fowty years younger, lad,' the old pitman had said, indicating a black model in Jackie's magazine who was bending over a cocktail counter with a hot-pink thong pulled up in the cleft of her buttocks and smiling over her oiled ebony shoulder at the camera, 'aa'd give haw some stick an' aall, divven worry aboot that.' They had gone on to talk about this and that – changes in the district, the number of teenage pregnancies and crack dealers and the unemployment, always chronic and getting worse – and then by way of nothing the old pitman had suddenly said, 'There's nothing as dark as the darkness down a pit, the blackness that closes in on you if your lamp goes out. You'd think you would see some kind of shapes but you can see nothing, nothing but the inside of your head. The darkest place on orth.'

Jackie had turned and looked at the man's head and wondered about the darkness in it. The customer in the barber's chair with the plastic sheet tented up to his chin and the Kleenexes stuffed in his collar gave him a strange look in the mirror then. The old man's cranium stuck out quite unpleasantly far at the back. Jackie noticed the faintest trace of a scar, like the tramline on a tennis ball, just beneath his already short silver crop. He remembered a fight of his where the outcome had been about sixty staples in his head, and his head had been half shaved and swollen. All he could think about was looking normal again.

He had got caught in the first round of the fight and didn't box the same after that. To begin with, he thought he was just having a bad day at the office. But they let him out for the twelfth and he got hit with three or four shots straight away, and then, when he went down, he knew there was a problem. He began to experience the dull euphoria, that carelessness, the giggly incomprehension. He thought about that: the blackness that closes in on you if your lamp goes out. 'In boxing,' Jackie told the old man, 'they say when you get hit and hurt bad you see black lights – the black lights of unconsciousness.'

'I think everybody should go down the pit at least once to learn what darkness is,' the customer who was currently in the chair said, belligerently, as if Jackie hadn't spoken. The man had had his hair washed, which didn't happen at Barnet Fair very often. His face was still blotched and raw-looking. He had backed up to the sink and Tony, the owner, had worked up a lather on his scalp, and then massaged it and rinsed it, cradling the man's neck in his arm, expertly sifting his hair through his fingers, and Jackie had reflected on what an intimate thing this was to happen. 'Are yi on a promise the neet like, Norman?' the older man had asked, and the man called Norman had winked back at him gruesomely in the mirror.

Jackie had grown up knowing the curious close intimacy of the gym and the training camp, the camaraderie of the changing room. On a number of occasions, gloved up and ready for a fight, and finding he needed to make another visit to the bathroom, he had had to rely on somebody from his corner to do the necessary for him, to aim him, to wipe him like a father tending a child. In one fight his second, a man he trusted more than his father, had been forced to lance a swelling under his eye with a razor blade and suck out the clotting blood to save him from blindness.

The longer he had lived in the village the more Jackie had become aware of the parallels between the two old, virtually extinct, worlds of the pits and boxing. In both worlds there was the ever present possibility of unexpected and violent death. And the continual presence of danger made the physical and instinctive contact between men very highly developed. It also brought them together to drink. Then as now champion boxers used their prize winnings to buy public houses, which usually proved their ruin. It is the way with a lot of fighters, as Jackie hardly needed to be told: he had seen it all, and many times over; from the Café Royal and the Regent Palace to sleeping rough and drinking wine at bonfires. He had seen men he could remember being as quick and sleek as greyhounds blotto on boiled-up shoe polish and flagons of cheap scent. Up from the carnival booths and back to the booths and the only end then being a pauper's grave. Most fighters led foolish private lives.

'Taking the cage down into the pit and being lamped in front of two thousand people,' Jackie had said in the barber's that day, speaking aloud something he'd only just thought, 'they're both about going into yourself. You can never be sure you're going to like what you see.'

Ellis was still wet from the lake and leaving a trail of water behind him all the way up the path through the woods. Telfer was lagging behind, limping, and Stella had also developed a limp which disappeared as soon as Jackie used his finger to prise out a stone that had lodged itself in the pad of one of the terrier's shilling-sized front paws. Jackie looked at his watch: 10:11. A time of the morning when, back in the years of full employment and never-had-it-so-good when you could job-hop on a whim, not many men would be around. Ray and Jackie had always been aware of their unusualness in that – of keeping hours not usual for a man. Of keeping hours *inappropriate* for men is how they sometimes used to feel, especially in the northern industrial towns where masculinity was identified with grime and hard graft and Jackie would stop the car at a chemist's to stock up on things they needed (razor blades, make-up remover, Vaseline – his purchases were often far from hairy-chested), or at a baker's for fresh rolls for their lunch, and experience a sense of unease at being the only man at large in a landscape entirely populated by women. In an area where nearly half the men were 'economically inactive' though, as they were around Rusty Lane and West Allen, Jackie had no reason to feel out of place at all.

His watch was one he had had for many years, with an anti-quated, slightly unsteady digital display. He pushed the button and the digits went from green to orange: 28:02:01. And back to green again: 10:12. He knew that Ray would be standing at his bedroom window with his breakfast by now, taking in the pass-ing show on the Moor. He knew that he would be showered but unshaved and in a grump because of the horse manure, as Ray never failed to refer to it, that was in the diary for the afternoon (a decision on new carpet tiles, wrinkles in the new rota-shift system to iron out, the meeting with Alan Harries, the former outside left known to supporters as 'Gladys', to discuss pool table revenues and wet sales). Jackie knew all this because it was his job to know it. And yet he also knew he was going to call Ray (it was now 10:14) the way he did at exactly this time every morning to make double sure he was up and about. But he felt his heart lurch when he reached around to the part of his belt where he normally carried his mobile phone and realized instantly the phone wasn't there. He felt the blood rush to his face, and then he felt it ebb away again as soon as he remembered he'd left it behind at the house to get some juice in it because his *shtarka*, shit-for-brains DJ son Barry had been speaking on it and texting on it and playing zombified games on it all night.

Barry was a 'mixmaster' or 'trancemeister' DJ, according to the druggy clubbing magazines with, to Jackie, incomprehensible titles like *XLR8R*, which he left scattered around the house. The captions to the pictures in these magazines – Barry 'bang on it'; Barry 'really having it off' – identified him as 'Jaxon', which was how he was known professionally and to his loyal followers in the house and techno clubs that apparently (it was true, but Jackie found this personally hard to believe) were always a sell-out whenever he appeared.

'Jaxon' was what Barry was also called by the under-age girls Jackie had started to find at the house. He had arrived back from work at three that morning to find a sharp-spined, skinny figure curled up asleep on the sofa in the living room and a local girl he had seen around sitting up at the table with Barry. Their thumbs were working overtime on the pads of their respective phones, and their eyes were out on stalks. Playing low in the background was music that seemed to incorporate church organ music and baby gurgles with crowd chants and the bloops and bleeps of a nuclear power plant or a NASA launch; at intervals this was punctuated with a line of commentary from a natural-history film – *When lava flows underwater it flows differently* – and Hannibal

Lecter's sibilant *tssss-tssss-tssss* salivating-over-human-liver sound.

Barry Mabe was thirty-seven, and as much of a stranger to his father as his father was to him. After an ill-judged night in a private London square with a woman and another man, he had been arrested and charged with rape (which he denied). After two-and-a-half months in Wandsworth Prison, he had been given police bail and had then immediately fled northwards to his father's house to 'chill' until the trial. For the first six weeks he had shut himself away in his room, where he guzzled Coco-Pops and illicit chemicals ('the illicits' as he called them) and took care to make sure that, even when he was wearing headphones, all the walls pounded evenly with a deep blood pulse to relentless pro-grammed music, like an artificial lung. He had emerged under cover of darkness in those first weeks only to take possession of the telephone and to have his weekly shower. So the current state of affairs, give or take the odd teenage crackhead and schoolgirl runaway, as far as Jackie was concerned, showed movement in the right direction from there.

An hour earlier when he'd left the house, Barry and his little friend had still been up and wide awake. A grainy, black-and-white documentary about shipbuilding was on the television, with Barry twiddling knobs and spinning decks, spinning the records back, chop-mixing them to supply his own soundtrack of electronic bleats and cascading strings. Interspersed with these were gales of recorded drunken laughter and a man's voice intoning the same words over and over – *'s all for this time seeee you next time 's all for this time seeee you next time 's all for this time seeee you next time* – which Jackie of course knew was Ray taken from his live in-performance video, *Ray Cruddas Live at Bobby's Back Yem.*

As Jackie and the dogs emerged from the woods into Back Church Lane he saw that white-overalled officials from the Ministry of Agriculture, Fisheries, and Food – it announced this

52

on a sign attached to the side of a rented van: 'MAFF' – were in the process of sealing off the path. They were holding back the tape to allow an elderly man to transfer some bottles from the basket on the handlebar of his old bike to one of a row of big metal recycling bins as Jackie approached, feeling like somebody going into the Nothing-to-Declare channel with a kilo of Chinese heroin hidden in a secret compartment in his suitcase. He knew he shouldn't have been in the country where he had just been walking the dogs. It was selfish and stupid, and one of the MAFF men seemed about to say something along these lines as Jackie cut through their little group, but the man in the white Baby-gro held himself in check at the last minute.

The route Jackie had taken had brought him in nearly a full circle around the back of the village. A succession of pale rendered bungalows on the main road screened off the houses of a pre-war council estate. The bank in the village was open only two mornings a week now, and the cashpoint that had been installed was protected by two metal reinforced-concrete bollards against the ram-raid attacks that were an everyday hazard round there.

Until recently there had been three shops in the village: one had been converted into a private dwelling, with witchy lace curtains across the plate window; another was an estate agent's. Most people did their shopping at the giant superstore a few miles down the motorway. Now there was just a Nice Price huddled behind metal grilles with coils of razor wire glinting on the roof. As Jackie stepped up to the door – the dogs were tethered to the broken-down remains of a horse trough – the door opened and a woman wearing a candlewick dressing-gown and carpet slippers came out clutching a four-pack of Scandinavian lager close to her chest.

Nice Price had been taken over by the Khans, and Mrs Khan, who wore the traditional vermilion mark in the centre of her forehead as well as bright lipstick and Western clothes, was sprinkling fish food into a large, floor-level plastic pond as Jackie came into the shop. The fish were clouded and lugubrious and rather sinister-looking, but the Khans had inherited them from the previous owner who specialized in koi and small household pets such as terrapins and gerbils, and the Khans, to the surprise of most of their customers, had kept this part of the business up. The back part of the shop was devoted to everyday hardware requirements and pets; the front part to groceries and confectionery. Jackie took his usual newspaper off the counter and walked over to the plastic Lottery lectern to do his lines for the Wednesday draw.

It was standing here the previous week that he had overheard three light-complexioned black girls and a darker black man he assumed was their pimp buying condoms, cottonwool, vodka and microwave meals. He had experienced the dull pang of excitement he'd imagined you'd get from writing something indiscreet or disgustingly explicit on a lavatory wall. He had gone close enough to smell the funky/musky scent of their skin and the stiffening gloop on their fruits-of-the-forest-smelling hanks of shiny hair and to establish that under their coats they were wearing bare midriffs and thin scooped-neck tops in February.

He tried to blank this from his mind as he handed Mrs Khan the Lottery slip and watched as she fed it efficiently into the machine. An inconsequential exchange on the chances of winning would have been in order at this point, but unusually Jackie had winnings to collect: £36 for matching five of the six numbers, to be divided equally between Ray and himself. Mrs Khan counted the notes on to the flat of his hand and beamed as she did so. Jackie folded all of the notes into his wallet apart from the five-pound note, which he handed back to Mrs Khan with a gesture that indicated it was for her.

'Good-luck money,' he said, when she took a step away from

him behind the barrier of the counter, aghast. 'Go on,' he said. 'It's a tradition. It's like . . . It's a present. I'm giving some of the luck back to you.'

But Mrs Khan continued to look alarmed and, he thought, even slightly afraid. 'Tell you what,' Jackie said then, anxious to bring their relationship back to its former friendly but always formal footing. 'I'll buy another five cards with the money and go evens with you if any of them come up. Then you'd never have to sell another hamster again, God willing.'

'You have heard the expression I am sure, Mr Mabe.' (She sounded the 'e', pronouncing his name 'maybe'.) '"Every man thinks God is on his side. The rich and powerful know he is."' Mrs Khan passed him the counterfoil with the numbers of his five new Lucky Dips. 'Be lucky,' Jackie said over the noise of the bell on the end of a strip of sprung metal that exploded into life when he jerked open the door.

The Miners' Club and Institute in Rusty Lane, a big building with a grandiloquent sandstone and granite Victorian façade, was somewhere Ray Cruddas had performed in the early fifties in sweetly old-fashioned light-entertainment concerts that had been recorded for radio transmission in the North of England only by the BBC. He had been the second-spot comic on bills that typically featured local choirs – the Low Fell Ladies' Choir, conductor Molly Peacock; the Shildon Youth Choir, conductor Harold Pletts – singing popular favourites such as 'Blow the Wind Southerly' and 'The Bells of St Mary's', and local songs like 'Bobbie Shaftoe' and 'The Bonnie Pit Laddie'. As he had grown in experience, and his producers had come to appreciate that he was a performer with channellable domestic charm rather than larger-than-life appeal, Ray had been allowed to act as compère at the shows, which were put on in different working men's clubs and miners' welfare halls in the area every week. Standing at the black coffin-shaped radio microphone in his penguin suit, over humming of 'The Stars Look Down', he would reassure audiences both in the hall and gathered round the radio hearth: 'Whatever the change these modern days may bring, there's no pleasure more lasting than that of voices combining in harmony. Tonight it's our privilege to present seventy girls who are as lovely to listen to as they are to look at. Under its conductor, Bill Armstrong, here's the Whitley Bay Girls' Choir.' And then Ray and the audience, in hearty unison: '*The people sing!*'

The Rusty Lane Club and Institute had been gutted and was currently undergoing conversion to loft-style apartments and studio flats. Manor Grange – the New Kennels – the estate where Jackie lived, was situated behind the Institute in an interlinked series of culs-de-sacs which, if viewed from above, would have formed a uniform star ratchet shape. The houses were small and semi-detached, with leaded lattice windows and white weatherboarded fronts. The front garden plots were postage-stamp-sized and unfenced, although Jackie's immediate neighbour (Barry's bugbear) had made a Japanese meditation garden with purplish washed pebbles and a set of jagged slate standing stones.

The house interiors had been fitted with a considerable amount of ornamental plasterwork and dado rails in the living rooms with timber panelling below and (usually) scumbled or floral-patterned wallpaper above. Jackie had some sepia mementoes of his fighting life hanging from one of the picture rails on yellow brass chains.

His house stood on a corner plot with a small wetroom just inside the back door where he normally left his heavy shoes and his old waxed jacket. He was just turning into the space at the side of the house when his knees collided with a running three-year-old in a Spiderman mask and a Superman outfit. This was OJ, sprog offspring of Barry's little gas-sniffer friend Eleanor, known as 'Choo-Choo', who Jackie knew had been sent round by Eleanor's mother to fetch her home.

'High-fives!' OJ turned and screamed at Barry, who had stood back to let the dogs rush past him and was following Eleanor along the path barefooted. 'Don't leave me hangin'!' OJ had his little hand up in the air and Barry high-fived him. OJ whooped with delight. 'Go some!' Barry shouted as OJ and his mother, who was bedraggled and a little unsteady on her feet, tottered off in the direction of home.

Inside the house, Jackie tried Ray on the phone although he knew he would be out on his run by then, and there was no reply. He disconnected his mobile from the recharging cable and noticed for the first time the small, sticky patch where, sometime during the course of the night, the phone had been put down in a pool of drink or had had drink spilled into it. It was something – another thing – he would have to go into with Barry, but not now. Barry was too much out of his tree, simultaneously dead-eyed and agitated, gnawing on the knuckle of a thumb, jaw muscles popping. He was wearing jeans with holes ripped at the knees and what looked like a white cabled county cricket sweater except that the solid band of colour around the neck turned out under closer study to be a pattern of hundreds of tiny inter-locking couples fornicating.

The video about shipbuilding that had been playing before Jackie left the house had been replaced by one showing muggers and robbers and other swamplife caught on police surveillance cameras: the pause button had been pushed and the screen was filled with angrily effervescing streaks and smudges. Barry flicked a switch on his keyboard. *Welcome, stranger, to the humble neighbourhoods*, a voice said several times, reverberated for several seconds, and then desisted. This was followed by gentle ocean sounds and a blast of screaming white feedback. Then a sample from what Jackie recognized as one of the monologues of Joyce Grenfell: *No, George, don't do that . . . G–g–g–georrrrrrge, don't do that.* Then nothing.

Barry, already calling himself 'Jaxon', had started out DJ-ing at the first acid-house parties towards the end of the eighties, never thinking that the simple act of putting one record on after another could take him where it had taken him. Up to that time disc jockeys had been regarded as the sherpas and pack animals of the music business – or as juke-boxes with chest wigs, as Barry liked to say. But the 'rave revolution' brought huge, instant changes, mostly reflecting how easy it had become to get ripped and wrecked and really messed up – 'Getting dressed up to get messed up' enjoyed some popularity as a slogan for a time – on increasingly ingenious permutations of drugs.

On more than one occasion Barry, who was always looking for ground on which to build a good relationship with his father, had tried to tell him that there were connections between the rave scene and prize-fighting in *its* pioneer days. Prize-fighting was unlawful, and zealous magistrates sometimes took considerable trouble to prevent matches being held and to arrest the organizers, Barry said. Important prize-fights might be widely advertised but the venue was announced only at the last minute, and the crowds were forced to race across the country, *exactly* (Barry argued) like acid-house parties in the nineties.

Jackie had protested, but Barry had stood his ground. He knew that several times his father had fought out in the open, once in a fight that was famous in its day. It took place in the meadows of the Isle of Ely in the flat country of the Fens where Jackie had grown up in an unruly sprawling family who much later had taken Barry in and looked after him when it was his turn. The fight had happened on a summer night at dusk with the twelfth-century crenellated towers of the Cathedral as a backdrop and naphthalene flares burning around the ring and stewards (some of them the welcomers and vergers of the Cathedral) with naphthalene-doused, bare-flame torches to guide people to their places on the bales of hay that had been brought in for seating in the darkling sweet-smelling pasture.

Barry had watched jerky ciné film of his father taken on that night, shadow-boxing in his corner as he waited to be called to the middle of the ring to touch gloves with an opponent announced as 'a good clean-living man and one of the gamest fighters to ever enter a ring'. (Jackie's footwork on that occasion by common consent was beautiful; his feet skipped sweetly; he moved lithely; he punched fast and hard and won a marvellous victory on points.) Barry had watched the flickering film of his father waiting for the call of 'seconds out' in a field on the watery edge of England, skipping on the spot, determined and muscled and very young, ducking and feinting and loosening up, all alone up there surrounded by family and neighbours and supporters who had come out together to cheer on 'Nipper', the local boy.

And Barry had been forcefully reminded of those images on the morning of his arrest, brought to a police station and ordered to strip naked and step on to the big square of white paper that had been opened on the floor and requested to jump up on the spot with first his legs apart and then his arms so that any debris or forensic evidence relating to the serious charge of rape (the woman's pubic hairs and imperceptible particles of skin and so on as well as his own) could be loosened and fall away from his body and be collected by the police doctor who was present throughout this humiliating ordeal, and witnessed by the female officer who was also in the room and the prying eyes and sniggers which he was sure – he was *sure* – lurked behind the mirrored strips of the fly-blown, nearly-wall-sized two-way mirror.

Instead of a sickle moon and a cooling breeze sifting over from Wicken Fen on to his sweating body and the admiration and even love of strangers that his father had enjoyed, for Barry only this: a fetid windowless room with dirty stain patterns on the carpet and waxy dirt and grease in the mouthpieces of the phones and his genitals providing mirthless entertainment for hidden strangers. As his unoffending (he was quite sure of this) penis slapped up and down and the black imprints of his feet blotted off on to the stiff white paper, Barry encouraged his mind to stray to a tale he had heard from many sources about his father on that faraway fight night in the Cambridgeshire fens. As the time approached to announce the fight, it was established that his father had gone missing. At first the powerful promoter, Mr Solomons, had put on a cigar and tried to look unconcerned. But as the time grew nearer with still no sign of the star of the evening, Mr Solomons and his partner in this venture, Mr Hulls, had begun blustering around, blowing their tops. Eventually, running out of places to look, Mr Solomons snuck behind the bales at the end of the meadow and approached the main turnstile. And there, lo and behold, sitting on the top of a gate, scanning the faces of the people as they came in, was the 'Nipper'. 'What the fuck are you doing here?' Mr Solomons yelled at him, which was unusual because Mr Solomons was not known as a yeller. But the relief at seeing Jackie was so great that the powerful promoter, usually as bland as butter and so affable he had become known to one and all as 'Jolly Jack', almost lost control of himself. 'I'm waiting for my pals,' Jackie said. He had asked permission to invite two boys from his village he had been at school with to see him fight, and was waiting to give them their tickets.

Barry had gone to be brought up in the same village, and the gang of his friends and cousins had made their personal domain the castle mound and the meadow and the monastic precincts that crowded in around the Cathedral. Entry to the Cathedral itself was free and unticketed in those days, and a trippy thing, especially in the summer they all first discovered mushrooms, was to loll around in the polished seats they called misericords and gaze up into the Gothic dome of the famous octagon, constructed from the largest oaks available in England, and get off on the exalted light and mote-filled space and the freaky colours of the probably prehistoric religious wall-paintings. There was a tall, table-top mirror on wheels to facilitate examination of the high-up artworks and ceiling frescos; you bowled it along the nave and looked down into the mirror instead of looking up for a view of what was directly overhead. And the best thing when you'd got a bit high was to stare down into the wriggling psychedelic depths with your spacey eyes until you believed you were really up there down in that lighted hollow lagoon, swimming with Judas and Jesus and all the Apostles.

Under the scrutiny of the arresting officer, Barry had continued to jump up and down, shaking loose all the unseemly evidence from his body, while he kept his eyes fixed on a certain tray of fluorescent light set into the suspended ceiling and in his mind in those direst circumstances travelled to Ely and the heart of the Cathedral and the timber lantern high atop the octagon and the small life-sized carving of Christ in Majesty that resided there, a representation of Christ drawing us upward towards Him, up and up and up and up, while our feet remain solidly on earth.

Barry had tried to convince his father that drugs and the drugging habit were now as English as fish and chips, but his father (no angel, it has to be said, and no stranger either in his younger days to the hit to be had from chewing the filling of a Vic nasal inhaler, or a bit of pot at the notorious all-nighters at Cy Laurie's trad-jazz Mecca in Windmill Street, in Soho) – his father wasn't having it.

'I've boiled up some chicken to give to Stella with some rice if you can manage that,' he said to Barry, as he gathered together his things in preparation for leaving the house to collect Ray.

'Cool.'

'I'm going to see if I can get this phone working in the car. I shouldn't be too late in tonight. Wednesdays are pretty slow.'

'Excellent. Whatever.'

The picture on the television had unfrozen and two men in

balaclava masks were staring up into the camera. Behind them people were lying face down on the floor.

Jackie, a young-looking older man who had known his way around a ring, had changed into a zip-up jacket and smart-casual light-grey slacks and trainers. The trainers, which he had acquired of course from 'Magpie' Jeff, were midnight blue with a pale blue plastic membrane like the veined surface of a haggis or blood sausage fused to the uppers.

On the television the villains were backing out of the door with their swag bag filled and their gun arms extended as if they were on television. Jackie could hear the shepherds quietly whining and whistling and sniffing in the space under the door. He heard their paws skidding frantically on the lino surface as he approached them, and was reminded that he had forgotten to pack the sick dog's sample when he saw several patches of nearly black blood on the marbled tile squares. He turned to go to the kitchen to bring water and disinfectant, but Barry was right behind him and he had brought both of those things already. 'Got it, Dad,' he said, trying to get a focus with his fathomless dilated eyes on his father. ''S fine. All sorted.' Stella tried to make a bolt for the door to follow them, but Barry grabbed him by his scrawny, chicken-thigh hindquarters and he let out a tired yelp.

The events of the morning had made Jackie late for his appointment with the vet. The practice was in the pedestrian shopping precinct in West Allen, sandwiched between a Cash Converters ('Your personal cheque cashed today and not banked for up to eight weeks – no credit checks') and Tanzmania. That part of the precinct was mainly tenanted by discount butchers' shops and pawn shops whose windows glowed dimly with sovereign rings and watches and other unredeemed pledge 'bargains' set out on nylon-velvet trays.

A disinfectant mat had been put down at the door because

Kevin Wilkinson, the vet, was on constant call in the current crisis and, in the days and weeks ahead, would relate to Jackie the horror stories involved in diagnosing and disposing of animals already suffering from, or judged to be in danger of catching, foot-and-mouth: the awkwardness of the marksmen waiting to be given the signal to begin the dirty work; the terror of the cattle, sensitive to the smell of death; the abjectness of the farmers and the farm families, forced to stand by and watch the work of several generations disappear on what were now officially designated 'Infected Premises' – 'dirty farms'.

Wilkinson had had to go out to a nearby farm that morning to condemn a dairy herd of 320 cows, and all his non-urgent appointments for the early surgery had been cancelled. The only other person waiting was a woman in a business suit with a blue-and-white plastic cat carrier on her knee who flinched visibly when Jackie came in with the big Belgian shepherd on a lead. But Telfer immediately cringed under Jackie's chair, reducing himself to half his normal body volume, and Jackie gazed for a while at the mosaic that had been made of the snaps that grateful customers had sent in of their happy pets. He heard a telephone ringing downstairs where the kennels and recovery cages were, and then a door slamming. The smell of Jeyes Fluid was sharp in his nose. He idly picked up a leaflet which was a police appeal for information relating to a recent rash of attacks in which a total of fifty racing pigeons had died after their feet were cut off for their identity rings; the police, it said, believed the birds were mutilated by teenagers, who wear the rings.

After a while the surgery door opened and a teenage boy came out with a schnauzer that had a plastic-bucket-like contraption around its head. Jackie motioned to the woman, but it became clear she was only waiting for her pet to be destroyed. She became too upset to be able to finish telling him this and the receptionist indicated to him to just go in.

'Let's have him up,' Wilkinson said, and once he had Telfer on the table inserted a thermometer into his rectum. 'Just hold his head. That's it . . . Good boy . . . He's a good boy . . .' The vet pressed his fingers deep into the tender places of the dog's stomach and a single bead of blood splashed on to the rubber coating the top of the table. There was an information poster about the procedures for obtaining a dog passport on the partition wall and Jackie let his mind wander beyond the wall to where presumably, even on a winter Wednesday morning, people in bikini briefs and goggles were kebabbing themselves on tanning beds and in stand-and-tan booths, imparting that golden glow which speaks of vitality and health and fends off the journey of degeneration and ruin the genes are pre-programmed to make – the phenomenon of your body dying while your mind looks on, wondering why it's all happening. 'All life is a process of breaking down.' Cancer, heart disease, arthritis, dementia: we gradually fall apart.

'I'd like to keep him in for a while and get some pictures done. I'd like to see what's going on in there,' Wilkinson said. 'Alrightee.' He opened the surgery door and called for the receptionist, whose name seemed to be Shirleen. He handed her Telfer's lead and the dog slunk silently away, turning briefly to give Jackie one last betrayed, beseeching look as he was led down the stairs and around a bend in the stairs and out of sight. Kevin Wilkinson had turned his attention to the now silently sobbing cat-carrier woman by the time Jackie reached the door. 'WE BUY, WE SELL, WE LOAN' a banner sign said on the opposite side of the precinct.

The accident involving the spillage of many thousands of gallons of disinfectant and the other hold-ups attributable to foot-and-mouth had all made Jackie uncharacteristically late. He had connected his phone to the cigarette lighter in the car, but it still wasn't working and so he had been unable to warn Ray about the delay. Less than two miles outside West Allen, traffic had been funnelled into a single slow-moving lane, and it had remained like that, bumper to bumper, most of the way.

Split up from his partner, Ellis had been restless and audibly unhappy in his space behind the dog guard, hyperventilating and changing position frequently with sighs and muffled hollow thuds. As far as Jackie could remember it was the first time Telfer and Ellis had been separated in their nearly four years together; it was why he had brought both dogs home to stay with him, rather than leaving Ellis alone to patrol the club. Now he worried about how the older dog was going to adjust, for the foreseeable future at least, to being on his own.

Jackie had switched the radio on briefly, and then switched it off again. Having Barry around had made him appreciate silence, and it was in silence that he stalled and hiccuped towards Ray.

A drive-through KFC with a modesty screen of plaited willow around it to protect the blushes of the suburb where it was sited was his personal marker for the beginning of the city. Then the tracts of new budget-opulent business parks; and then quite suddenly the tubular metal trusses of the football stadium rose importantly on the horizon and he knew he was nearly there, exactly an hour and ten minutes late.

There were only a few of the regulars camped outside the tea van when Jackie came to a halt at the place where a little while earlier the ambulance had been. Ray was on his feet and pacing, his blue baseball cap pulled low, his face grey and pinched in a way that Jackie had long ago come to recognize: Ray's do-you-know-who-I-am-this-had-better-be-good face. Jackie leaned across and opened the passenger door.

'Watch out, flower, he's worked up to top doh,' Mighty called to Jackie from the window of the Scran Van. She was laughing. 'Look at the face on it. Berra be careful the day mind, Jackie. He's got a face like a well-slapped arse.'

65

Ray got in the car and said nothing. After a while he twisted round and examined the collars of some shirts which were hanging under plastic covers in the back; his shirts went to the laundry every day because of the make-up he wore; they must never be starched. There had always been these rules: 23 sports jackets that he liked to have hanging a certain way, shirts that had to be carefully laundered and exactly folded, 21 pairs of shoes he insisted on lining up in a long, even row on the floor. He pushed aside a newspaper and a clipboard and some other clutter on the rear bench seat.

'I'm looking for socks. I hope you didn't forget the socks I asked you to bring.' Ray had a perspiration problem. Very bad foot odour, exacerbated by the trainers he had taken to wearing. He got through a lot of socks.

'I forgot the socks,' Jackie said, slowing at some lights. They were in one of the main shopping streets in the city centre and pedestrians coursed off the pavement on to the road, intent on their deep-filled sandwiches and good-intention, calorie-counter meals. It was the first day of Lent. The lights changed and Ray directed his attention to the front of the car and the phone which was still connected by a cable to the dashboard – Jackie's phone, claimable as a business expense, paid for by Ray. Ray put it against his ear and heard what he expected: nothing. He had spotted the gluey drink mark on it straightaway.

'Fucken Barry. Excuse me – "*Jaxon*",' he said. 'The sooner his frickin' trial comes up and they send him down the happier I'll be. Bang him up.' Jackie ignored this. It was nothing he hadn't heard before. They sat in the silence that they both regarded as the natural condition of them being together. The two of them could sit there together, saying nothing, savouring the darkness, as Dean Martin once said of himself and one of his close Cosa Nostra companions, of one another's solitude, in a silence more comfortable, and in a way more expressive, than conversation. They had evolved a way of communicating that didn't involve talk. When they were working, they were able to turn this to their practical advantage. For example, Ray playing with his tie indicated that a complimentary bottle of wine should be brought to that table; Ray toying with his pocket handkerchief indicated that there would be no bill; Ray running his hand through his syrup alerted Jackie to the fact that he wanted to be relieved from having to talk to the bores who had buttonholed him.

As they drove along Jackie dug into his pocket and brought out a tight ball of notes and coins which he gave to Ray.

'What's this?'

'Lottery. I thought I told you. We had five numbers come up Saturday. Another one and we would have had it away.'

Ray said nothing, but the mood of gloom that had been sitting over him lifted slightly. 'I've thought of a way to turn your Barry's frown upside-down,' he said eventually. 'Tell him the one about the acid-bollocks-for-brains-house DJ who was arrested for rape. He went on an identity parade and, as the victim was led into the room, your man shouted, "That's her!"' Jackie had heard it before. He knew it was originally about an Irishman, and a Polack in America. But it was still funny. Jackie could be Ray's best audience.

They drove on. It occurred to Ray for the first time to wonder about the dogs. With Telfer and Ellis both absent from the club overnight he had had to put an extra body in, at added cost. At the mention of his name, Ellis's tail thudded dully a few times against the hollow tyre cavity, and then stopped.

As they turned out of Trimdon Street on to the Quay, Ray wound his window down and looped the useless mobile over a line of parked cars with expert aim, arcing high and dropping clean into the river.

3

In turn-of-the-century New York it became fashionable to 'honour' the poor. At palaces on Madison Avenue and on Fifth Avenue overlooking the Park, the walls covered in red silk damask, old-master paintings glowing behind glass in heavy frames, people gave poverty balls. Guests came dressed in rags and ate from tin plates and drank from chipped mugs. Ballrooms were decorated to look like mines with beams, iron tracks and miners' lamps. Theatrical scenery firms were hired to make outdoor gardens look like dirt farms and dining rooms like cotton mills. Guests smoked cigar butts offered them on silver trays. One hostess, according to accounts written at the time, invited everyone to a stockyard ball. Guests were wrapped in long aprons and their heads covered with white caps. They dined and danced while hanging carcasses of bloody beef trailed around the walls on moving pulleys. Entrails spilled on the floor. The proceeds were for charity.

Mondays at Bobby's had a 'washday' theme: bed sheets, frequently darned and patched, and long-johns and lumpy elasticated knickers, similarly worn and darned, were hung low from washing-lines stretched across the club, and hatpins with gnarled decorative heads were provided to keep the 'washing' pinned back out of the food and the faces of the diners, who were greasy-chopped and fiery-eared and dressed in drab austerity suits and broken-nebbed caps and, in the case of the women, serviceable aprons and knotted Aertex turbans and other garb associated with the impoverished working class.

Bottles of white wine at Bobby's, on Monday nights as on every night, were brought to the table in handsome Edwardian chamber pots replete with gilding and transfer prints of the old King and Queen and the Royal Standards, and traditional old-rose patterns. Wine and beer were kept cooling behind the bar in pot-bellied zinc poss-tubs packed with ice. The heavy-headed wooden possers that would have been used to pound the dirty washing in the tubs, in dark backyards and poky sculleries, were also in evidence as part of the decor at Bobby's, along with three-legged crackets and clippy mats and several sets of heavy mangles.

None of this had been done, however, in an excessively knowing or cynical way, or in a spirit of mean parody. Ronnie Cornish, Ray's principal financial backer in the club, had had his own mother's well-worn mangle stripped down and reconditioned and installed in pride of place in the drawing room of the pilastered country mansion which his business success had bought him. The mangle – at which he had watched his mother toil, bringing her full body weight to bear on the broad wooden handle in order to inch leaden sheets all the way through the rollers, which over the years began to bear the imprint of this struggle, becoming withered and indented in the middle – this back-breaking washday aid, framed now by lofty casement windows and many metres of bunched and swagged William Morris fabric, had become the emblem of how far Ronnie Cornish had travelled: from respectable poverty to a home helipad, a Bentley Azure, local eminence and a quote he claimed was from Rudyard Kipling that always tripped easily off his tongue: 'Like he said, "You can play among princes, but always keep your feet on the ground." I don't forget where I came from.'

In this, Ronnie Cornish was no different from the hundreds who came to Bobby's every week to be reminded, when the circumstances of their lives sometimes seemed to be conspiring to make them forget it – the ninety-five channels, the call-waiting, the multi-tasking, the compound interest accruing on the credit-card bill – that they came from a specific place with a long history and a unique identity and were not in fact unrooted particulate individuals free-floating in infinite space.

It was the great rush to rediscover roots and the sedulous piecing together, in local libraries and over the Internet, of family trees that had originally given Ray the idea for a club that would celebrate a communal identity and a frankly romanticized Geordie past. The aim – in addition of course to getting the tills ringing and the profits flowing – had been to provide a place dripping with the texture and particularity that had been largely drained out of the modern world, and to allow the paying customers to reconnect with a missing vital part of themselves. People were no longer embarrassed about their humble origins, as they once were (as Ray had once been), but boastful of any connection they were able to make between themselves and their rough, long-disappeared proletarian backgrounds. 'My great-grandfather committed a murder on the Shields Road,' a man (admittedly well in his cups) had recently told Ray: well-dressed and well-spoken, he had tears in his eyes as he spoke.

In an unlooked-for development, which had caught the public imagination and garnered a good deal of valuable coverage on television and in the local press, the walls at the club had turned into a gallery of ancestor portraits brought in to be hung there by the clientele. Instead of the wall enamels advertising meat extracts and ointments, shoe blackings and hair oil that had been put up originally, the walls at Bobby's were now home to scores of vignetted portraits of bewhiskered fellows in stiff wing-collars and curl-brimmed hats, and ample women sharing the same stern, unwavering gaze – great-great-aunts employed as rabbit-skinners by a company that made hats for the quality of the city; the great-grandmother of a second cousin in a sandwich board advertising the suffragette journal, *The Common Cause*.

Every night at Bobby's brought people who had clearly come slumming; groups of businessmen, in particular, in the North for a bulling session or a sales conference, came prepared to smirk. But after half-a-dozen rousing choruses of 'Keep Your Feet Still, Geordie Hinny' or 'The Gallowgate Lad' and (especially) a dozen pitchers of Radgie Gadgie strong bitter, they tended like everybody else to be content to be cast back to a time when nobody spoke of 'community' and everybody belonged to one, and nearly always went away with a souvenir T-shirt or a video or a picture of themselves taken with the star of the show (£8.50 incl. de-embossed self-stand cardboard frame) at the end. Jackie was in charge of the merchandise, which he sold from a kiosk in the main foyer, where he was also occasionally asked, usually by a fellow former denizen of the boxing racket, to sign an autograph himself. Like most places of public entertainment, the club was cold and rather bleak-looking when it was empty. 'Sharp warms up when people come in, like,' Blanche, the general manager, would reassure new members of staff as they stood in the hangar-like, vaulted space with their collars up and their hands plunged deep in their pockets, watching Blanche's breath pluming in the twilighted darkness. Voices echoed in the building in those pre-opening hours and something like a clattering ladder detonated with the shock of an explosion, and even the old-stagers sometimes allowed themselves to be teased by the thought: What if no one ever came? What if all the customers of Bobby's had decided against it and found somewhere else to go in the future?

Normally it was a thought that could be immediately dismissed rather than morbidly chewed over. There was a thick bookings register made thicker by Post-its and business cards and elastic bands that Blanche fussed and clucked over, endlessly entering new names into it and rubbing old names out, briskly dusting the crumbs of rubber away with the heel of her hand. There was a bookings book and usually the book was full a month or so ahead.

But when she had got in just after ten that morning there had been messages on the machine from Bulls Hill Farm at Dunstan, and Emrick Farm at Yarm, cancelling their tables for that night. And all through the morning all the other farmers who had been coming in with their families for what was turning into a much-looked-forward-to, once-a-year occasion – Cleughfoot Farm, Cambo; High Highlaws Farm, Marlish; Startup Farm, Halt-whistle – had had to cancel their bookings on account of foot-and-mouth disease. (Blanche soon started to recognize the jumpiness in the voices and to appreciate that people were calling from already quarantined places where unknown, and possibly unen-durable, circumstances lay ahead.) By the time Ray arrived, the page for that day was striped with rulered black lines. There were still some private bookings for couples and small groups of four or five. But the only block booking remaining was for a party of sixty associated with the Ephphatha League of the Deaf, a social club exclusively for deaf-mutes. It had already been agreed that a signer would stand at the side of the stage during Ray's set, to sign the jokes.

'Candy is dandy but liquor is quicker,' Blanche said, poking her pencil into the airy pillow of hair at the side of her head.

'This should be interesting,' Ray said and headed for his dressing-room, where they both knew his first drink of the day – a generous Jack-and-ginger – would be waiting on the table by the sun-bed.

The club was a simple industrial shed, a part-brick, part-prefabricated structure on a small industrial estate on the western fringe of the city centre. With the 'BOBBY'S BACK YEM' illuminated sign switched off in daylight hours, Bobby's was indistinguish-able from the other small businesses – mainly body shops and one-man-and-a-lad grease-monkey outfits – that occupied the unexceptional plain shells. The previous owner had been a sanitaryware manufacturer, which gave rise to the inevitable jokes, in the early days when Bobby's was first being mooted, about pissing money up the wall and shit-for-brains and watching it all going down the pan. (To which it had since given Ray and his partners inordinate pleasure, whenever they ran into a disinvestor, to – with equal inevitability – go: 'Have a drink. Have a bottle. I'm feeling flush.' It was a line that Ronnie Cornish, in particular, couldn't hear himself saying loud or often enough.) The club's closest neighbours, separated from it by the car park on one side and a reinforcing wall of wire cages filled with rocks on the other, were Metal Morphosis, suppliers of quality jewellery and medical equipment for the piercing and tattooing industry, and Tip Top Light Vehicle Crash Repair.

Because of its exposed position on a bank high above the river, the fences on the industrial estate were constantly festooned with shredded plastic and rooted in an ever replenished build-up of refuse. Every day when Ray got out of his car he left instructions for Paddy the odd-job man to come with his broad broom and clear it away. And every day it was back, a deep drift of cigarette packets and rubber gloves and lager tins and syringes and dirty sculpted dunes of dog-ends, arrived, Ray could only suppose, on the wind. That day he had been able to ask Paddy to go and see to it himself: he had come across him on his way in, swilling out the row of brick toilets in the yard – the 'ootside netties' – which had originally been put in as a gimmick, but which had proved surprisingly popular, especially with women, who rhapsodized about the memories they brought back of lagged pipes and hanging icicles in winter and nipping in there late for a last cigarette and a snog. (And who, Ray had had pointed out to him, wrote far fruitier things on the walls than were ever found in the men's toilets.)

On arrival, Jackie had changed into his blue janitor's trousers and gone off to drain the dregs from the barrels in the cellar and stillage the beer that the brewery had delivered that morning. Ellis had crossed the yard, sniffed around for a long time in the place where Telfer would normally be, and retired miserably to his kennel.

It often seemed to Ray that he'd spent two-thirds of his life in a state of stupefied suspension, just waiting. Like everybody in his business he had evolved strategies designed to cope with the empty, dragged-out time leading up to the brief time – an hour and frequently less – when he had to be 'on' and performing. At the height of his popularity, when it had been difficult to go any-where without being recognized, he had whiled away the hours playing board games and endless hands of poker and rummy for matchsticks with Jackie. It was in the course of these long hours which turned into weeks and then years that they developed the ability to be alone together, *da lontano*. 'Success is a peculiar thing because you stop living,' one of the great stars of the day had told Ray when he was just starting to get a foot on the ladder. 'You don't tend to get into scrapes, and then where's your material? Things don't happen.'

At one point in his desperation Ray had even given needle-point a go, encouraged in that direction by Dora Bryan during a summer season in Weston. But he had quickly come to feel that he might as well be sewing mailbags for sixpence a day and a snout ration, and that was the problem with all the sedentary pastimes he'd dabbled in in the confines of his dressing-room cell: he felt like an old lag just noodling away his life until the parole board next met to decide that he continued to pose a threat to society and therefore to return him to his cell to go on rotting.

For one happy summer at Paignton on the 'Devon Riviera' he had learned the rudiments of bell-ringing from the theatre chaplain there. Most theatre chaplains, Ray had found, were just frustrated performers having to make do with camping around in their mitres and best frocks on Sundays, or elevated autograph-hunters looking for the sprinkle of stardust to rub off. But Pastor Bernard was a former communist agitator and organizer of flying

74

pickets who had been gathered in by the Lord, as he put it, during a spell in solitary in Armley Gaol in Leeds. Encountering Ray in one of his periodic lows, he had extolled the virtues of bell-ringing on the body and the spirit and had persuaded Ray to join him and his happy band on their ringing trips into the outlying countryside, when they would do three or four churches in a day – off the coach, up the cobwebby stairs into a bell tower with a resident bat colony and gaps in the unrestored tiles showing the sky, sending a carillon across the sun-baked fields and – best of all – no need to talk because it was impossible to talk inside the confined aeons-old space choked with dust and banging with noise. Ray learned to play the changes from Pastor Bernard, and the reverberations seemed to stay in his arms and in the air for a long while afterwards, making pretty little picture-postcard villages such as Berry Pomeroy and Stoke Gabriel and Ipplepen feel as lonely and desolate as the Bay of Funday and the river Hooghly. His back ached and his hands trembled when the ringers gathered round a table tomb for tea and biscuits after the last bell had been rung out, but he looked back on those months from the perspective of his later years as a time of almost total contentment.

Now that he was not so young Ray filled most of his dead dressing-room hours with routines connected to his health and his appearance. He was coming to learn, as so many others of his age had come to learn before him, that at no other time of life is existence so intensely physical. A small infarction caused by some interference in the blood supply and resulting in the right-hand side of his face going south for a week or two had brought on the jogging and a new, rigidly observed low-cholesterol, high-protein diet. (The admonitions about his drinking he was largely ignoring.) He took vitamin B12 complex in capsule form and six-teen drops of oil of echinacea in his second drink (ruining the taste but not the kick) and zinc and calcium supplements and put on restful music and lay on his sun-bed for thirty-five minutes every afternoon. He did a gentle work-out using leg weights and barbells. Jackie came in some time after that and massaged warm olive oil into his back, pressing into the flesh to find the knots of tiredness and stress. He had his remaining hair cut and coloured and blow-dried in a way that cleverly disguised its uneven thinning condition. It was washed and styled for him every afternoon by Julie, one of the front-of-house staff, who returned later to help him fix his hairpiece correctly and do a finishing comb-over at the sides and back to ensure that no joins were showing. Jackie, who knew to the millilitre how to pace him, kept drip-feeding him drink.

Calm and quiet, that was the idea. *The silence that is in the starry sky, the sleep that is among the lonely hills.* Except that today, all day, he kept having his quiet time eaten into by extraneous noise and interruptions and what he considered unreasonable demands on his time. The band was auditioning a new singer, which he had forgotten was going to happen, and so the soothing music on his CD was drowned out by a voice that could strip paint, belting out club concert-room standards like 'New York, New York' and 'Mack the Knife'. He had had to skip his massage when Alan Harries, the brewery rep, overran by nearly an hour, bending his ear with his tale of woe about how his wife was leaving him for another woman, the mother of his daughter's best friend, and how their affair had been going on for years under his nose without him realizing, de-dah-de-dah. (Jackie had got it in the neck for this. 'If he wants to talk, he should see a priest,' Jackie said. 'That's all you had to tell him.' 'Don't make me use rude obscenities, Jackie, you know it gives me indigestion.')

And then in the late afternoon he had had to jam his baseball cap on over his still-unpolymerized hair in an attempt to put out Typhoon Eddie, which was blowing through the kitchen. The chef, 'Eddie' Edmunds, was a big man in all directions, with a proud stomach and a broad red floreted nose which turned white when he got angry, which was often. (His nose had earned him the nickname 'Traffic Light' among the younger kitchen workers, a fact he didn't know.) He wore his thinning hair in a pony-tail-with-scrunchie with two fuzzy brackets of hair, which turned into lank *hasidim*-like ringlets in the wet heat, framing his ears.

Some of the waiting staff were folding cutlery into paper napkins and watching an afternoon soap on the big scroll-down television: the drilling Australian accents boomed around the empty room and even a door opening or closing cracked like thunder. 'Chef's off on one,' a voice called to Ray from out of the gloaming. But Ray could already hear him, roaring and erupting and violently banging about.

'Whichever yi lay yor hands on forst, hinny. Aa divvent mek a pet o' me stummick,' an elderly woman had said a few nights earlier when she was asked if she would be having the tripe and onions or the Tweed salmon. Her family and the waitress serving her had thought that was very funny, but when it was reported back to him in the kitchen Eddie Edmunds had just grunted that it was typical. The menu at Bobby's mainly consisted of cow-heel brawn, saveloy dips, leek-and-bacon roly-poly, sheep's-head broth ('the eyes will see you through the week'), stotty cake, pease pudden and other authentic local dishes which the chef took pride in preparing. But recently rumours had been flying about a plan to add the kind of eat-all-you-want Chinese hot table that was proving to be such a popular draw in the restaurants of Chinatown, and Eddie Edmunds had already resigned twice that month.

'Haddaway, man, I've enough meat here to feed the fucken five thousand and still have enough left over for half the Hoppins.' Eddie was fulminating by the pastry station in the centre of the kitchen. He was wearing a tabard top which was heavily, almost heroically, soiled, and red-and-white (his team's colours) chessboard trousers. Sweat coursed down the back of his neck into his collar; his strawberry nose glowed white. But while

Eddie continued to blow his stack, all around him was an oasis of uninterested calm: two acned youths were hunched over a board game that Ray could see was called 'Social Insecurity'; a dreamy, dark-haired girl was sitting cross-legged on the floor, caressing one of the satinized industrial surfaces with a mutton-cloth duster and baby oil; another girl – plainer, plumper – was idly pushing the orders carousel round and round with her finger.

'Whoa,' Ray said. 'Whoa there. *Whoa!* Hey, Eddie, why don't you just shut your mouth for a minute and give your arse a chance?' What was exercising Eddie, it seemed, was the fact that the wholesale cancellation by the farmers' group had left him with a meat mountain to get rid of. What Eddie couldn't say was that it was 'moody' meat bought off a pal for a fifth of the price he would claim for it and that it was already a day past its sell-by.

Ray talked a good fight. He had put-downs to deal with any kind of heckler situation or audience loudmouth. But he hated confrontation. 'Pagga! Pagga!' – the cry that went around the playground when a fight was brewing – had always made him feel physically sick as a boy. It set off a loud alarm in his fear centre, right in his gut. He could feel his heart race and his legs weaken underneath him; a dry throat and his heart going crazy. He felt that standing in the kitchen's thick-walled, room-size refrigerator where Eddie Edmunds had brought him, surveying the hanging carcasses of sheep and pigs, registering the blood smell in the air, listening to the generator fan running. He looked at the larded tattooed sides of beef and thought of Daisy and Dolly roaming Allotment Field, responding when their names were called, harried by dogs, mechanically cropping grass. And then his thoughts had turned to gory gangster films and heavies using beef carcasses as punch-bags and bodies hanging from hooks on moving pulleys, and at that moment somebody had started singing in the club.

Are you lonesome tonight?
Is your brassiere too tight?
Are your corsets just drifting apart?

He had noticed that Eddie was wearing wooden-soled clogs and that the tight cuffs of his trousers made his feet look like pig's trotters in them. He noticed the rime of sweat around his chef's paper hat and the pitted, grapefruit-like texture of his skin; the fact that his neck was thick with fat.

Are your stockings well laddered
And shoes wearing thin?
Do you keep up your knickers with a safety pin?
Are your teeth old and worn?
Do they slip when you yawn?
Then no wonder you're lonesome tonight.

Ray realized he had been gradually manoeuvred into a place where his view of the door was blocked and that the animal bodies hanging within a foot of where he was standing had residual hairs that you didn't notice from a distance and were giving off what seemed to him a sour bad smell. And he had just gained the impression that Eddie was about to snatch at his cap, exposing the even grid of scars that he had been left with as the result of an early, failed hair transplant (the crown of his head looked like a scrubbing brush that had been worn down to the wood and the stubbiest bristles – a domino with chickenpox, as Jackie described it), when he heard Jackie's voice in the kitchen and felt time whirr back up to real time and heard cheers and a smattering of ironic applause as the Presley impersonator – he had an idea it was one of the young waiters – came to the end of his song. '*Thankyouverramush.*' Something solid – a head or a hand – collided with the microphone, sending out a loud amplified crack followed by a squeal of feedback.

'Is everything OK here?' Jackie was standing with his legs

under him the width of his shoulders instead of spread wide and dug in, which is the mistake that many amateur fighters make. It was all about balance. Balance meant leverage; leverage meant speed; speed meant power. Jackie's strength as a boxer had always been in his determination, his courage, his will to carry on. It wore opponents down.

'I wanted to talk to the engineer, not the shitey rag,' chef said to Jackie, but in a way that indicated he knew the fun was over, and Ray had taken that as his cue to escape from the cold, back into the kitchen where the two boys were still bent over their game and the girl with the duster was busy examining herself in the dimmed surface of an oven and it was as if whatever it was that had happened inside the big chilled room had never taken place. The other girl had momentarily dis-appeared.

'I've got one forya on the mad-cow disease if you want,' the less crater-faced of the two crater-faced boys said to Ray when he was nearly out the door. He had turned red and his acne scars looked sore and livid. 'There's two cows in a field. One says to the other, "What d'you think of this mad-cow disease?" The other one says, "It doesn't affect me. I'm a fucken duck."' His friend sniggered, and the boy who had told the joke, exceedingly red now, sniggered as well. '*Fnarr.*'

'Eddie wanted to make it a BSE day,' the friend said. '"Bit of Something Extra".' And they were off again, laughing with their mouths closed so that their shoulders rocked and tears welled in their innocent eyes. They reminded Ray of the two fire-lighters on the Moor that morning, which was already beginning to seem an awfully long time ago.

'The mad-cow disease was last month, son,' Ray said, 'haven't you heard? Now it's the foot-and-mouth. But thanks, I might be able to find a way to use it, you never know. Thanks anyway.'

*

It was nearly dark by half past five when the 'BOBBY'S BACK YEM' sign stuttered into lurid life, colouring up the dusk. Its blue and yellow neon flourish could be seen from the other side of the river. At quarter past seven a switch was flicked and the tape of an old wireless programme from the palaeolithic age of radio started to be streamed as background into the club.

This is the North of England Home Service [a double-breasted BBC voice announced]. Presenting the people to the people. *Bob's Your Uncle*. Featuring Bill Robinson and the Northumbrian Serenaders in the songs that live for ever. [The sound of the Serenaders humming 'Roses of Picardy' swelled in the background.] And starring Bobby Thompson in the life and hard times of a plain working man as heard through the ears of his neighbours. Ladies and gentlemen, tossed on a sea of trouble stormy enough to wreck the happiest home, but riding it all with a nod and a wink, meet the comic in a million, Bobby T–

In his dressing-room, Ray rose and touched a button near the Tannoy speaker which faded out the sound of his younger, starchier, painfully ingratiating self, strangely isolated in time.

When he was new to the business and still wet behind the ears, Ray had broadcast with Bobby Thompson from many working men's clubs, works canteens, corporation halls and drill halls in the North East of England. And it had been his idea to name Bobby's after the Geordie comedian whose trademarks were a flat cap, a tab that was continually dribbling ash down his sloppy jumper, and a style of comedy that was rooted in his own hard upbringing during the twenties and thirties, when you had to fight for your bite, as the saying went. 'The Little Waster', as Thompson became known for his jokes about running rings around the rent man and the Assistance and life on the dole, was born in 1911 in the pit village of Penshaw Staithes in County Durham, and in a long life hardly ever left the North East.

He was a comic in the great eccentric tradition of Billy Merson, George Robey, Rob Wilton and Frank Randle in a way that Ray Cruddas, for all his national reputation, had never been. But the combination of an impenetrable accent and material that already had whiskers growing on it in the sixties meant that his comedy didn't travel. He was given a chance to break out of the working men's clubs when Tyne Tees Television gave him his own sixteen-week series in 1959, in its first ever season. But after a storming beginning, *The Bobby Thompson Show* rapidly ran out of material and turned into a ratings calamity. It bombed spectacularly, the broadcasters looked like fools and he was an outcast after that, a pariah in the new world of slick patter and canned laughter in which Ray Cruddas was just beginning to establish himself. (It was the period when he was heavily in demand for judging beauty competitions, opening swimming pools in civic centres and giving bouquets to the most glamorous grannies of Hull or Gypsy Hill.)

But back in the mechanics' institutes and the fag-end, back-of-beyond clubs, Bobby Thompson was welcome. Poor people would always laugh at his well-worn routines. When Bobby said of his wife, 'Yes'dee I thowt she was havin' a bubble bath an' she'd been eatin' mushy peas,' he got howls. When he told the one about how he telephones Neville Chamberlain to see how he can help in the war effort, only to find himself talking to Mrs Chamberlain who responds with the epic line, 'Can you haad on a minute, Bob, I've got a pan of chips on,' they roared and banged on the tables.

He used his humour to show his deep affection for the people and places he had been surrounded by all his life, and inspired a strong regional loyalty in return. 'I suppose you could say that I represent something special to people, something that is more meaningful or more personal, because of their background, than history,' he once said, in a rare recorded utterance. '"You don't know what you mean to my mother . . . My father was saying your jokes when he passed away . . ." It's like they look at me and they see something in themselves they're afraid they're going to lose, or mebbe they've already lost. I feel almost a desperation in their love for me.' When everything else got corporatized and homogenized, Bobby Thompson stayed the way he was, preserved in amber.

'Eee, aa'll tell yiz. Yi naa why I keep the tropical fish, divven yiz? So aa've somethin' entertainin' to watch when Ray Cruddas is on the tellyvision. He should buy a barra an' orn a decent livin'.' Bobby had said this on one of the last occasions the two of them shared a bill together. The local press had tried to make something of it and build it up into a bitter feud. But Ray felt sure that nothing was meant; that it was just part of the professional give-and-take. He remembered the occasion well. It was in 1961 or '62, the bridging period between the hard, sombre days of the war and rationing, and the more dashing, mobile times that were to come. There was a feeling of modernity and adventure. People were buying their first car and booking their first Continental holiday. DIY was starting to boom. Young couples were putting hardboard on doors to cover up panels whose edges were dust-collectors, and pulling out old Victorian mouldings and sconces. People were trying to bury the past, and all the reminders of deprivation and poverty. And Ray felt he reflected the new spirit in his clothes.

On the night in question he had been wearing one of the new Terylene drip-dry, non-iron shirts in a pale buttercup yellow, with a metallic, fat-knotted tie and a pale metallic suit with double vents and a faint windowpane undercheck. This had naturally raised suspicions that he was a bit light on his toes. (A wolf-whistle greeted him as he walked on.) But what drew most comment among the audience of miners and their families was his shoes. These were made from the softest kid leather of the

83

sort only ever usually used for making ladies' gloves and, as with gloves, you could make out the faint outline of his toes. They had concealed tongues and parallel lacing and an almond-shaped toe. What was most startling about Ray's shoes, though, was the colour. They were a delicate dove grey, and then somehow overlaid on the grey was the kind of pearlized sheen that was just starting to be seen on the new laminated bathroom and kitchen surfaces. In an area where most footwear was utility-wear, protected against corrosion and fierce indus-trial processes and, even when it was being bought for 'best', was bought for durability rather than appearance, Ray's shoes were something.

He had been booked to appear with Bobby that night at the Miners' Club and Institute, Percy Main. It was a benefit for spina bifida. He could remember clearly them being in the committee room, which had been set aside for the use of the artistes, as a pencilled sign said on the door. There was a lot of dark wood panelling and heavy, dark oak furniture and a round port-hole window with rich stained-glass and leaded lights. 'Nice ti naa if I gan oot there the neet an' die, like,' Bobby said, 'thi can bring iz back here ti the chapel a rest.' He had black boot polish in his hair and kippered nicotine fingers and was eating the 'bait' of clammy beetroot sandwiches that his wife, the fearsome Phyllis, had put up for him and that he slurped like poor man's oysters, the white bread dissolved into a purple paste on the slippery purple beets, *shhhlurrrrrrp*, through his best teeth.

His whole attitude to life was distilled in a one-liner he bor-rowed from probably the most famous case of a comedian who was idolized in the North but who remained incomprehensible to a southern public, the Wigan-born Frank Randle: 'She says to iz, she says [assuming his still Geordiefied version of a cut-glass accent], "Ew, you're not polished enough, Berbby." So aa gans, "What di yi tek iz for, like? A coffin?"'

For his first set of the night at Bobby's, Ray put on a sharp suit and a wide tie and a pair of pale shoes made from ostrich or emu or crocodile or salamander, selected from the long row of shoes lined up along one wall of his dressing-room.

For his second set, he pulled on a flat cap with a lick of Brylcreemed hair fixed to it, a baggy Fair Isle jumper with a hole in the elbow, a pair of baggy trousers and some soft-soled carpet slippers shiny with grease. Just before he went on, Jackie passed him the Player's Weight that he had started for him in order to authenticate his impersonation of Bobby Thompson.

An irony not lost on Ray was that, in the last years, the Bobby Thompson who put on the cap and the jumper and the flattened gutter snout was by then a wealthy man with a fine house at the seaside, a car with a driver and whose greatest pleasures, indulged at every opportunity, were days at the races with a full wallet in the jacket of his bespoke silk suit with the satin Paisley lining, and nights at the gaming tables playing roulette and blackjack.

For forty years, up to his death in 1988, the Little Waster was locked in a love embrace with the North-East working class.

'Your voice', somebody, an important man in the industry, reaching for a compliment, had once told Ray, 'has a little quality of being reassuring in it.' This, he knew, is what he amounted to.

Counting the house was an old tradition, and one that Ray, a traditionalist in most things, nightly observed.

Every night around eight o'clock he walked the few yards from his dressing-room and inserted himself into the space between the blackout cloth at the back of the stage and the high rear wall of the club. The back flat was studded with lights which objectively everybody knew were plain household bulbs coated in a thin layer of dust but were nevertheless prepared to accept as a representation of a twinkling, starry sky. The back of the flat was a confusion of spaghetti leads and electricity ducts, and Ray climbed on to a platform of wooden crates to press his eye against the peep-hole that had been inserted in the cloth slightly above the part of the stage where the band sat.

From this vantage point he was able to encompass the entire panorama of the club: the communal tables arranged in rows radiating out from the circular dance area in the well of the room, with smaller tables, each one with an amber lamp glowing on it, rising in tiers; the long brass-rail bar stepped down the right-hand side of the club in all its promise and bottley glitter; the five-hundredweight chandelier hanging on tension wires anchored high up in the roof; the faded Coronation-era bunting and colours; the waiting staff assembled at their stations all along the middle tier, clean and scrubbed and ready to go. From day one they had stuck to a hiring policy that discriminated in favour of workers who had been made redundant from the old heavy industries, which meant a preponderance of men and women in their forties, fifties and even sixties, most of them without any previous waiting experience. But it seemed to work. They were less inclined than the waitresses and bartenders that Ray had come across in other establishments to treat the customers as turkeys to be housed, fed and stripped clean with a minimum of violence. He had watched many former rivet-slingers and conveyor-belt overseers develop performance skills and learn to project a character in keeping with the nostalgic tone of Bobby's and earn big tips.

Occasionally, standing on his platform of splintered pallets and crates, listening to the band play an old standard from his youth, Ray would allow himself to be engulfed in a fondness and a nostalgia for his own life. Nostalgia, or homesickness, is never about the past but about felt absences or a sense of something lacking in the present: even primitive peoples are said to dream of an even more primitive past – the original, unspoiled season (described in so many myths). And, watching from the secrecy of his blackout screen while men in corduroy britches and bicycle-clips and canvas braces like his father's and women in hairnets and curlers and sensible sandals like his mother's were brought to their tables, Ray could sometimes imagine he was seeing a parade of dead relatives descending the tiers like players at the final walk-down in a pantomime – uncles who worked as lighter-men and emptying the bins; grandmothers who pushed wicker baskets and zinc bathtubs of washing up to the wash-house on old bogeys and prams on Mondays and laboured for hours in the life-sapping heat and steam.

He was also constantly surprised by the number of young people who came dressed in ways they could never have seen, except in period TV dramas and faded family pictures. A related phenomenon was the local talent competitions Ray was asked to judge which were invariably won by teenagers impersonating people – Bobby Darin, Matt Monroe, Norman Evans, Sammy Davis Junior – who had been dead before they were born.

By eight o'clock, he normally expected to see the bar brimming with people and the main room beginning to fill up with buzz and noise. Tonight, though, he could hear the brushes and the kick-drum of the drummer, who was immediately below him, with the eerie clarity of a record and, in the quieter moments, hear the band cracking wise among themselves. Even with one eye he could see that the bar was about a third as full as it was supposed to be.

Blanche usually supplied him with a crib sheet which set out the who and where of the party bookings so he could work some local or topical reference in during his first spot of the night. Most nights this didn't tax him. The hen parties and ruby-wedding groups, the sewing circles and pigeon-fanciers and stags; the domed eccentrics of the Antiquarian Booksellers' Association and the nervous nellies from the vast Ministry of Pensions gulag to the east of the city – these were all easy, requiring one or two one-size-fits-all gags from his mental Rolodex. But the Ephphatha League of the Deaf posed trickier problems.

Clipped to the sheet that Blanche had given him had been a note, written with a broad-nibbed pen in blue ink, from the organizer of the deaf-mute club's trip to Bobby's:

> The deaf live in a soundless world – a world of deadly silence [it began]. The singing of the birds, the inflections of the human voice, beautiful music, and the confusion of noises that proclaim life are lacking. Many things are in motion, but there is no sound.
>
> If you were wondering: 'Ephphatha' is a word that Jesus spoke when he healed a deaf man. You'll find it in St Mark. It means 'Be opened'.
>
> If it is possible to bring this to the attention of Mr Cruddas I would be very grateful.

Ray knew instantly now that the first thing he had to do was stand down Alexis, the dumb waiter. 'I spill beer on people, bump into them, step on their feet, and hit them in the face with my elbows,' Alexis, a former circus performer, had told Ray when he came to be interviewed for the job. 'All the time I look dumb. It is a very funny act to people with a keen sense of humour. Of course, some people just don't have a sense of humour.'

'What do they think of your act?' Ray had asked.

'Well, I tell you,' Alexis said, 'look at this scar on my forehead. And I suppose you noticed that I walk with a limp.'

Ray had hired him on the spot, and on many nights Alexis was the star of the show. People liked having Radgie Gadgie slopped down their necks and pease pudden dropped in their laps by an apparently well-intentioned but accident-prone waiter, it transpired. ('Aah naa, 'e's canny, man.') It helped them to lose their inhibitions and have a good time. But tonight, Ray decided, Alexis's brand of slapstick couldn't be risked.

When Jackie went looking for Alexis in the bar he found it largely populated with people dressed the way Ray dressed every night, in dead people's – their own mother's or brother's or somebody else's – clothes. They were having pre-drink drinks before the serious drinking, and there was an air of expecting the place to fill up, everybody both spectator and part of the spectacle, not knowing yet that tonight, for reasons beyond anybody's control or contrivance, the spectacle was going to be curtailed and limited to just about all those who were there now – about ninety in total and two-thirds of that total being the deaf-and-dumb people using signs to small-talk and joke and gossip with one another. They closed and unclosed their hands in the air, wriggled their fingers and made complicated gestures.

Some had come as ladies' maids and land-girls; others as farm labourers and Jarrow Marchers. Jackie himself was wearing a dark lounge suit and a plain crew-neck sweater. As he looked around for Alexis he was approached by a tall, slightly stooped man dressed as a miner who was carrying a spiral notebook at the level of his chest. 'Do you work here?' he had written on the first blank page. Jackie nodded yes, that he did, and the man flipped the page and started writing. He was wearing breeches that hung just below his knees and had a red sweatcloth hitched to his waist. When he reached the bottom of the page, he tore it out and gave it to Jackie. 'Hello. Glad to meet you. My name is Mark Douglas. I'm the organizer of the deaf group's outing. Perhaps it would be helpful if I write down a couple of things about the group that you may care to pass on to whoever's in charge of things this evening.' Jackie saw that there were two upraised hands printed on the piece of paper. The hands represented letters in the manual alphabet, but obviously Jackie didn't know what the letters were. 'For one, the deaf are top dancers. A1 dancers. None better. We don't hear, but when we dance on a wooden floor most of us feel the vibrations of the music. To watch us dancing, you'd never guess we didn't hear anything at all. Even have a few jivers!'

Jackie side-stepped to his left and reached around and under the bar counter where the new order pads were. 'Dance floor hear glass.' Jackie wrote everything in awkward block capitals whose interstices didn't meet up and which lay on the page like broken branches on the forest floor. 'Also hi–' He scored that out. 'Hay–' The word Jackie was trying to spell was 'hydraulic'. They had a hydraulic dance floor made from strengthened glass, salvaged from one of the first clubs to open in the city in the fifties. Mark Douglas wasn't paying any attention to him anyway, but continuing to write in his notebook. He had a sharp, very pronounced Adam's apple which bobbed in and out of the neck of his collarless pitman's shirt as he wrote. Presently he tore out another leaf and gave it to Jackie. 'We also "sing". We love singing. We have choirs who sing in sign language and we are all looking forward to singing tonight! We take part in many activities as a group. We prefer our own company because most hearing people have a tendency to look on us as peculiar, or mysterious, or unnatural. We are always stared at. Because of this we like to go about together. Do you find these facts interesting?' Jackie was smiling politely; nodding and smiling. But what he was thinking was: The inside of your head. The darkest place on earth.

From conversations he had had in his village, Jackie knew that the job everybody dreaded when they went to work at the colliery was being put on the belts – the conveyors from which the stone was picked from the coal before it was loaded into railway wagons and taken to the docks. When the belts started up at five in the morning you could hear them all over Rusty Lane, and it was a wet, filthy, demeaning and most of all a head-wreckingly noisy job. The noise was so great and incessantly terrible that speech was impossible. 'That's why you had the deaf-and-dumb people working there,' a man he met on his walks had told

Jackie once. 'Then you had subnormal people, criminals, child molesters, very ugly people, outcasts – the sort of people who couldn't get a job anywhere else. You'd be standing there, black, freezing, surrounded by these people. You were fourteen, and you wondered what you'd done to deserve it.'

And perhaps because of some folk memory, sleeping but not extinguished, which associated deaf people with criminals and outcasts, Jackie could tell that the presence of the deaf-mute club bothered certain of the hearing customers, who had mostly come dressed not in costume, but in their normal going-out clothes. As the communal hum, the strange fluctuating excited moan of the Ephphatha people grew louder, these were the ones going small and tight in their seats.

On his pad Jackie stabbed out, 'Scuse plse - back in a sec.d.' He held this up to show Mark Douglas and then aimed himself at the clown waiter Alexis who he had just seen was about to jolt the elbow of a man on the point of taking his first glug of a big wel-come gin and tonic at the far end of the bar. He got a hand to his arm just in time and was able to explain to Alexis that he was being retired for the night. There was no resistance, just a shrug. 'You am de boss, boss. As a matter of fact I've just rolled a number.' Alexis indicated his jacket pocket. 'Two fat numbers, to be precise. This stuff is pretty mellow. Dope you can reason with. If you want me I'll be in the bar.' Then he executed a pratfall over Jackie's left foot.

Ray was gargling with mouthwash when Jackie got back. He was wearing a striped towelling dressing-gown over his shirt and trousers and touching his dress-hair with the fingers of one hand as he tipped his head back.

'How did that old Monkhouse opener go?' Jackie said. ' "How do you open a cabaret act . . ." '

' ". . . when you'd rather open a vein?" '

The band was just finishing a Joe Wilson medley. Ray's play-on music was next. Jackie checked his watch, kicked some balled-up socks under the sofa with the side of his foot, and freshened Ray's drink. He took a small swig from the bottle himself then wiped the top of it with the palm of his hand. He sprayed powder deodorant into Ray's shoes. 'Funny teeth in? OK. You're on in three.'

The anxiety of playing a half-filled house on a dead matinée in one of the lesser halls in one of the smaller towns had never left Ray: walking on to the sound of his own footsteps, talking for ten minutes into the echo of his own voice, and walking off covered in flop-sweat. It was at these times, dying in front of a small and apathetic or actively hostile audience, in a depressed mill town in Lancashire or a filthy smelting centre in the Black Country, that he would travel in his mind to the Moor and the trees and the slow-moving, unchanging life being lived within and without the little grove, and for a while rest there as if that place could speak to him and begin to carry a meaning other than the simple fact of its existence. 'If I had to live my life over, I'd live over a decent Chinese restaurant,' he'd find himself saying – and nothing. The fat man in the third row passing the bag of sweets to his very fat wife. The door at the back of the stalls flipping open briefly to show a bus passing; a woman stooping to pick up a baby's dummy; a slice of light, and the raindrops bouncing merrily.

As a young comic, like all learner comedians, Ray had tended to talk too fast and rush his gags. Lapel-grabbing was never his style; he was never a gagster or a zany or one of the Loony Lunatics. His natural style was to underplay, and aim for a low-pressure success – that 'carefully studied nonchalance'. But as an apprentice he tended to charge towards the end of his jokes and stampede all over the punchlines. The reason he did it was simple: it was fear. The fear of going for a minute, more than a minute, without a laugh. To play for one minute without a laugh was murder. He got the dry lip then. The incipient panic. The more he pushed to make an audience laugh, the more they would clam up on him. He was dying from trying, as the saying went.

The recognition had dawned on Ray early on that he wasn't going to be loved. He had always been too afraid of audiences for that, and had always protected himself against them, even as he craved their attention. When a comic loved an audience, they knew it. Ray didn't love them and they could sense it. He was afraid of them and so he wanted to outsmart them, to convince himself he was smarter than they were. In the end he had settled for simply being personable and commercial: a pro comic telling pro-comic jokes who still had a terror of corpsing.

Because of the shortfall in numbers, body heat hadn't warmed the club as effectively as it usually did. It was significantly cooler than it usually was, and Ray could sense that. Maybe something about his voice. His voice sounded thinner or more remote or in some way different to him when it found its way back after perhaps a tenth-of-a-second delay over the PA.

He had mentally disconnected, but he knew that he was still talking because in his peripheral vision he could see that the woman was still signing, standing several feet to the rear of him on the far side of the stage. A pin spot illuminated her hands so what she was saying with them could be clearly seen. And the spectre of the signer's hands, soft-edged and swooping and mag-nified, played across the gallery of framed ancestor portraits along the left-hand wall. The light from a ring the signer was wearing sprayed out coloured rays and all this unaccustomed movement was caught and held in the smoked mirror behind the bar, where Jackie was sitting on a high stool, swivelling. Jackie was sitting at the bar, discreetly yawning.

Ray had got off to what he considered a well-judged start with a joke that seemed to him to address the situation in an unsqueamish, but not a callous or a crass way. 'The last time I worked in a place as quiet as this they drew back the curtains and buried my grandad.' Nothing. The sign for curtains is both hands raised, palms inward. Projected on to the wall, the translation looked sombrely literal.

'I walked by a funeral parlour the other day. They had a sign in the window that read: "Closed because of a birth in the family".' A sound of crashing came from the kitchen. Then chef's voice. Then more crashing of pans and trays. In the dark recesses of the club, movement sensors glowed red and then dimmed again, something Ray had never had occasion to notice in the past. They came on red, just pinpoints of light, and dimmed.

A waiter passed in front of the stage, carrying a tray of drinks. 'Evening, Ted. Some men are built like Greek gods. Ted's built like a Greek restaurant.' This raised a jeer from the band. 'Oh.' Ray did a half-turn, bringing the microphone lead with him. 'So rigor mortis hasn't set in . . . Have you met the band? One on key-boards, one on bass, one on drums, two on cannabis and all three on probation.' Boom-boom on the kick-drum and the kind of loud scoffing laughter from the band that greeted this joke every night. The laughter from the members of the deaf-mutes' club, who were seated at the long tables, was involuntarily subdued – a kind of strangulated, breathless ululating or wailing, mirthless and agonized-seeming. But they were smiling and signing and many of them were clapping enthusiastically.

But it took Ray to a cheerless place, and he was present only in a physical sense after that, spilling out the jokes and doing the bits of corny stage business he'd done ten thousand times in his life while the translator signed and Jackie yawned and chef raved and ranted and the mirror continued to throw sooty shadows like a television, and the Ephphatha Club – it meant 'Be opened' – opened their hearts and their throats and released a sound Ray knew he would be happy never to have to hear again but also knew he was going to have to hear again in his second set in just over an hour.

'What an amazing audience – you have fantastic self-control.

As I call your names please pick up your belongings and get on the truck.' An extended drumroll from 'Dodgy' Rodge Dyer, followed by a crash of the hi-hat which only a small fraction of the audience could hear.

About ten minutes into his flat-capped and raggy-ganzied Little Waster routine Ray had seen Ronnie Cornish come in. He often came in around that time after he'd wined and dined elsewhere, quite often with people in tow, and a table on the upper tier was always kept open for him. Keeping an eye on his investment is how 'Big Ron', as he was generally known, liked to explain his fondness for the nightlife at Bobby's. But the truth was that, after a lifetime in the construction industry, which he had spent breathing in brick dust and being covered in dust – he owned a brick-making company that had diversified into demolition and architectural salvage – he was attracted by the glamour that, late in life, the club had come to represent to him. This also partly explained Ronnie's involvement with the football club, where he was a director, and which had similarly opened up doors that previously would have remained closed to him. In recent years he had extended his circle to include sports stars and show people, industrialists, entrepreneurs, journalists and politicians. He had become something of a powerhouse locally, which he didn't feel he needed to apologize about to anybody. He was pleased with his success. He wanted it, he worked for it (more or less) honestly, and he'd got there eventually.

The 'Big' in 'Big Ron' referred to his height as well as his girth. He was on the tall side, and heavy set with silver hair worn in a youthful fringe that sat oddly with his facial features, which were as chipped and fissured as brick. Brick ran in the family. His grandfather and great-grandfather had been brickies; his father had run a brickworks where the clay had been hand-drawn and the moulds had been crafted from wood and the bricks – beautiful

95

bricks: tactile, textured and grainy; bricks that had built or been patched into some of the finest buildings in the city; brick that breathed easily and naturally and grew old gracefully; that matured and improved with the passage of the years – the bricks from the old Cornish factory had been hand-thrown, hand-coloured and hand-fired in a process that seemed to have been untouched by the Industrial Revolution. Now, under Ronnie, Cornish Bricks were thrown not by hand but by computer in the country's most sophisticated plant.

Computer-designed bricks have the faults built into them. They can be programmed to look not only chipped and cracked, with the corners rubbed off, but also to give the appearance of being mildewed and streaked with soot marks. And, miraculously, Ronnie's complexion, which for all the years he had worked with brick had remained dry and reddened and cracked like brick, now looked more like the computer-generated, synthetic product his company was putting out and shifting by the shedload; it was this post-industrial product that had bought him the Bentley and the two-door Mercedes 500 CL and the chopper and all the other good things of life. After a concerted campaign conducted by Nikki, Ronnie's daughter, and Hope, Ronnie's wife, Ronnie had finally relented and recently had gone under the needle for a series of Botox treatments which had plumped out his frown lines and smoothed away other signs of wear and tear on his façade and all in all gentrified his appearance to the standard of the very popular, top-of-the-range, heather-mixtures brick.

'Brick is the most English of the building materials,' Ronnie was apt to tell gatherings both intimate and international, quoting from his one great set speech. 'Concrete, the wonder material of the age, turned out to be rocking-horse shit compared to brick. The age of brick began in this country – *this* country, England, not Ireland or Scotland or Wales – with the Fire of London in 1666 and it's still going strong. Brick is English – honest and down-to-earth, plain and unvarnished.' Exactly, as Ronnie hardly needed to add, like himself.

Ray had come to join Ronnie as soon as he'd showered and changed and fixed his chestnut hairpiece back in place. 'I hear you phoned your performance in the night, kidda,' Ronnie said as Ray dropped into a seat. With Ronnie was another man, a business associate called Warren Oliver. Warren, sometimes referred to as Ronnie Cornish's 'sleeping partner' because of his quiet, almost shy, demeanour, was another, smaller investor in the club.

Ronnie had had bottles brought to the table. The waiter had brought brandy, vodka, sambuca and Ray's favourite Jack Daniels, and Ronnie had indicated to leave the bottles there. He was in an expansive mood, as he tended to be by that point in the proceedings, and apparently not over concerned about the impact the restrictions brought in to contain foot-and-mouth disease were going to have on his business. He could see there was a killing to be made ('Sorry, like! Nee pun intended') in supplying the transporters that were going to be needed to move the bodies. Also in barrier mats ('Load a coconut mattin', splash the fucken stuff on the fucker, an' Bob's your uncle') and disinfectant sprays.

They had been talking for about a quarter of an hour and the audience was singing along silently with their hands to 'Cushie Butterfield' when there was a flutter of excitement among the people sitting closest to the door, who had spotted five of the United players coming in. They were quietly ostentatious in designer clothes and in boisterous good spirits as they moved up through the bar. They sat a few tables away from where Ray and Ronnie were. Ronnie pantomimed some tick-tack signs in their direction, and a couple of them tick-tacked back. A big defender called Darren Easby pointed at the Ephphatha people and mouthed the question, 'What the fuck?'

'Yi divven have to whisper, man,' Ronnie shouted. 'They're all deaf as posts.'

With the group was a recent signing from a German club, a Paraguayan or Chilean with the unlikely poetic name of Triste-le-Roy, although it had been announced he would be wearing the single name 'Roy' on his shirt. Also in their company were two local girls they had hooked up with in the course of the night. The girls were dressed almost identically in semi-transparent lace tops and tiny skirts made of scraps of denim held together with white laces criss-crossed through brass eyelets up the sides. Both girls had lots of elaborately piled and twisted blond hair and jewelled bolts in their navels.

Colin Shales, the captain, came over. He squeezed Ray on the shoulder and shook hands with Ronnie. 'All right, Mr Cornish?' 'Not bad for a Wednesdee neet, bonnie lad.' They talked football and motor cars for a few minutes, and then when Shales turned to walk away Ronnie seemed to think of something and called him back. He whispered something confidential in the player's ear, and when he was finished Shales laughed. He went over to where Alexis was playing on one of the pool tables and, after a brief conversation, Alexis disappeared.

When he reappeared he was wearing a long white apron and carrying a tray which was loaded with an ice bucket and an assortment of snacks and drinks. He approached the table where the players were sitting and, while unloading the tray, managed to spill some ice into the new player's, Triste-le-Roy's, lap. He apologized very nicely and then, while fussing around him with a napkin pretending to clear the mess up, caught him with his elbow in the ear. When 'Twisty', as he had quickly been nicknamed ('Triste-le-Roy'/'Twist again'/'Twisty'), stood up, he dragged a bowl of piccalilli and a bowl of olives to the floor, and Alexis trampled heavily on his feet while pretending to brush these up. He tripped and dumped the contents of the dustpan over the player's shoulders when he was seated again. And it was at this point, with the two girls giggling and Ronnie gulping and reddening and his team mates falling about, that Twisty went for Alexis big style, as they would all later say.

'Initiation, son,' Ronnie said, when the ex-fitter waiter who had been lurking in the shadows finally stepped in and pulled them apart. 'You've got your traditions where you come from, we've got ours. Thi' probably drink the blood of ten-year-old virgins ower there. Dee funny things wi' chickens. People up here will always mek you welcome. They'll always ask yi back to their place for a fight. Welcome, Twisty, if I may call you Twisty, welcome to the North.'

Ray had been called away while all this was going on. Suddenly Ronnie realized he didn't have any cigarettes. He looked around for somebody to fetch some and, failing to see anybody else, called over to Jackie. 'Jackie, man! Jackie!' He used a slightly impeded, high-pitched voice like Jackie's. One of the footballers half turned and faced Ronnie, squeezing his crotch. Ronnie called Jackie over again, in a normal voice this time. 'Ah howay man, Jackie, divven gerrin a pet.' He always talked broader when he was drunk. 'Has somebody tekken your baal, or what?' Jackie came to the table and asked Ronnie what he wanted. When he wanted something Ronnie always wanted it quick fast in a hurry. 'Kish mir 'n tushes,' Jackie said under his breath when Ronnie told him he was out of smokes. Yiddish is a language rich in insults and curses. 'Kiss my arse.'

Jackie had learned the rudiments of Yiddish from Mr Solomons', 'the potentate's', black-veiled, mahogany-coloured elderly mother who he used to secretly bring waxed cartons of jellied eels and other forbidden treats in to from the stall outside the Knave of Clubs pub on Club Row in Whitechapel.

What Ronnie Cornish should have realized, and perhaps didn't, was that Jackie had been in some bad company. He knew a lot of the 'chaps' who used to hang around Jack Solomons' Soho gym in the fifties. He knew that Tony Mella in those days. They were both boxing for Solomons. Mella had been badly cut by Mad Frankie Fraser, whose services Mr Solomons on one or two occasions employed to cut some Americans who were clouding his horizon. Tony Mella had ultimately been offed by his partner in the Bus Stop Club in Dean Street, after Mella had humiliated him in front of some of the girls who worked there. He had been shot and died in the gutter outside the club with the girls all screaming and half naked around him.

In those days when Jack Solomons reigned supreme over the fight game, a boxer had really arrived when he appeared at either the Albert Hall or Harringay Arena. And towards the end of his career Jackie had appeared on a Solomons Christmas promotion at the Hall, as it was always known in boxing circles, which had all three Kray brothers on the bill. Ronnie fought Bill Slimey of Kings Cross; Reggie fought Bob Manito of Clapham; and Jackie got the oldest of the three, Charlie. In the week leading up to the fight, he had been leaned on very heavily by one of the razor gangs who ran the betting to lose it; he had got his fingers severely stood on when he went to try and pick up the 'nobbins', the loose change thrown into the ring, when the fight was all over. But he had stood his ground and refused to box at less than his best, and all the Krays had continued very friendly towards Jackie afterwards. Ronnie Cornish was purely one hundred per cent a lightweight compared to some of the mad crazy deviators Jackie had known.

When he came back, Jackie saw that two of the footballers and one of the girls had gravitated towards Ronnie Cornish's table. Ronnie was doing one of his party pieces for them that Jackie had seen him do many times before. He put a napkin on his head and pretended to be Queen Victoria.

Jackie placed the cigarettes on the table in front of him. He had brought them on a plate, with the Cellophane taken off and the flip top tipped open in what Jackie considered to be a subtle fuck-you gesture. '*Khob im in drerd,*' he said as Ronnie went on playing to the table without acknowledging him. And a strange idea occurred to Jackie then: it was always almost like jealousy on Ronnie's part; almost as if Ronnie Cornish was jealous of him.

Heading back in the direction of the pool tables, Jackie spotted Alexis slipping out of the men's toilets and sauntering knowingly back to the table where he had been playing for the last hour with one of the younger United players.

The hand drier in the Gents came on automatically as Jackie walked past it and he felt the whoosh of warm air. In the chrome paper-towel dispenser, he found a small packet of cocaine. Jackie slipped it into his pocket and walked back into the club.

After he'd closed the souvenir stall and cashed up Jackie took Ellis for a walk. It was a fresh night with some dampness in the air. Nothing was moving on the river, but the lights from some buildings on the opposite bank were reflected in the black water. A set of construction cranes towered above the buildings and their night lights were points of roiling light reflected in the river. There were still a few cars left in the car park and the boy car-park attendant was still in his booth. The light was on and a radio was playing. Ronnie Cornish's driver was sitting in the front of his car with a low light on, reading. They were working late at Tip Top Crash Repair. The radio was playing a song that Jackie knew was called 'Here Comes That Rainy Day'. It was the Peggy Lee version. The metal roller gate was raised a couple of feet and orange light with the blue light of metal-cutting torches in it seeped through the gap on to the baulked and lightly circling litter.

The industrial estate where Bobby's was situated was high up on the side of the valley. Once the streets here had dropped precipitously down to the shipyards at the river. Clara Street, Violet Street, Aline Street, Helen Street. Streets named after the wives and daughters of the bigwig industrialists and shipyard owners. There were big blown-up pictures of the streets of the former neighbourhood on the walls at the club. It was a neighbourhood that, in its heyday, had been famous for the number of licensed premises per head of population. There was a pub on every corner, and the names reflected the industries for which the area had won world renown: The Gun, The Hydraulic Crane, The Vulcan, The Forge Hammer, The Blast Furnace. The Forge Hammer had stood on exactly the spot where Bobby's now was and had long enjoyed a reputation for providing everything the visitor could require: a barber shop, women for sale, stabling for horses. Bare-knuckle boxing took place in a ring on the first floor. For generations 'a fuck or a fight' was the Saturday night promise at The Forge Hammer. In the twenties, the pub had been managed by the former world heavyweight boxing champion, Tommy Burns, a Canadian who lost his title in Australia to the first black champion of the world, the American, Jack Johnson.

A giant mural photograph of The Forge Hammer hung in the foyer at Bobby's. Blowing up historical 'views' and plying the nostalgia industry was what Warren Oliver, Ronnie's sleeping partner, did for a living. Many of the computer-enhanced, hand-tinted family portraits hanging in the club had passed through Warren Oliver's Photoshoppe. He supplied images to pubs, supermarkets, railway stations, motorway eateries, showing what had been cleared away or trampled under in the march of progress. The more completely the environment in a photograph had been destroyed, the more sought after the picture. After a trail of false career starts involving mothballs, bubble baths, prams and fridge magnets, Warren had finally struck lucky with the retro-imaging.

The eastern boundary fence of the industrial estate followed the path of a stream. The stream had once run through the grounds of a grand house built by one of the illustrious Victorian empire-builders. Both house and stream, along with a considerable acreage of the original grounds, were, surprisingly, still in existence. They had been bequeathed to the city by the spinster daughters of the great man whose name they carried. The house had become a hostel for the homeless, the grounds were overgrown and choked with ivy, and the stream was clogged with refrigerators, supermarket trolleys and other rubble. As Jackie approached, two women workers were having a cigarette break on the steps outside the hostel whose windows were protected by ominous metal grilles. It was a creepy, Gothic building standing well back in the grounds and the women looked horror-show ghostly in their white uniforms and clinging cocoons of swirling smoke. As he got nearer Jackie smelled the Jeyes which had permeated the fibres of their clothes. He thought of Telfer sedated in the vet's basement in a shopping precinct in West Allen and called Ellis's name. The dog came instantly, bounding through the thorny undergrowth, panting and wagging his tail.

When he returned to the club, Ray was with Ronnie and Warren and the footballers, messing around with a drink that involved trapping ignited alcohol fumes in a glass and inhaling the fumes through a straw. Alexis and the two girls, who seemed pretty drunk now, were also included. It was 4 a.m. before Jackie could persuade them all to leave.

The sky above Allotment Field when Jackie dropped Ray off was bright and clear. The moon and stars had never been as brilliant as in the blackouts during the war. But tonight the stars were out and you could see the mountains and craters of the moon. With his key in the door, Ray turned to wave cheerio to Jackie and saw that one star appeared to be particularly bright and seemed to him to be blinking in the clear dark sky. 'It's a new satellite. It'll be leaving our orbit in a few days' time,' he was certain he heard a woman's voice say – a girl's; only a girl – although he couldn't see anybody in the road or in any of the gardens.

Same trees, same stars, he thought, as he went inside.

After satisfying himself that there were no cows near by, Jackie released Ellis on to the Moor for his final run before taking him home. He took off towards the Park with his ears flattened and his rich fur parted and flying. And then he suddenly stopped and smelled the air. He was used to being a pair, and kept running and stopping, looking around and waiting for his partner to come.

4

One night towards the end of January 1947 when he was still sixteen and cycling home through the night to his village at Chatteris after a fight which had been a close-fought thing at Mr Solomons' converted church-hall club in Hackney, Jackie felt what was to be one of the harshest of all English winters start to blow in.

A north-east wind started blowing that night and blew for a month without stopping. Weeks passed and the temperature never rose above freezing. The Thames froze. Coal boats, bound for London, were ice-bound in the North East ports. Coal was frozen at the pits. There were no trains to shift it. People worked in offices by candlelight; fires and traffic lights went out; lifts stopped. Thousands were laid off work and went home to houses that were dark and freezing. The newspapers reported queues of professional women with buckets waiting at a stand tap in the road in St John's Wood, like a night after a blitz. Big Ben was silenced, its mechanism frozen solid.

In the early hours of 24 January 1947, an area of high pressure somewhere above Archangel began moving in an arc over Scandinavia and down towards England, sucking Siberian cold with it, and Jackie was one of the first to feel it. It cut through the layers of vests and shirts and two corduroy jerkins he had put on. It even penetrated the impractical heavy topcoat Mr Solomons' book-keeper at the Devonshire Club had wished on him and stabbed through his trousers and his long-johns to the satin Lonsdale ring shorts he was still wearing.

The road from the West End ran more or less directly from 'the square mile of vice' past Hackney and round the Epping Forest borders to Essex and Cambridge and straight past Jackie's door in the flat country of the Fens. One road, and a flat one, from Chatteris going south past the Isle of Ely and the great floating mothership of the Cathedral, riding high in a dead line above the marshes and mud flats and the sucking peat fen, past the steam-pump houses and the ruler-straight and geometrically patterned rivers, and then along between old fields choked with thistly weeds and brambles until the isolated single houses started to become attached to other houses one by one, and the houses became a terrace, and the terraces darkened into rows of dark brick terraces and the smells of that part of London came in – glue and paraffin; paint and bonemeal, the 'stink industries' as they were called – and Jackie, leg-weary as he was, couldn't wait to get in and get the fight behind him and climb aboard his bicycle which he would have parked outside the hustling matchmaker Mr Solomons' Devonshire Sporting Club in Devonshire Street, Hackney, and head back along the long straight road to where he felt he belonged.

It was a strange landscape of the Fens. But it was the one he had looked out of his window and seen around him all his life, bare trees edging the fields like stamp perforations against the sky; islands sticking out of the sticky fen floor. And the road was raised up and it was an area well dotted with memorials to the Great War in every village and medieval steeples and cemeteries where the white shapes of the gravestones would suddenly become visible in a break in the straggling privet hedge bound with vines and climbing plants of cat brier, trumpet creeper, morning glory. And so Jackie did not feel alone the way you could suppose he might with the night and pitch darkness all around and unaccountable noises and animals shifting in the dark and in fact would say that he could feel more by himself in a room with people all talking or in a ring going after a man with the intention of smashing his face and people on their feet shouting the odds than he ever did on his long rides home to Chatteris with his ribs sore and his knuckles smarting and a ten shilling in his pocket after a fight.

The snow started falling just outside Duxford in the first hour of the famous freezing winter of 1947, and snow stood an inch deep on Jackie's body and two and a half inches deep on his woollen balaclava when he finally reached home. The double doors of his father's smithing shop were open, and he could see his father inside stoking the fire of the furnace in his long leather apron. He shook hands with his father, who poured out a cup of beef tea for him, and was glad to be able to give his father three of the four heavy half-crown pieces that had been his pay for the night.

Jackie was a country boy. His mother, a local Chatteris girl, drank. She was a common drunk and a bloody scandal of a wife to Jackie's father, who asked her to stop, and begged her to stop, and did all he could, went to doctors for advice, tried this, tried that, but she wouldn't stop. It was a mystery to everybody, because Jasmine Drake as she was before she was married – 'Jass' – was such a cheerful, pretty person. But eventually she took up with a man travelling with a road-laying gang and one day, when the gang packed up and moved on, simply disappeared. The only thing that anybody could find that she had taken with her apart from items of clothes was a small schoolboy trophy Jackie had won for boxing with an argent tin-plate figure on the top which his mother had always insisted, with its wild thicket of hair and brave fisticuffs stance, reminded her of him. His father had gone on to have a number of other children with several other ladies in the village, but nobody had seemed to regard that as particularly unusual at the time, and his father's attitude, and the attitude of the ladies themselves, as far as Jackie knew, had always been: 'Who's countin'?'

Jackie's father, whose familiar name was 'Bunny', had tried for a jockey at Newmarket in his youth. But he had grown too big-boned for that and had settled for blacksmithing where he was able to maintain his association with his beloved horses, and two in particular – Bill and Billy – in the one-horse village of Chatteris. Bill and Billy were the hearse-horses for the hearse owned by a man with the funny Dutch name of Woglom who owned the general store and also had an icehouse. The horses were shiny and Bible black and on duty they stepped sombre and slow just the way Bunny Mabe had tirelessly trained them to, with windows on both sides of the hearse so you could see the coffin.

All the men on Jackie's father's side of the family had been horsemen and he could claim an unbroken link stretching back to the distant days of the early nineteenth century when generations of Mabes worked at the stables in Newmarket Heath and, in a time before the railway, walked horses for up to a week across country to the towns where they were going to be raced. Stories had come down to him about walking highly strung thoroughbreds through the coolness of the night along roads as quiet as garden walks and not encountering a single living soul, because few people travelled after sundown then, unless there was a full moon.

It was this history that, when he first started showing out as a boxer, made Jackie think nothing of getting on his bike and cycling the 72 miles to East London, punching somebody sense-less, and cycling the 72 miles home. Sometimes, riding back to Chatteris after a good win at the Devonshire, he would think of his Mabe ancestors leading some snorting Skylark or Gallant Lad home from a win at Goodwood or Epsom or Ascot. Going into a field to relieve himself, he would watch the steam rising and feel the breeze on him and experience the sensation of time collapsing or spiralling in on itself. There was a painted sign outside a church in a neighbouring village he used to pass as it was coming light: EVERY MORNING, THE WORLD ANEW. He'd look across the fen to the towers of the great Cathedral just beginning to become visible in the distance and he'd revel in being alive.

Although they didn't know each other in those days, Ray and Jackie made their first visits to London at around the same time, when bread was rationed and bacon was a commodity changing hands on the black market and the city was still patched with bomb sites.

But these were things that, in all their years, Ray and Jackie had never talked about with each other. Oh, this and that. The odd bit here and there. But never the full story (inasmuch as there can ever be anything like a full story). Never very much about the years of their lives when one lived in the North and one lived in the South and both were foreign lands to the other and London, the teeming Babel and Babylon, was an unexplored alien universe to both of them.

Around the beginning of 1949, when he had just turned seventeen, Ray had been invited to audition for the BBC in London.

This was a momentous occasion, and his mother, Betty, who was earning her living as a barmaid then, had asked the advice of one of her regulars, a gentleman with an attaché case and a dark overcoat with a clerical air who, in his conversation, seemed to be quite familiar with the capital, and whose opinion she valued. Learning from him that the BBC was located at Savoy Hill, she had booked Ray and herself into a small private hotel in a narrow street between the Aldwych and Covent Garden market.

The other guests were mainly commercial travellers who in appearance looked very much like Mr Harris, which was her gentleman regular's name. But Mr Harris had been inaccurate with his information: the BBC had decamped from Savoy Hill to new purpose-built headquarters in Portland Place and Betty discovered, to her alarm at first, that they had booked themselves into rather a raffish area, shadowed by theatreland and the all-night market on one side and the down-and-outs of the Embankment on the other. (On the opposite corner to where they were staying was a tiny, one-roomed shop which, when his mother sent him into it looking for hairgrips one morning, Raymond discovered sold, in addition to *Film Fun* and *Breezy Stories*, postcards from Paris in sealed envelopes, American and French magazines, and books on flagellation in paper jackets. His cheeks caught fire, and he slipped quickly away.)

At home, the whole town went to bed early: the picture theatres closed at ten-thirty, and a quarter of an hour later everybody had left the centre by tram or bus. Here, though, there was a sense of relentless activity and purpose; the streets were thronged day and night with men wearing the checked sports jackets, the pullovers and the flannel trousers that were then the uniform of the spiv, and women wearing the kind of bright brazen make-up that would stop the traffic back home. But Ray's mum couldn't say she didn't like it. This, Betty believed, was 'the very elixir of life', as she had heard it referred to many times on her favourite programme, *In Town Tonight*, which she settled down to listen to at six-thirty every Saturday evening without fail: the announcement 'This is London!' and the flower girl murmuring 'sweet violets' and the chimes of Big Ben. '*We stop the roar of London's traffic to bring you the men and women of distinction, the stars of stage and screen who are . . . In Town Tonight!*'

They looked across at 'Little Ben' from the window seat that quickly became their favourite at the Corner House opposite Charing Cross station. His mother liked to pore over the long list of sweet iced drinks, of parfaits and sundaes and coupes and splits. Her particular favourite became a tall layered concoction known as an 'Alpine Glow' which had something called kümmel poured over it. Ray liked to eat brown bread and butter and drink Horlicks.

Betty gazed in awe at the rippling steel façade of the Savoy, whose bands, the Savoy Orpheans and the Savoy Havana Band, her bastard lying husband Tommy used to play along with on the wireless in the little front room of their house in Turkey Street before Ray was even born. Ray tried to get her to go with him to a tea dance at the Waldorf, which also was very near to where they were lodged, but she said they couldn't afford it, they weren't made of money and he couldn't even persuade her to step across the threshold to sneak a look at the famous sunken Palm Court.

Ray's audition comprised two parts. In the morning he was shown into a sub-basement deep in Broadcasting House and left there in front of a hand-painted notice which informed him how to proceed. This was a 'listening room'. A lot of comedians died a death on radio because they were so visual (or because southern audiences couldn't understand their 'cloggy' accents). Here was the programme-makers' chance to hear them before they saw what they looked like or how they moved. A disembodied voice asked Raymond to state his name and his sponsor and then he stood on the scuffed orange mat as instructed and waited for the green light to come on and proceeded to be mirthful. He pressed the black button under the light switch by the door as the sign told him to when it was over.

Afterwards he returned to his mother, who was sitting upstairs in the churchly commissionaired foyer where he had left her. She said she had seen the band-leader Vic Oliver, who was married to Churchill's wayward, alcoholic daughter Sarah, and a woman who she remembered had done funny voices on *Band Wagon* for 'Stinker' Murdoch and 'Big-Hearted' Arthur Askey, whose face she was sure she recognized from the *Radio Times*. She was light and flushed with pleasure and would have been happy staying there doing that all day.

The afternoon audition took place in front of the BBC's Deputy Head of Variety in the Wigmore Hall near Oxford Street. It was

111

velvet-draped and sepulchral and so quiet that you could hear London going about its business outside. Somewhere in the street at one point there was a loud bang, and the sound of air escaping. Ray began perspiring and very soon started to wish he hadn't let his mother make him wear the new lovat-green jumper she had knitted and his leather-buttoned, cavalry-twill jacket.

The famous Harley Street was near by. And as Betty Cruddas walked as she waited, it seemed no matter where she walked, or how she tried to avert her eyes, her eyes bumped up against surgical stockings and haemorrhoid preparations and cold, saw-like surgical instruments and unblushing displays of medical supports and flagrant, dusty-looking pink trusses. 'DAMAROIDS, THE GREAT BRITISH REJUVENATOR' was a sign that Ray pointed out to her using an oily American advertising-man accent and that they both had a laugh over afterwards.

Ray emerged from both of his auditions with respectable results and went home with a promise of future work from the Corporation. Broadcasting on the BBC in the radio days was a sign of prestige and arrival. They employed him steadily for three or four years as the number-two comic and then the compère of variety programmes ('presenting the people of variety to a variety of people') made specifically for and broadcast only in the North East region. The problem was that, because the North East had lost its own wavelength at the end of the war, they had to share a wavelength with Ulster, and North of England Home Service programmes were heard only on the whim of Broadcasting House, Belfast. More often than not this meant that, when Betty's and Ray's friends and family gathered round a set to hear him on *Workers' Playtime* or *Wot Cheor, Geordie,* he'd be faded out to make way for long dreary hours of Irish jigs and sports news from Ulster.

He wouldn't hear the call from London again for a further six years. By which time he had comprehensively Italian-Americanized his appearance and deregionalized his accent and become personable, prosperous, ochre-faced, slick. They were years that gave him the chance to get his ducks on the pond, as he would later (often) say.

There is a respectable chance that while Ray and his mother were sitting over their austerity-busting luxuries in the Corner House in the Strand, Jackie was in the Coventry Street Joe Lyons not far away, where he was liable to be mixing with the prostitutes who worked the pavements of Shaftesbury Avenue and Lisle Street ('You'll always find a smile in Lisle Street' was the joke there), and the Cypriots and the 'Malts' who were their ponces, and visiting Americans in forces bands who were exempt from the Musicians' Union ban, and men who fancied themselves on the cobbles but who you would never get in a ring, and junkies clutching their scripts for the all-night chemist in the Circus, and servicemen and brasses fresh in from the Potomac Club or the Bouillabaisse or the Fullado, stumbling on doctored whisky, and Tubby Hayes and Stan Tracey and other young English players who would congregate at the all-night Coventry Street Corner House to meet the American jazzmen there and listen to their stories about being in Benny Carter's band and playing with legendary figures like Dexter Gordon in unattainable meccas like Memphis and Chicago and glean ideas from them. They had a band in the gallery in the all-night Joe Lyons and the waitresses all wore smart little black dresses and were known as 'nippies', presumably because they nipped in and out smartish to take the orders and get the food for the faces and the chaps, and all human life was there in those days really, as the saying went. A thousand stories under the sky.

But, after Chatteris, it was Hackney that for Jackie on his first visits had seemed like the big beating heart of the West End. And for a while they had managed to convince him that the West End was where he was. There were quantities of drink and women, strings of Christmas lights, pungent and exotic smells; the press of bodies, the occasional flashes of bright modernity in the close huddled streets. And, hick that he was – carrot-cruncher, shit-kicker; he knew the words – Jackie had been taken in. There had been distraction enough to keep his attention for a while.

As a boy, when he came from Chatteris to the East End, he loathed London so heartily that he would cycle home through the night after a contest, or bribe a lorry driver with half his purse to give him a lift home. As a prospective champion, and even as a prospect whose brilliant future was irretrievably behind him, the bright lights could not be too bright for Jackie, the dance bands could not play too long or too loud; the party could not be too frolicsome.

After a bout at one of Mr Solomons' celebrated smokers at the Café Royal, for an example, he would take the pats on the back and pocket his nobbins and then after a few drinks in the company of the punters, managers, corner men and boxers who jostled each other in the bar at the Regent Palace Hotel, which was dependably a maelstrom of fight chat on those nights, he'd take off with his pal, another young fighter called Sammy Silver, for Toliani's Latin Quarter or the Café de Paris or, occasionally, depending on how the spondulicks was holding up, such a place as the Empress Club in Berkeley Square where the lardee went to tear up the rug. After that it was on to the Corner House or one of the tea stalls that ringed the piazza at the all-night market and then sometimes, if he was very lucky, Jackie would end up going home with one of the nippies from Joe Lyons, a lively little brunette called Greta. Greta was half on the game, but if she didn't have a paying customer she'd let Jackie go back with her to her place in Phoenix House, a rabbit warren of tiny apartments above the Phoenix Theatre in Charing Cross Road, where she'd let him have one on the slate.

Afterwards, with the dawn coming up, he'd walk through

Soho, where the last stragglers from the spielers and near-beer joints would be sharing the pavements with people going to work in the snack bars and kitchens and the newly delivered ice blocks which would already be starting to melt. The seen-it-all, white-overalled dairymen would be making their deliveries and the Continental butcher could be receiving the day's horse sections.

In a few hours, men would be forming a straggling queue along Great Windmill Street in front of the Windmill Theatre, whose boast during the war had been 'We Never Clothed'. By 11 a.m., the peeping Toms would have gathered on the corner of Archer Street opposite the hallkeeper's office at the Windmill hoping to catch quick flashes of the girls running up and down the stairs to and from the stage in their plumed head-dresses and pasted-on tassels and stars. (A narrow window on the last half-landing before you reached the Solomons gym looked straight across Great Windmill Street to the 'undressing rooms' of the theatre's lovelies and was also always heavily subscribed.) There was a convent a few doors along, and sometimes as Jackie washed up there in that pre-dawn hour it was possible to hear the nuns singing Gounod's 'Sacré Cœur'.

He had been entrusted by Mr Solomons with the key to the gym. And, after cadging a warm roll or a sweet-smelling cinnamon Danish from the still-shuttered 'Nosherie', which occupied the ground floor of the building, Jackie would climb the stairs to the 'Palace of Sock', as it had become widely known, and flop down on the old couch in the laundry room under the picture of a platinum blonde in a pea-green bathing costume stuck to the wall with a piece of soap, and wait for 'Jolly Jack', the boss, to arrive and announce with the bravado of his arrival that it was time to commence getting into another day.

Actually, on most days, 'the motley throng', as Mr Solomons called them, would have gathered around the whisky cabinet in his inner sanctum by the time he rolled up, the motley for the most part consisting of the boxing writers for the daily papers, give or take the odd *shvartzer* or provincial promoter. The scribes themselves would have been beaten to it by several hours by the boxers and trainers and the various gym rats and hangers-on who would already be spilling sweat sparring, working on the light bag, the heavy bag, the tattoo ball, etcetera. The gym would already be loud with the kind of effort befitting its reputation as the forcing house of champions and giving the sense that it was a place of serious endeavour. But it was only with the arrival of the nabob of the noble art himself, Mr Solomons, every day with a bang and a crash that the Solomons gym could be said to truly spark into life.

Mr Solomons never simply walked in anywhere. Mr Solomons pushed his way into offices, conversations, all through life. Big, blustering, fast-talking, fast-living, glint-eyed, bulbous-nosed, Mr Solomons (motto: 'All the world's a fiddle!') was one of the most controversial, colourful and supremely sure-of-himself members of the managerial ranks. Habitual wearer of a snap-brim trilby, a tie that needed volume control and a suit with enough padding in the shoulders to pack Harringay (these were his own lines, it's why he got so much ink; he was very good), he also unfailingly wore a yellow rose in the lapel of his camel's-hair topcoat and had another waiting in a stem vase in his inner office to be sniffed and turned and finally threaded through the button-hole of his suit jacket.

Where to begin with this Mr Solomons, who the Game hadn't seen anything like since the days of cigar-smoking Joe (Yussel the Muscle) Jacobs, Hymie Caplan, Dumb Dan Morgan, Jimmy (The Boy Bandit) Johnston, Billy McCarney and other managers with more colour than their fighters? And the aforementioned were all Yanks. Perhaps the oddest thing about Jolly Jack was that, despite all the best efforts of himself and his fastidious wife, Fay, and in spite of the masking masculine odours of cigar smoke and the high-class (black-market) 'Tweed' cologne which he took care to splash on, he always smelled faintly but unmistakably of fish.

'King Cod' was Jack's other nickname away from the ring, based on the early-morning business he ran with his brother Maxie at Billingsgate, wholesaling prime mackerel, haddock and hake. 'I started on the up and up slapping fish on a slab. And as with fish, so with fights. Only more so. If you sell fish – as I do – give 'em big fish. If you promote fights – as I do – give 'em big fights. Stick to this way of doing business and you can't go wrong. Maybe! *Kin-a-hora!*' (Which means: 'May the evil eye not fall on me'; 'Touch wood'.)

Almost all of Mr Solomons' first wave of visitors, in a phrase coined by one of his cronies, the *News of the World*'s boxing man, Frank Butler, were men who were 'tenpercental'. Milling around in the gym and the outer office when the boss breezed in would be club-owners, bouncers, bruisers, burglars, ex-boxing champions, con men, ponces, pickpockets, fences, racketeers, car salesmen and visiting Americans in dark glasses; all desirous, all itchy and soliciting a piece of his time.

Jack, the archetypal *alrightnik*, liked a good villain. And, if they were respectful, then, seated behind his desk and talking around a large cigar, he would express sympathy, ask encouraging questions, and finally tell them that everything possible would be done. If necessary, toes could be stepped on.

But if one of the desirous ones was pushy, antagonistic, demanding instead of imploring inside his teddy-bear coat, or if they were bold enough to be critical of Mr Solomons, to blame him for their problems, he would rub his hands together, harder and harder. In a long, difficult meeting, his hands would get raw. His voice would grow lower, softer, and the corner of his mouth would turn down. At this point, those who knew him would back off. They knew what was next. But the foolhardy would mistake

117

his lowered voice for nervousness or weakness. Then he'd blow and it came in a frantic roar which made its way to the bookies hanging around the telephone box on the corner and had the Windmill girls holding their pretty beringed little fingers over their pretty little rhinestoned ears in mock shock and alarm.

It had been a red-letter day for Jackie when he had climbed aboard his bike and directed himself towards the club the hustling matchmaker Mr Solomons had made in that funny little building in Devonshire Street in Hackney, sevenpence in the balcony, one shilling downstairs, the big promoters in on Sunday mornings, sitting at the ringside eating kippers and watching the boxing. Jackie's brief amateur career had ended with a suspension at fourteen for taking ten shillings for a bout in Chatteris. He had enjoyed a string of victories against small-timers for small pay at the Dev, and Mr Solomons was coming round to the opinion that there was something a bit right about Jackie. Only he couldn't believe this boy skedaddling on his bicycle back home to the sticks every time without even seeing the inside of the new shower bath he had gone to such great lengths and nearly done his money (so he claimed) to install. So Jolly Jack had a notion. He put forward a plan.

Mr Solomons loved and doted on his aged mother who, when he was a year and a half, had joined the wagon trains of Jews with pushcarts leaving Eastern Europe and trundled him out of her marshes village in White Russia. Judah, Booba's husband, had arrived first with other *landsmen* from the village, and had found employment in a rag factory, sorting rags, a filthy, terrible job, and then as a cap-maker in a workshop in the East End. He had been able to save enough money to rent two small rooms above a wardrobe-dealer in Pearl Street, Spitalfields, behind the Cambridge music-hall. A couple of years later they had moved a few streets north, to two rooms in a teeming, dark, three-storeyed tenement, only ever called 'the Buildings'. There, Booba started to take in work for Bryant and May's, making matchboxes. Bryant and May supplied the labels and the pieces of cardboard. She had to buy the paste – flour and water and a bit of soap – out of what she earned. There were strips of sandpaper to stick on. The work was paid daily, and Jack or one of his brothers and sisters – in the final there were six of them: Jack, Maxie, Barney, Harriet, Asher and Cissie – would take the matchboxes into the receiving depot in Bacon Street for their mother. In later years, the girls would buy lace curtains in Caledonian Road and sell them or rent them for sixpence a week to the neighbours, but they never had more than the two rooms for all of them.

By the late forties and Jackie's arrival, Judah Solomons was dead. Jack's brothers and his sisters, like him, had taken a step up in the world and moved away from the old East End. Not very far away: only to the double-fronted houses and two-car garages of Stamford Hill and Hendon which they had decorated in the new-style *goy* way. But, try as they may to persuade her, Booba had resolved to end her days in the Buildings and was determined that she couldn't be budged. So, in truth, lodging Jackie with his mother was a very Jolly Jack way of filleting several herrings at the same time.

For sure, exchanging the flat and empty fenland he had grown up surrounded by for the stewed enclosure of the tenement came as a jolt to Jackie's system. The whole court or alley – it was an L-shaped cul-de-sac – had been congested to a small dimension and was about a hundred years old. It was surrounded by the backs of two timber yards and the railway arches. It seemed that the Council was not proud of the Buildings and had encouraged the builders to hide them from the public view so that not even the sunlight could brighten the gloom. The only entrance to the alley was in Brick Lane. A pub called the Jane Shore had made a small passage into the Buildings so that the people could get their beer from the Jane. This passage formed a perfect escape route for the many thieves who began to rob passers-by of their purses, watch-chains and other valuables, although anybody who carried the Solomons name or was known to be able to call on the Solomons brand of retribution was exempted from these activities. The pickpockets (called 'whizzes') and the *gonifs*, as the Jews called common thieves, hung around the entry to the Buildings and the back of the Jane. And what impressed Jackie most was the conceit and vanity of their characters. First and foremost everybody wanted to be regarded as belonging to the highest ranks of the criminal fraternity when all they mostly were was a collection of small-time, coarse and common *grober yung* ripe for any mischief.

Before the war, Jackie would have been the only *yock* in the Buildings. But now there were other non-Jews, Romanies and Irish who used bottles and *shiv* knives against each other and bred cage birds and vicious pocket-sized terrier dogs for sale on Sunday mornings in Club Row. It was a quiet night when the peace was disturbed by only one eruption of *goyishe midas* – one eruption of screaming and the exercising of very foul tongues.

But Booba – her given name was Lenah, but nobody had said the name Lenah in her hearing for very many years – was feather-bedded too deep in her memories to hear. To step into the two rooms she had shared with her husband and her children and filled with her smell and her spirit and her life for fifty years was to step back into the Russian *shtetl* of 1904, or even 1804. Town called Pridneprovsk. Minsk region. Pripet Marshes.

Booba had always been happy to deny herself the delights of freedom and the possibilities of the city; outside the home, the focus of her existence was the *shul*, the synagogue. She informed herself of what was happening locally through the pages of the Yiddish daily paper, *Di Tsayt*, which ceased publication soon after Jackie moved in to live with her, in 1950. Booba had a dark face, black eyes, vigorous hair. Her old-country Jewish dignity was very firm and strong.

She had been born in a small wooden house with caulk walls and a stove chimney and the icy press of space bearing down on all four walls. She had been able to construct Minsk region, period of the May Laws, of the pogroms and persecution, with the beads, the mantel ornaments, the brasswork in the fender, the eight-branched candlestick on the mantelpiece, the linoleum-green blinds.

This was especially the case on Friday evenings when Booba's children and in time her grandchildren returned to the old home before the Sabbath came in. Then she would light the candles and bring the fish and plaited bread she had prepared and Jackie, feeling not at all *mishpochah* yet but strange and like an intruder, ignorant of the words and the manners, what to eat with this, when to sit and when to stand, would squeeze a chair up to the table wearing unfamiliar new clothes and watch while Booba stood up to cover her face with her apron and say grace.

On high holidays again all Booba's children would come home, although these were always times of stressfulness and ripe for misunderstanding. Before the Day of Atonement every year, for an example, Mr Solomons resolved to take Booba to pay respects at the grave of her husband, his father. But always something intervened. A deal. A lunch. A transatlantic call he had to be there to take. He would send a car with a driver around to one of his sisters, and Harriet or Cissie, with their children if they were available, would go with Booba to the cemetery in Golders Green and look out from the maple interior-veneered Armstrong-Siddeley (Booba smelled stale cigarette odour in the upholstery; noted the slovenly smears on the window) with their mother's flinty, disdainful eye. She always brought a bunch of blue carnations and the late Judah Solomons' prayer shawl with its black stripes and shredding fringes with her on this day of visiting the dead and forgiving the living – forgiving and asking forgiveness.

Jack would make it to the Great Synagogue on the corner of

Fournier Street for the *Kol Nidre* service with wine and whisky on his breath, and then make his way along Brick Lane in the dark past the 'brides' as the prostitutes at that end of the Lane were known, coat collar up, trilby down, tea-rose wilted, to try to make a respectable show of eating (having already repleted himself at Murray's or the Ivy) the old-country food his adorable, demanding mother had prepared.

On the nights Jackie went home with Greta and catnapped at the gym, Booba would make a show of ignoring him and be distant for a while. But sooner or later, he knew, she would appear and slide a plate of biscuits and pickles or *challah* bread with cold mutton with *chrayn* in front of him and then retreat to her chair to watch him eating, wagging a finger when he chanced to glance in her direction. He was her *lobbes* then, her lovely rascal. And she would call him this fondly before she retired for the night. She slept in a corner alcove on a high bed which she had to raise herself on to backwards, her crochet shawl around her shoulders, her side hair in plaits. She pulled a curtain across with a deep sigh before she went to sleep.

Booba couldn't of course countenance to see Jackie fight. But on fight nights when he came back to her from the Dev she would fuss around him, running her fingers over the nicks and bruises on his face, turning his hands over in her hands, *tsk*ing over the purple and yellow patches that were already appearing, blooming and spreading, caressing the hurt-delivering, hurting reddened knuckles. Examination over, she would direct him to the table where a starched snowy cloth would have been draped, half folded, over the fireplace end and set for one. Then she would proceed to feed him the meal of Yiddisher food that she had deduced to be his favourite – *matzo*-meal dumplings in soup, the sweet carrot stew called *tsimmes*, apple strudel – until he would go *oy-oy-oy* and *ay-ay-ay* and Booba would blush and beam to see him becoming native *vayttshepl* in her caring.

Booba's Buildings were famed locally for being the tenement where the great welterweight champion of the twenties, Ted Kid Lewis, had grown up. Lewis, born Solomon Mendeloff, had started at the world-renowned 'Wonderland' only a short step away, and gone on to become one of the most popular British fighters ever seen in North America. From America, news of his fabulous exploits – his epic series of battles with Jack Britton, his car crashes with chorus girls – winged their way home, and he became an idol and nothing less to the young Jews of White-chapel, and a famous figure out in the wider *goyim* world. He appeared in advertisements, penned columns, punched a golden bag and skipped silken ropes twice nightly and three times on Saturdays for Stoll Moss Empires, and amassed a considerable fortune. For a while he was everywhere, and knew everybody, and everything he loaned his name and his gold-toothed image to prospered.

Booba remembered this little Mendeloff as *prost*, utterly common, and reserved her right not to join her neighbours on the open staircases and common areas of her Buildings to see the conquering hero return in his white fedora and diamond stick-pin and his white gangster suit and spats, his middle girded in multiple gaudy Lonsdale belts. Booba was orthodox and old school in this as in all else and referred Jack and his cheering brothers and squealing sisters, who for the occasion had some-how acquired an illustrated cover of *Boxing* magazine dated 1915 which bore the caption 'Kid Lewis, his new coiffure, his golden smile, and Zalig Goodman, his guide and supervisor', when she could get them finally on their own away from the *kocheleffel* and the vulgar mayhem, to the teachings of the rabbinical authorities and the rules of their religion which condemned sport in general as a pagan activity and decreed that striking the Other and shed-ding blood was mores of the heathen. Jewish fighters were 'bums' or 'tramps'. To respectable Jews such as she was and they were, such men were to be considered a not-to-go-near area and an embarrassment.

Her effectiveness may be judged by the fact that Mrs Solomons' little boy, as the potentate cutely liked to refer to himself in later years, by the early thirties had spaded his fishmongering profits into the Devonshire Sporting Club accommodated in an old church building in Devonshire Street, Hackney. It was perhaps to reassure his mother in the matter of his moral probity that, for years after he was established, by virtue of his control of the heavyweight championship, as the world's 'fistic Parnassus' and set up as a big-shot in the West End, he continued to rise at four o'clock every morning and invite anti-social odours to swarm on to him by putting on a white store coat and white wellingtons to wade amongst the guts and entrails amongst slabbed and bucketed smelly freshwater fish. 'They're all alive!' was Jack's famous shout, which could have been the shout of the doormen at the strip clubs and clip joints that were his near neighbours in Soho. 'They're lovely!'

Booba's misgivings about the little Mendeloff Yiddle were borne out when Kid Lewis became associated with Oswald Mosley's 'New Party' in the thirties and stood as a fascist candidate in East London. By the end of the war, though, he had been put on the payroll of Solomons Promotions and was functioning as Jolly Jack's aide-de-camp and right-hand man. Lewis, sometimes known as the 'Sphinx' for his cruelly sharp wedge face and his narrow eyes that never betrayed elation, was still unpredictable and in condition at fifty. And, Windmill girls and hangovers permitting, he would climb through the ropes to do some sparring and shadowing and put Jackie and some of the other fighters in the lower divisions through their paces at the Great Windmill Street gym. 'You still look tough,' Jackie, cruciate and medial ligaments untorn and intact, ambitions undaunted, congratulated the Kid. 'Tougher than a night in jail,' came the reply just like that accompanied by an armour-plated 24-carat grin.

One day in 1948, when he had just turned eighteen, Jackie was summoned by the gymnasium major domo Nat Sellers and instructed to shower and be ready to accompany the boss and his sidekick Lewis on an errand in two shakes of a lamb's tail if not sooner and make it snappy. Jackie threw himself down the flights of chipped stone stairs with his hair still wet and his shirt-tails flying. He ran against the stream of up-coming traffic still headed for the heavy wooden door of the outer office marked 'BUSINESS ONLY': boxers, managers, referees, rival promoters, matchmakers, doctors, actors, politicians, police, nobility, respectable citizens, spivs and drones. They had all come soliciting Mr Solomons, to bend his ear, to seek a favour; and Mr Solomons had asked apparently particularly for him, hick from the sticks who didn't know night from day it seemed about just a minute ago or (this was Mr Solomons' personal assessment of how wet Jackie was behind the ears) how many has-beens make five. The boss and Kid Lewis had already taken their places in the back of the car when he reached pavement level. The Kid was holding one of the thick plaited leather straps, legs crossed, pinkie ring glinting; Mr Solomons, Havana'd and hatted, was leaning forward having a conversation with the driver, who was seated beyond a sliding glass partition. Jackie let himself in on the driver's side and took one of the kick seats which, through an ingenious arrangement, could be set facing backward towards the passengers or forward towards the driver and turned out to be covered in a luxurious soft velvet with leather piped between the ridges. The carpet was pale and deep and luxurious and Jackie watched with pleasure as his feet sunk down into it, displacing each immaculately valeted twist pile individually. He had elected to face away from Mr Solomons and Mr Lewis so as to vouchsafe their privacy. But as the big car purred – this was the word; the rough world was a mute pantomime going about its rumbustious business on the other side of the thick, slightly green-tinted glass – Jackie could see the two important men into whose circle fate had brought him, facing away from each other, communicating with their individual thoughts, reflected in the sliding glass panel behind the driver.

It was a glorious early-summer late morning at that time when pleasure motoring continued to be curtailed because of the rationing on petrol, and they glided through St James's and along the Mall in the direction of Westminster virtually unimpeded, with the whole of London laid out about them. The gold and blue leonine Standard was flying at the Palace and people were relaxing in deckchairs in the park and the air on that morning it seemed to Jackie was marked with the sense of anti-climax at having survived all around.

It was only when they had crossed Westminster Bridge into Lambeth and then Vauxhall that he started to notice the craters, sometimes crudely walled off behind advertising hoardings, and the bomb sites with groups of wild-looking children playing on them, lush and overgrown with weeds. South London was unexplored territory to Jackie and so unlike the West End and Whitechapel and other parts that he was growing to know as to not seem part of London at all.

In their stately way, like royalty themselves in these surroundings, they cruised past war-scarred streets and blighted buildings, Mr Solomons taking the occasional nip from a silver flask which Jackie knew contained whisky combined with milk for his ulcer problem ('I need a stiff milk!' was one of the boss's jokes guaranteed to get his regular court yokking and laughing), and Kid Lewis would take a more animated slug from his own smooth silver flask shaped to curve with his upper body and not conflict with the drape line of his jacket. And watching them by their reflections – Mr Solomons so brainy intelligent and well fed even through all these war-time restrictions; the Kid, who never wore shoes until he was ten years old and seldom had enough to eat and whose face was still all hollows and chalk-like and whose

ribs when he was stripped still stood out like dulcimer keys –
watching them then Jackie was moved to see these two products
of the Brick Lane Buildings who had taken such steps up and
wore the clothes and rode in the purring car that showed the
world by what increments they had bettered themselves. It made
Jackie, now a denizen of the Buildings himself, fasten on with
hope to the coming prospect of his own future and reflect on the
small rewards he had staggered home to his father with as an
amateur boxer – glassware, canteens of cutlery, and so on; on one
occasion a huge armful of leather-bound volumes of the poets,
from Milton to Masefield – and were still there gathering dust in
his old house in the empty Fens now as far as he knew.

Mr Solomons only forty-eight hours earlier had disembarked
from his latest trip Stateside on the *Queen Mary* where (Jackie had
half heard him saying just now to Kid Lewis) the top stateroom
cabins had been occupied – in addition to himself and Gus Les-
nevich, who he had inveigled to come and make sweet turnstile
music for him by putting his title on the line against the people's
champion Freddie Mills at Harringay Arena – the onboard VIPs
had included the newspapering legend, Lord Beaverbrook; the
Liverpool football team on their way home from a profitable tour
of the United States and Canada, and the Duke and Duchess of
Windsor, who the boss had missed being given an introduction to
by that much thanks to the gawping useless parties at the next
table. Kid Lewis, no stranger to the upper-tier sun decks of the
Atlantic routes, only answered by gruffly mumbling that he had
noticed VIPs was 'spiv' spelt backwards.

After toiling up a hill of dull suburban villas, Jackie observed
the sky open up before them as if they would soon be approaching the ocean. When they crested the hill he saw that they had
come to a wide flat public common which the road took off
around in both directions, it was just a case of which. The driver
slid the partition along a few inches and enquired of Mr

Solomons if he had a preference or knew his way in these far-flung parts. But the boss said nothing, just handed a ragged-edged but (from its unyellowed and quite crisp condition) recent newspaper clipping to Jackie with the instruction of communicating the relevant information contained within it to the driver. 'If you've brought your reading glasses, my old chum-china.'

The piece of newspaper unfolded three or four times to reveal a lot of writing which was attached to a picture of about the same size. The picture showed a gathering of coloured persons in numbers that Jackie had never before seen photographed together. In the background was a ship and in the foreground was the dock at Tilbury with dressed-for-best West Indian men and women (although they were mostly men) crowding every available inch of every surface. The people in the picture seemed both shy and bemused by all the fuss their arrival seemed to be causing. The men wore pork-pie hats and roomy, peg-bottom suits and carried cardboard suitcases secured with canvas belts and lengths of raw twine. The focus of the picture was a handsome, lighter-skinned man with an oriental cast and dark almond-shaped eyes who the caption identified as 'James Li, 26'. Li was holding aloft a two-handled silver cup which was the boxing trophy he had evidently won onboard, *en route* from Jamaica to England.

The headline above the article open in Jackie's hands said: 'HAPPY TO BE HERE! FORMER TROOP SHIP DOCKS AT TILBURY WITH FIRST WAVE OF 500 IMMIGRANTS FROM CARIBBEAN. COLONIAL OFFICE UNPREPARED'. Certain key sections had been underlined or circled. In addition to Li's name and nationality (half West Indian and half Chinese), and his status as flyweight champion of Guyana, these included: 'Clapham Common Deep Shelter' and 'Clapham South Station', which is where, Jackie saw from a sign, they had now adventitiously arrived.

The common extended away from them with trees on both sides. Across the street from where they parked was a tumble-down encampment of khaki ex-army tents. There was a line of trestle tables with two monster tea-urns squatting in the overhead sun. Groups of coloured men were lounging in the shade of the tents and gathered under trees. A thin horse-hair mattress had been thrown over a branch of a tree and a group of hard-muscled men were taking it in turns to give it a pounding with their fists. Card games and games of dominoes were in progress and much guarded, languorous watching. This was the advance guard, 'the 500 Sons of Empire' as the *Daily Mirror* had hailed them, come to that distant place where life was wider, bigger, more significant; the London whose streets from Trenchtown and Kingston and Marine Square in Port-of-Spain in Trinidad had seemed gleaming and beckoning – the site of creation and riches and power in the modern world. They had been there four days and had been allocated a former air-raid shelter as a place of emergency accommodation and they were bored.

There was a style among the men for trousers worn very high up in the waist with the ends of skinny belts hanging down. A number of them had Vaseline in their hair. A group resplendently got up in broad-brimmed hats and suits of unlikely purples and pinks was gathered around a man who was leaning against a tree playing a guitar. 'Mr Lord Kitchener', as he would eventually introduce himself, was strumming and singing in the middle of a softly humming circle.

'Give us some bad song now, man.'

'Some little evil tune, Lord Kitchener.'

And in a flamboyantly distorted British calypsonian accent Lord Kitchener sang as if he was truly making it up there and then:

> This little Miss Coldharbour Lane she say to me,
> 'I can't spend much more time in your society.
> I know you keep me warmer than my white boy can do,
> But my mother fear her grandson may be black as you.'

Amid the cackles, the singer disengaged himself from the group and extended a large hand to Mr Solomons. 'I embrace the rotundity of conventionality and wish you a good day.' This went down well and even Kid Lewis managed a bleak smile. 'That must be one of the most belligerent neckties ever seen in London,' Jolly Jack kidded the Jamaican, who was tall and tightly built into his suit. 'I see's you a smart fellow, not rich in ignorance.' They proceeded in this manner for another few minutes and then Mr Solomons got Jackie to show the newspaper picture of the boxer James Li who had brought them to this, to them, very unknown part of town. 'Probbly standin' on him this minute now,' Mr Lord Kitchener said, 'deep down where I don't go. No no no no, your honour. Shelter down there way too hairy-scary for me. I rest my case up here where I'm sure I'm only breathing my own air.'

Clapham Deep Shelter was in the bowels of the earth. It was half a mile down and some of the new immigrants were wary about getting in the lift. The entrance to the shelter was in a circular concrete structure situated several yards on to the Common. And Mr Solomons had started walking in that direction flanked by Kid Lewis and Jackie when the calypsonian called him back.

Every time he crossed the Atlantic, Mr Solomons went to great pains to avail himself of the latest American cure, the absolute end-all, for ulcers. He carried the pills in a small tortoiseshell box engraved with his initials and a pendant boxing-glove motif. He kept the box in the ticket pocket of his jacket. And it was Mr Solomons' precious pill box that Mr Lord Kitchener was offering back to him now. 'Ferdganef!' Jack said, wagging a finger and sipping on his cigar and laughing, somehow all of this at once. 'See if you can work that into one of your how's-yer-fathers. It's Yiddish for you light-fingered little son of a son of a howitzer. Like the style, pal. Like it a lot. Be good. An' remember: if you can't be good, be careful.'

'Please to make your acquaintance,' this long-streak Jamaican said.

When they found Jimmy Li he was stretched out on his bunk, shaving the hairs off his chest with a safety razor. The shelter was a tunnel which had been bored parallel to, but deeper than, the tracks that carried the Northern Line underground trains. The walls were curved and noise from the trains reverberated through them thickly every few minutes. The bunks were painted metal and stacked in tiers and there was a sense of packed earth pressing in all around like water packing a submarine. 'Jack Solomons!' Jimmy Li sat up, his feet dangling in mid-air. 'Mr Solomons.' He had grown the traces of a goatee beard but he was still recognizably the good-looking man in the newspaper picture. 'And Mister you got to be pure joking me I don't believe this do not believe this Kid Lewis. I've seen nearly all your fights with Jack Britton on the newsreels. "The most colourful clouter ever seen." Oh man. Man-oh-man.'

Part of Jimmy Li's purpose in paying the £28 10s for his passage to London had been to put himself on the powerful promoter's radar. But now, through the lucky break of a picture in the papers – the power of the press – Mr Solomons had come looking for him.

'Oh.' Mr Solomons had forgotten Jackie. 'This is Jackie Mabe. Nipper. Ring name "Nipper". The next flyweight champion of the British Isles.' It embarrassed Jackie to hear himself being spoken of in this way by the silken-tongued, snake-oil salesman Mr Solomons, reputed to be able to sell ice to the Eskimos, moheek to the Mohicans and so on and so forth if you believed the papers. Jackie's ears burned red as he shook the hand of Jimmy Li.

'Jackie, man.'

'Welcome to England.'

They took Jimmy to a gym in Brixton to see if he lived up to his advance billing, and on the way he told them his family had had to sell three cows to pay for his trip over, about how strange he

131

had been finding it in London to see daylight at ten o'clock at night, and about how he loved walking in the parks in the evening sunlight. Above all he talked about his new-found taste for fish and chips. '*Gute ta'am*,' Jackie nodded. 'Tasting good.'

At the gym, Jackie and Jimmy stripped off and put on the 16-ounce 'pillows' and sparred a few rounds under the critical eye of Kid Lewis, who was Mr Solomons' once-and-for-all arbiter in these matters. 'I am the head man around the dump,' Jack liked to say, 'but one word from me, and the Kid does as he likes.' They stood toe to toe and traded punches, Jimmy Li at one point hanging a beautiful right-hander on Jackie's chin, and old stone-face showed no reaction. But when in the car afterwards Mr Solomons said he would like, without plastering him with promises, to sign Jimmy on a manager's contract, Jimmy knew that he must have impressed.

What Jimmy Li hadn't yet fully discovered was that in London, as in the rest of the country at that time, a colour bar was in operation. Something else he didn't know was that Jolly Jack had spotted a business opportunity in the same place that had given hundreds of pub comedians the easy punchline 'No dogs, no Irish, no Coloureds'. Jews vs. non-Jews had been big box office in the Mosleyite thirties, when a number of East End boxers worked as bodyguards for the British fascist leader. And now, in these hangover years after the war, with a different kind of racial tension brewing, Jolly Jack had intuited that there was a market for Black vs. White promotions. Many of the best black boxers had gone home to the Caribbean on assisted passages after demobilization. Which is why, when he had spotted Jimmy Li's picture in the paper, he had been quick to pounce. He had left a business card with his good new friend Lord Kitchener at Clapham Deep Shelter and was anticipating many calls to the office.

Jimmy stayed in the car and sat tight all the way into the West End with them. And that night, for the first time ever, Jackie joined the 'jimmers', which was the name they gave the men who went with their flasks and their sandwiches and sat through several performances of *Revudeville* at the Windmill Theatre, clambering forward over the rows in front as the seats closest to the footlights became empty.

Each 'edition', as Miss Van Damm, a gym regular and the rally racing-driver in charge of the Windmill operation called them, started with a lively song and ended with the cancan. In between were the balancing acts and the comedians and the conjurers and – all any jimmer ever wanted to see – the living, light-washed flesh of the girls in their historical tableaux and classically inspired immobile *poses plastiques*.

Kid Lewis (who eventually pulled the very few strings that needed pulling to gain Jackie and Jimmy admittance) was scathing that two such fit young men in their prime would want to join the old peepers and under-their-hat masturbators with their Spam sandwiches in their pockets and not a Chinaman's chance of ever coming within sniffing distance of one of those half-brass Windmill girls who'd all been promised by the old bird that taught them tap dancing since they were knee high to a grasshopper that they were going to be the next Vivien Leigh. 'Them mugs in there have probably never seen a woman undressed. Probably never even seen their old lady without her flannelette on. What is it, you're so *shmegegge* – so *brenda* – you think it's just to piss through?'

The West End was still shadowy at nights; still 'dark' as the theatre people said. The law allowing the famous rippling signs to be switched back on and neon lights spelling out names in a perpendicular way wouldn't come in for nearly another year yet. From the landing window at the gym Jackie had watched the nests of individual bulbs that filled each big hollow letter of the word making 'WINDMILL' grow dusty and black and for this reason had imagined the shows going on inside the theatre being similarly low voltage and dimmed.

That this was not the case he discovered as soon as he and Jimmy tiptoed in and took their seats behind the jimmers. The band, for a start, was loud and brassy, and the spectacle of light and colour it was accompanying, featuring high-kicking show-girls and bare-chested dancing boys, seemed too much to be contained on the small stage. As they settled down, each with his copy of the Windmill programme which, with its pictures of near-naked girls, was the closest you could get to a dirty magazine in those days, the big production number was brought to a conclusion and they believed they might be going to see something then. Instead two men came out in front of the curtain, one of them pushing a piano. 'Hello, music-lovers,' the piano-less comedian said, and Jimmy and Jackie both thought this was very funny, but nobody else laughed. The audience seemed to have heard the jokes before and dozed or rattled the pages of their newspapers pointedly while the double act was on. As they came to the end of their five or six minutes, though, the newspapers were put away and the men in the stalls sat up in their seats as the curtains drew back to reveal a 'Grecian Frieze' of three models posing like statues on ivy-covered plinths towards the rear of the stage, while a song-and-dance item went on in the subdued 'artistic' ultra-violet haze that drifted around in the foreground. The Olympic Games were due to open in London in a few weeks, and Jackie supposed that this was meant to be some sort of topical tribute to the Olympic ideal: one of the nudes posed with a discus, another with a spear, while the third, who had noticeably the largest breasts, held a plaster torch which began to sway slightly after a while. The dancers wore approximate net-gauze swimsuits and gymnast leotards which, in accordance with the strict rules laid down by the Lord Chamberlain's Office, teasingly outlined the figure but never glaringly showed details of the human form.

The effect was oddly erotic and, although they didn't join the move stagewards, Jackie and Jimmy found themselves sitting on until the next tableau, and then the next one, came around in the anticipation that something more explicit might be shown. The truth was that Jimmy Li had never seen a white woman unclothed. A man a few seats along in the row in front watched furtively through a pair of heavy black binoculars whose warm Bakelite casing Jimmy could smell.

They left when the lights came up on the old sheepish pervs and the pattern of black chewing-gum pressed into the carpet of the centre aisle.

Kid Lewis had palmed a big wadded white five-pound note to Jackie when they had parted company with him outside the theatre. And Jackie had kept dipping into his pants pocket and satisfying himself of the note's increasingly soggy presence throughout the performance. Five pounds could be made to go quite far in the summer of 1948, and as they emerged on to the darkened streets that promised much but that didn't easily give their secrets up to strangers, it pleased him to be able to lead Jimmy Li away from the clueless milling crowd of rubes and out-of-towners to the places that only somebody like himself with the inside dope would know.

In the space of not quite two years he had become a well-known figure, and Jackie nodded his 'good nights' and 'be goods' to a number of dubious characters as he guided Jimmy through a network of echoing courts and alleys to their first pit-stop of the after-hours and quietly revelled in what this said about his change of station.

They were still in June, only a week or so past the longest day. And it was one of those sunlit nights that Jimmy had spoken of earlier, with the sky still blue and the newspaper-sellers and flower stalls still open for business all along Coventry Street between Piccadilly Circus and Leicester Square. The Potomac and the Princes were two clubs situated back to back between

Jermyn Street and Piccadilly. One was run by a Belgian trumpeter called Johnny Claes, the other by a glamorous local heart-throb tenorist, Reggie Dare. They blew twenty-five shillings in the Potomac listening to Claes's Claepigeons playing a kind of boop-de-boop jazz music that wasn't strictly to either of their tastes, and then slipped through a service door at the end of a passage by the kitchens into Dare's place, where the boss stood them their first round. (Not very many years later, when Jackie went to visit Booba, who was dying in Homerton Hospital, the gatekeeper there was Reggie Dare.)

The place all the faces went in those days was the Modernairre, owned by the big gangster Billy Hill's sister, Aggie, in Greek Court. So they made their way round there and had one, and had another two for the road somewhere else, then went into Lyons Corner House where Greta made out she didn't know Jackie and the upshot was that at the end of it Jackie and Jimmy, acquaintances of a little over fifteen hours, were dead friends.

Jimmy Li was robbed of the first fights he had in London because of his 'paint job'. The nearest Labour Exchange to Clapham Deep Shelter was in Coldharbour Lane in Brixton. Most of the people Jimmy had come over on the boat with had gone to live there and Jimmy had joined them in Brixton because it became the place where in a city of called-out monkey noises and constant unaggravated violence he could feel comfortable and most himself.

He rented a bed in a house with a dozen other fellows from home, and on many nights they would gather together to drink the cheap ginger beer and whisky-based punch they called 'lunatic juice' and listen nostalgically to recordings of the Senior Inventor, the Caresser, Lord Beginner and other favourite calypsonians, and relive memories of the street marching, the costume floats and steel-pan music that dominated Trinidad Carnival in the four-day 'mas' leading up to the beginning of Lent. Mr

Solomons' acquaintance Lord Kitchener started to play regularly in the saloon bar of a local Brixton pub, singing the new calypsos he had composed in Britain, about Britain, and then at the dance clubs, cellar bars and semi-legal bottle parties that Jackie started to go to sometimes with Jimmy.

These, Jimmy assured him, were the nearest proximity you could get in London to the gaiety and happiness back home. 'Is weed, man,' Jimmy said to explain the uninhibitedness of the party-makers who had dipped into the little brown-paper packets that Jackie had seen surreptitiously changing hands. 'Rockin' high with charge.' And Jackie became aware of feeling an aloneness again in the midst of people with manners – ways of saying and doing things; music they liked and clothes they wore – that he didn't and could probably never hope to comprehend. To the best of Jackie's knowledge – but what did he know – when he was with him Jimmy stayed clean.

Black vs. White, as Mr Solomons had seen coming, became a major draw. And because he was needy for the money and there was little he could do about it, Jimmy Li was one of the 'bodies' put in against white boxers who were sometimes a stone or twenty pounds heavier than him. Occasionally when he was over-matched Jimmy upset the betting and won. But even in winning one of these uneven contests he could sustain a severe amount of punishment. 'The only good fighter is a hungry one,' Mr Solomons, who had much fatter fish to fry, would tell him on those occasions when Jimmy tried to raise a protest.

Jackie and Jimmy often ran together and sparred and trained together at Windmill Street under the eye of Nat Sellers. There wasn't much weight difference between them but they were different physical types. Jimmy was like a perfect take-apart teaching hospital model, lithe with long, elegantly defined muscles attached to a fine powerful frame. Jackie was squatter, more clenched, with the milky, transparent, sun-starved English skin that takes a cold blue undercolour from the skeins of surface veins. In training, and during fights, a hot red flush came up under the blue in a way he had been told many women liked. Jimmy's supple brown skin was perpetually slicked with sweat. Jackie hardly seemed to sweat and sometimes actually seemed to emit a ghostly glow in the gloom of the cracked dark leather and the dark wood of the gym. Jimmy liked to jab and dance; he punched above his weight and his fighting philosophy had always been a simple one: 'When you see an opening, just put your fist through it.' He had a snapping right and tended to fight every fight to the same pattern: to punch, keep punching, and punch some more. Jackie was an in-fighter, kidney-punching and pummelling and preferring to fight skin to skin. He liked to keep coming and wear opponents down; his style was to stay close and be all over them like a rash. Jimmy was a bleeder; he cut all the time. Jackie by contrast hardly bled at all. His fists were calloused but his face was barely marked.

They had never been matched against each other until Mr Solomons was drawing up the 'underneath' for the big show-piece set-to of 1950 between Bruce Woodcock, the reigning British heavyweight champion, and the American, Lee Savold, with Savold's world heavyweight title on the line. The glamour fights always drew a celebrity crowd to training sessions at the gym consisting of champions and former champions and show-business stars such as Danny Kaye, who was enjoying his triumphant season at the Palladium at that time, and Sophie Tucker, who was at the London Casino, and lesser stars of the calibre of Robertson Hare and Ann Shelton and Nova Pilbeam and members of the Crazy Gang, plus a couple of the racier High Court judges mixing and mingling with some of the top coppers from West End Central and the government hangman Albert Pierrepoint, who was also a boxing referee and came accompanied by a very powerful deathly aura which was heightened by his stark terror of a camera and the way he refused ever to speak for publication. 'Miss Tucker, let me introduce you to His Majesty's hangman, Mr Pierrepoint, who gave that wicked Ellcot boy the drop last week.' Jolly Jack loved all this celebrity *booshwah* of course and looked forward to big fight nights for the opportunity for blowing smoke up celebrity *tushes* as much as for anything that took place in the ring.

Jackie and Jimmy, who were both used to the small halls, were excited by the big occasion, although very few others at White City on the night appeared to be. When they went on many of the cheaper tiered seats on the far side of the greyhound track were occupied, but they made their entrance through row upon empty row of the dented metal folding chairs in the field that they themselves had helped to put out. Woodcock, the Doncaster piston-fitter, they knew was booked into the Strand Palace Hotel. The American champion Savold and his manager were staying at the Imperial, Russell Square, which had a Turkish bath in the basement. Jimmy was still sharing a room (and sometimes a bed; with a railway cleaner who worked nights) in Brixton; Jackie was still lodged at the Buildings in Whitechapel, and they had both made their separate ways to White City on the underground. In Jackie's satin dressing-gown pocket was the small leather box containing the set of *tefillin*, the sacred texts, with which Booba had solemnly presented him. Only a handful of the pencillers for the papers had bothered to claim their seats for this nine-stone battle of the minnows when the bell went for the start of the first round.

To his own amazement, and then with a slight sense of concern, Jackie won at a clip – 'without bedewing his brow with a single pearl of perspiration', as one of the scribes present would later write. Jimmy, at twenty-seven to Jackie's twenty, was giving away seven years. But he was more experienced, stronger and usually much faster on his feet. If the mood was on him he could win a fight by feinting and dancing and not letting his opponent come near. That night though Jimmy never seemed to get going.

Now and then he would buzz his way in to close quarters, land a flurry of punches and flicker off out of distance. But all in all he seemed preoccupied and sluggish and wasn't moving with any of his usual fluency and zip.

In the first round Jackie was able to score heavily to the body, and he caught Jimmy with a solid left hook about a minute into round two. Jimmy wasn't seriously hurt, but he was knocked off balance and slipped. He left himself wide open, hauling himself awkwardly off the canvas with the help of the top rope, and Jackie should have moved in then for the kill. When he didn't – he stood back and waited until Jimmy was ready and then sportingly extended his gloves – he noticed some of the old-timers and Mr Solomons, who had materialized at the ringside in his midnight-blue dinner-jacket, disgustedly shaking their heads.

The third round was about even. By the fourth, Jimmy's right eye was bleeding. He kept clinching, and his blood was on Jackie's head and chest. When they broke and Jimmy turned his head to listen to the referee, Jackie didn't hesitate. He heard the voice of Kid Lewis in his head: *Be ruthless. Never hesitate when you see your opponent is staggering but throw everything into the blow that will end the contest. When your opponent is cut never back off but deliver your hardest punches to the wounded area. The objective is to incapacitate your man. It is the boxer's job on any and every occasion to protect himself.* His right whipped out, connecting with Jimmy's temple, and Jackie's good friend Jimmy sank in a heap.

In his corner, Nat Sellers and his seconds tried to revive Jimmy with ice at the base of his skull. He remained unconscious for three minutes. It was seven or eight minutes before they were able get him standing between two of them and assist him from the ring.

Instead of leading, which was his right as the winner, Jackie followed. He saw the empty seats with the strips of white paper saying 'RESERVED' on. He looked up to the wide perspex window of the VIP room where none of them had apprehended what had just taken place below, but were only waiting for their name to be called on the public address and listening to hear the volume of cheering which would go up when they stepped into the light and formally bestowed their presence on the fight-goers from the badly sprung and blood-spattered ring. They had been speaking of this or this or looking around to have their drink freshened and had failed to catch the catastrophic moment when a man hurt his brain so badly that he would still be learning to walk and talk and lift a spoon to his mouth in a year's, even two years', time.

The brain is a jelly-like mass suspended inside the skull in cerebrospinal fluid. Think of it like this (the white-coated specialist in his dusty basement office explained to Jackie): the brain is like a blancmange in a box, connected by thin strings which are the blood vessels. As a punch shakes or rotates the head, those 'strings' are being ripped apart. The blood flow puts pressure on the surface of the brain and the pressure of the added blood compresses the brain, causing unconsciousness, coma, and sometimes death. Repeated 'sub-lethal' blows such as those sustained in training are more dangerous than one-time knockouts. But it is the devastating knockout that most often causes death.

When the end came for Jimmy six weeks later – an end that Jackie would always remain convinced he had contributed to – Jackie was there. It was another small-hall promotion at Caledonian Road Baths and Jimmy this time had been put in against a Welshman called Boyo Morgan who was a lanky, unmuscled, string bean of a boy, shy to the point of invisibility outside the ring, but lethal inside it, with a punch like a mule. Jimmy had complained of tiredness and occasional dizzy spells since the KO by Jackie but, always co-operative, amenable, whatever anybody asked of him, he was quite sure he wanted to go on.

It was a hot night at the end of an exceptionally hot summer. All the doors and the windows in the hall had been jammed open in an attempt to get some air flowing through, but the fight was fought in torpor and strength-sapping heat. (Jackie had a clear memory of glancing up at the dome above the ring and seeing several figures tilted in against the slatted glass and another cobalt summer-night sky.) A number of men in the audience were stripped to the waist by the close of the fight, swabbing themselves with their shirts.

Jimmy gathered himself. He weaved and swerved into and out of distance, and he scored cleanly and well and probably shaved the first two rounds. In the third, Morgan dropped him with a right cross and a left hook to the head, but he was up again after three or four seconds. Honours in the fourth were even, but Jimmy walked on to an arcing right uppercut in the fifth and by the sixth he was already looking spent. From the sixth round onwards every punch thrown by Boyo Morgan jarred Jimmy. In the eighth Jimmy was forced to take two counts. In the ninth it seemed more than likely that the referee would be forced to stop the contest to save him. At one moment he stood defenceless rocking on his heels as Morgan measured him again and again, driving hard rights and lefts to the jaw.

By the start of the twelfth round Jimmy had been on the canvas four times. For most of the audience it was a relief when Morgan chopped him with a hard, loping left to Jimmy's head, dropping him for the last time. He was unconscious before he hit the canvas and his relaxed neck muscles allowed his head to thud against the boards.

'It didn't feel particularly special,' Boyo Morgan told the reporters from the local papers who crowded round him afterwards. 'Just everything I had.'

Jimmy was in a coma for a month. He had suffered an acute haematoma, an injury most often seen in car-crash victims.

After a month, he started to show the first signs that he was coming out of his coma. By November, he was able to communicate by blinking, and in January moved his right arm and leg slightly for the first time. By May he was able to form sentences and respond to simple commands. After a year he was still paralysed and confined to a wheelchair, as he would be for the rest of his life. He was able to feed himself when not feeling too tired, and was learning to talk again although his speech would always be halting and slow.

Jackie brought bulletins on Jimmy's progress from St Bartholomew's Hospital back to Great Windmill Street, but he very quickly sensed Mr Solomons' interest melting away. He was a busy man and they were, after all, hectic times with, just in the year of Jimmy Li's personal tragedy, many wheels to grease and fires to stoke. Mr Solomons had Woodcock–Mills, Mills–Maxim, 50,000-seaters, fights that were energetically promoted to the status of national occasions. Then he had Mills's retirement which left him with no British-born fighter capable of drawing these full houses of on-the-nose paying customers. But then along came the infant prodigy Randolph Turpin, youngest of the three fighting Turpin brothers and, in spite of being half black, box-office dynamite.

In 1951, Mr Solomons had Turpin–Sugar Ray Robinson 1, an event complicated by the cross-examination of Robinson's camp followers following the disappearance and murder of a little girl last seen alive near his training quarters at Windsor, and further calamatized by Jack's brother-in-law Izzey Cohen taking a heart attack and dying ringside. He had the return, Turpin–Sugar Ray 2, and the headaches and *shlemozzel* arising from Turpin's arrest in New York for allegedly raping a girl in his shower. He had the former high-earning prodigy Eric Boon, who was down but refusing to declare himself out, and this one and that one and the never-ending daily parade of coat-tuggers and *mitt-glommers* pleading special cases for his time. Plus, Mr Solomons had never been under any illusions, as Jackie knew.

'They want to see it done to you, or you do it to the man. But they want to see it,' he had once told Jackie. 'Everybody likes to see the fights. You watch the faces in a boxing crowd when it gets exciting and you see expressions on people's faces you don't see anywhere else. It's a different expression. Motor-racing, the crowds are always on the bends. That's in people. You haven't got long enough to understand what's in people. The cameras are looking at you; the people are there howling for your blood. A guy is punching you to pieces. It's all very basic. There's just something in all of us.'

It was out in the open where Mr Solomons stood. It was spelled out on a plaque which hung over his head: 'WINNERS WIN. LOSERS MAKE THEIR OWN ARRANGEMENTS.'

'This Jimmy Li. Very nice boy. I'm very sorry what happened,' he said. 'But he knew when he came over it wasn't going to be no game of doughnuts. Nobody ever told him it was a top-hats and tea party. So?' He shrugged.

Jimmy Li was still learning to walk and talk when Jackie snagged his foot in the canvas and did his knee and had to stand and watch his own career go down the pan following his title eliminator at the Empress Hall against Alby Ash. He was handed the sponge and the bucket and delegated sole responsibility for Mr Solomons' wife's, Fay's, fight-night needs and hot-dog snack requirements.

So there it was: Jackie and Jimmy gimps and losers both; both relegated from being prospects to a future of small returns and the lowly, grubbing-around end of the food chain. At least Jackie had the compensation of being *mishpochah*; he was still regarded as family.

The fact was that, even when Jackie was being groomed for a champion and still training intensively, Mr Solomons had imposed on him to run little errands on his behalf – take to that person, collect from this person, and a here and a there, no questions. Jackie was part of the special intelligence-gathering operation that Mr Solomons referred to as his 'SI6'. 'Sooner or later,' he assured Jackie, 'every mug, pug and slug' – he really did talk like this, taking great pride in spieling his own script in colourful Runyonesque words occasionally stretching to more than one syllable – 'every mug, pug and slug finds his way to the cafés, pubs, milk bars, dance dumps and billiards barns within spitting distance of this office. A million tongues wag there every minute of the day and half the night and if I didn't plant a smart ear or two to snap up unconsidered trifles for me, well, Mrs Solomons' little boy would indeed be a sap.'

No matter how on the bottle and given up to the moment Jackie appeared to be at the Latin Quarter or the Modernairre or Club 11 or wherever he happened to have arrived on his nocturnal round, part of him still acted as the boss's ears, flapping for Jack in the snakepit that was the cradle of the noble art. If there was, say, somebody having trouble making weight for a fight and weakening himself with steam baths and laxatives and sucking on copper coins to make spit – that would come back. Or a boxer in training with a damaged eye or fist that he was trying to cover up. Or the wide boys saying for the benefit of the mug punters they had their money on x when they were in fact on y. Or some *mockie* manager facing up Mr Solomons for £250 for a fight when Jackie knew from Ben and Dolly at the Archer Street café that he would be overjoyed to sign for £150, because he had been in for a tea and a rock bun that morning, that would also count as valuable intelligence and be marked up as Brownie points. Jackie was authorized to slip the odd note to Greta at the Corner House and to any one of a dozen doormen and sharpies around town and had built up an effective, low-level network of his own.

He had been married to Tina from the Greek café in Frying Pan Alley for a little over six months at the time of the accident that forced him to hang up his gloves and living in faraway Streatham with Tina's mother and father, Mary and Hercules Metaxas, and the rest of the well-meaning but rackety Metaxas clan. Tina had lost the baby that he didn't know she was carrying while Jackie was in hospital recovering from the series of operations on his knee. And this, combined with the dip in his professional fortunes, had confirmed what they had really known since the day Herky Metaxas had made them legitimize their entanglement: that it wasn't going to work.

Metaxas wanted to bring his son-in-law into the family business but Jackie understandably wasn't keen to give up the eventful life he had found for himself in the West End in order to compete with various neck-bracelet-wearing brothers and hairy-backed little relatives to become chief olive-pitter or head griller of the aubergines or staying up half the night basting the slow-cooking knuckles of lamb they called *klephtica*. It was another greasy, heartburn-inducing food and another non-indigenous way of life and Tina was obviously destined to marry the ouzo-importing cousin she did end up marrying just as soon as her brief liaison with Jackie could be pronounced kaputted and officially over and done with, no hard feelings on either side.

His errands, and the closeness they had established, continued to take Jackie back to Whitechapel and Booba, still in the Buildings, still observing the ways of the old country with the exception of the salty brown shrimps and slippery monster bull-whelks in mustard malt vinegar that Jackie went out of his way to bring for her whenever nostalgia or Mr Solomons' nipping bad conscience put a visit to Booba on the programme.

Down the turning, into the court, up the stairs, on to the faintly urine-smelling landing into the warm encompassing murkiness, the familiar pall and penumbra and Booba's tin boxes and little candles and gas mantels, a trail of wax collecting on her single treasured Meissen candlestick with the painted pattern of bud flowers, the flames dancing on the walls and leaning and shifting in the wind.

Booba who did not want many pleasures in life; who believed the more pleasure you got out of living, the more fear you had of dying. Booba who was still attached to the economy of scarcity, despite the growing evidence of abundance all around (a labour-saving electric Teasmade invention in a box she had never opened; chests full of Egypt cotton, silk and satin, the finest stiff linen; a mink stole, retail value forty guineas, moulting in the wardrobe). Booba who was so different from her son the big box-ing man and loud presence in the world, always so unashamed, so colourful, so compulsive, and exhibiting such a lack of restraint. 'This clouding-out ego,' she called him now, agitated, black eyes flashing, tough chapped *shtetl* fingers on the table smoothing and smoothing. 'This bellying blister waiting to drop its dirty load over all our lives, mine and all his brothers and sisters. And yours too, Jackie. Jack was a happy baby. Jack had a normal life as far as I, his mother, is concerned. Never in criminal offences. But now with Jack is all big "I"s and little "you"s. He expects bow and scrape to his whims. Jackie, hear me, you are another being with another life to lead.'

It disturbed Jackie to hear Booba speak like this. Was she dying? Afflicted with an intractable ageing disease? Had some-thing happened? (Every grain of Mr Solomons' life, personal and business, was grist to the rumour mill, exchangeable currency, but Jackie had heard nothing.)

'He thinks he is good man. He is *rich* man, but this is different. Finance terms, yes – money – when it comes to money, we are all on velvet,' the old lady said, speaking half in English and half in the Yiddish that Jackie had come increasingly to understand. '*Pah!*'

She had been shocked by the recognition that such uninhibi-tion, if not exhibitionism, of her son's was allowed in the world; that here a completely different and new content was expressing itself. '"All world is fiddle." Hah! What you do comes back around to you. This I can say, *lobbes* Jackie. This I believe.'

Booba asked Jackie if he had heard of the Jewish legend of the *golem*; if he was familiar with this word. 'Was an artificial man. Mechanical man in a human image which stood and lived. *Golem* had the gift of memory and would obey orders mechanic-like, without reflection, provided they came at regular intervals. Chop wood, sweep the street and the synagogue, all diversity of menial tasks. *Golem* was servant, and servant that does not answer back. But when rabbi wished to destroy his *golem*, rabbi had power to revert his *golem* – *his!* always me me me! – back to straw and wet clay.

'I don't like to be *kibbitzer* here,' Booba said, slowly easing herself out of her chair, 'but boxing is over with you now. What is you do? You come with the bucket, you mop up the blood. You *shmooze* the mother. You prowl the night. You carry tales. Jack is Jack. Jack is his own story. But you are Jackie. Different story. What is Jackie's story? Where does Jackie go? Are your dreams *really* your own dreams?'

Booba started for the scullery, supporting herself by the knuckles on large pieces of furniture as she went. Jackie stood at the door and looked at what had been Jack's and Maxie's and Barney's and Asher's room (the shiny rub of their bodies was still imprinted on the walls), and then his room. The openwork window curtain weighted with a single lapis bead which frequently made a light tapping in the night; the wallpaper faded to an almost sepia brown; the swan-neck gas bracket for the hissing light. He saw a pair of shoes he had forgotten he ever owned peeping out from under the bed.

Booba brought pink veal, gherkin pickles, *challah* bread – a little *shmeck*. The candles guttered at a slant, gouging crater holes in the wax. Booba cupped her hands around the candles closest to her to shut out the draught. He ate. The knife rang against the plate. So it was agreed. He would move back here.

*

Life in London was such a rich density of living – so densely tex-tured and closely packed with the tight unpickable weave of detail and incident: the hanging yellow smogs of the traffic and the frying-onion smells drifting from the new hamburger bars that were now starting to spring up all over; the visual crash and com-motion, the roar and racket non-stop from neon-rise to neon-set.

It made that other life that Ray had been used to until then feel like a thin thing, thin as the sheets he liked to have his mother tuck in tightly around him at night while pretending to be asleep and unaware she was there. These sheets he remembered from childhood were frictionless and shabby and rubbed away to a slippy pilled near-transparency which was beyond patching. ('Even the patches had patches' – an old joke of Bobby Thompson's – for a while had been literally true in Ray's case. In Ray and Betty Cruddas's case: many times his mother would sleep with only a hessian-like rough blanket next to her body, or a dyed Service coat, coarse against the satin slip she slept in, and no sheet at all.) Every so often an elbow or a knee or a ragged toe-nail would catch in a sheet and Ray would become aware of a rasping tearing sensation which would briefly wake him up. The next morning his mother would rip conclusively through the sheet using her fists and (he particularly remembered) her teeth, demonstrating unsuspected pent-up strength, and he would recognize the colour or the pattern with a start or a pang some time later when she started using the sheet pieces for dusting and polishing and other tasks about the house.

The place Ray was always most likely to entertain thoughts about the interesting thickening of his life and the encouraging course it was taking was a small drinking club on the ground floor in Denman Street in Soho; the Mazurka it was called. It was also known as 'Ginnie's Club' after the woman who ran it and who had been a Windmill girl once: Denman Street was a narrow rat-run almost directly opposite the Windmill Theatre, and a lot of the girls from the show would get down there. Solomons Gym was around the corner, and the boxing fraternity came in to 'Ginnie's'. Occasionally it was the champions themselves, but more usually the managers and the sharpies and other supernumeries of the fight game. Mac's Rehearsal Room was in the basement of the Jack Solomons building, and the cool hip-hep jazz types from Mac's would also crowd in with their hair cut short in Perry Como 'college-boy' styles, duffel coats, pointed, elegant shoes, and skinny, horizontally banded ties. What you also had in Ginnie's at this point in the mid-to-late fifties was a group of ex-Guards officers who camply called each other names such as 'Miss Ann' and 'Belinda' and shouted 'Abyssinia!' at each other when they parted, and leggy gorgeous chorus girls who waved around Princess Margaret-style cigarette holders and addressed each other as, for instance, 'Brian'.

Standing on the good side of a stiff Scotch, Ray would loiter in the Mazurka and try to get to grips with this new world he was entering, in which nothing was ever totally what it seemed, or even close to what he would have imagined it to be just a few weeks earlier. There was a code to be broken, and he was intent on breaking it. The sense of things seemed upside-down. A curtain made of strips of garish coloured plastic hung in front of the door at the Mazurka. Where he came from, these curtains were put up in the summer to protect the outer paintwork from the sun and were generally considered common. Here, though, the plastic strips were out in all weathers and seemed to denote something witty or clever ('infra dig' was the vogue expression then), like the rum-and-peps and the brandy-and-Babychams Ginnie's regulars ordered, the Tia Marias and Rémy-on-the-rocks which Ray had believed were vulgar, unfashionable things to drink. It was like a joke everybody was in on but nobody ever mentioned.

The Mazurka Club was a single room with a utility bar and a star walnut upright piano; rose lights glowed dimly on the worn 'tapestry'-pattern upholstery of an oak wood and a drover bringing the cows home and fish swam in a tank above the old bronze-metal cash register which rang up every sale with a grating *ding*. The Mazurka would enjoy a brief notoriety four or five years later when it became identified as a regular haunt of the vicious property racketeer, Rachman, and Ward, the society osteopath at the heart of the sensational Profumo scandal. Ray apparently met both of these characters in his days going to Ginnie's, but he met so many people in those days he could claim no memory of them. Even when he saw their pictures in the paper, brooding and notorious, they meant nothing.

Ginnie's prided itself on being untrammelled and inclusive and madcaply come-as-you-are. 'The great thing about here is that no one, not a soul, cares what your class is, or what your income, or whether you're nobody or famous, or a boy or a girl, or bent, or versatile, or what you are so long as you can hold a drink and behave yourself and have left all that crap behind you when you come in the door.' Ray heard this, or something like this, on any number of visits to Ginnie's. In practice, of course, it actually wasn't the kind of place you could just walk into off the street unless you were with somebody who was already known there or you came with an introduction from a member.

Ray's open-Sesame to the Mazurka and the underlife of Soho had been a beautiful but rather strange girl called Pauline. Pauline – 'Reeves' was her second name, although almost nobody who knew her would have been able to tell you that; even her first name varied according to which special clique or demi-monde she was in: 'Christice' and 'Ruby' were among her aliases – 'Pauline', as Ray knew her and would always think of her, came from an ordinary, respectable, professional background in Buckinghamshire or Berkshire or somewhere else that he could never remember in the Home Counties. She had scandalized her parents by telling them when she was sixteen that she wanted to be an art student (a 'famous artist' she actually said) rather than apply for teachers' training or go to an approved secretarial college as her mother had, to learn shorthand and typing and begin the long task of scouting for a husband.

The stake would have been driven into their hearts even deeper if they had ever discovered that she was supporting herself and earning the college fees they refused to give her by working as a showgirl in a Beak Street club. The rules at the Cabaret Club, as it happens, were unusually strict. Discipline was in the hands of two 'matrons'. They were assisted by two 'head girls' who were helped by 'prefects'. The main offences were being late, missing a cue, or taking time off without permission. Lesser offences included forgetting to wear nail varnish, missing the free weekly visit to the hairdresser, and failing to cover light patches left by swimsuit straps after sunbathing. All this struck Pauline – as most of life did then – as being hilarious. She was sparky and fearless. ('Plenty of fun and gaiety but no sex silliness,' she would quote old man Murray who owned the club, collapsing in laughter.) But none of this could disguise the fact that she was living a hazardous life.

Many of the Cabaret Club's forty-five 'young ladies' were housed on the opposite side of Beak Street to the club. One of the familiar sights of Soho in those days was the girls tripping across the street in their exotic costumes to go to work, like the famous ducks at the Peabody Hotel in Memphis waddling in file across the lobby at a set time every morning to frolic in the hotel fountain. And, coming across it one night without warning, Ray was as riveted by this little Soho side-show as any of the northern businessmen and American tourists and Arabs and other gawpers who could always be found lurking in the vicinity of the club.

It was something imprinted on his memory. He was disoriented. It was dark. He was slightly drunk. He was just starting to find his way around. He turned the corner of Kingly Street and almost walked straight into the two Amazons who emerged arm in arm and chatting from a deeply recessed door. They wore tall silver head-dresses and silver sandals with high spiked heels and long, full-skirted street coats over their showgirl costumes. Pauline had a pale face and heavily mascara'd eyes and pouting lips and a big tumble of savage blond hair in the style of Brigitte Bardot. (There was a poster of Bardot in *Mam'zelle Striptease*, Ray would discover, pinned to a wall in Pauline's flat.) Her friend was a bottle blonde, taller, fuller figured and more conventionally pretty in the bathing-beauty mould. As they arrived at the edge of the red glow cast by the Cabaret Club sign, Dervla, as the friend was called, turned and unexpectedly flashed her tits at Ray by quickly opening and closing her coat. She was wearing a glittering stiff-ribbed costume which stopped just short of her breasts. Pauline bent down to pick up something she'd dropped and glanced quickly back at Ray and then a frock-coated doorman he hadn't noticed until then stepped from the shadows and ushered the girls inside.

On 20 July 1957, at an open-air rally at Bedford, Mr Macmillan, in his first year as Prime Minister, was reviewing the country's economy. He said: 'Let's be frank about it. Most of our people have never had it so good.' It was a phrase that caught the national imagination and even, perhaps, people said, its lust.

Ray had finally made the big move south that year. Over the previous few years he had established a solid reputation in the North through his long residency on *Variety Parade* which he recorded every two weeks for the BBC in Manchester. He did the clubs, a pantomime every year, a summer season in Blackpool or Scarborough. In 1953 he had been given a small part in one of the lousy pictures Frank Randle made for Mancunian Films in what was laughingly known as 'Jollywood'. He had had a crash course in power-politicking and brass-neck showbiz bravura by watching the off-screen performance of Diana Dors, who was the sex interest in *It's a Grand Life*. He had to learn to be more 'pushful' if he ever expected to get anywhere, she told him in their single, brief conversation. 'And for chrissakes get rid of the child-pesterer's haircut and that dopey goddam shirt and tie. Unless you like looking like the man who's come to read the meter. Didn't anybody tell you? The war's over. Get with it. Is it Ray, Roy? Self-respecting modesty never buttered any potatoes. You're in the business of show.'

It's a Grand Life led to nothing, but Ray thought he looked OK in front of the camera. He appeared on television for the first time in 1955, presenting *Top Town*, a talent competition between teams from Sunderland and Blaydon. He was 'discovered' when he did *The Good Old Days* in a matinée scarf and muttonchop whiskers live from Leeds City Varieties. The impresarios George and Alfred Black had been looking for a young comedian to present a new television variety show that was to go out on Saturday nights from the Prince of Wales Theatre. And after his first appearance on *The Big Show* in October 1956, Ray's career had caught fire. The Blacks (in association with the Delfonts) had booked him to appear with Tommy Steele, Dickie Henderson and the singer Jill Day in *Startime* at the Hippodrome in the West End, which opened in April 1957 and ran into the first weeks of the following year. He acquired an Austin Hereford, a flat in a portered thirties-modern block in Marylebone, and started to indulge his taste for hand-crafted, expensive bespoke shoes. He had to experiment with ways of using hats, scarves, heavy horn-rimmed glasses and other props in order to avoid being recognized and even chased in the street. He had a top West End agent who was quadrupling and quintupling his fees. Things looked swell; things looked great. Everything was coming up roses.

'"Light Entertainment." What is it meant to be the opposite of? Heavy Entertainment, or Dark Entertainment?' This was the first thing Pauline ever said to Ray. He didn't recognize her at first without the headpiece and the war paint and the trappings of her job at Murray's Cabaret Club. She was dressed all in black, which was unusual for somebody so young then. Black lacy stockings, short black skirt, little high-heeled black boots, high-collared black blouse, lots of black eye make-up, bushels of tumbling hair, pancaked white face, chalky white lipstick.

It was the first-night party for *Startime*, a week or so after he had seen her arm in arm with Dervla, jawing and clicking across Beak Street. The party was in a club close to the corner of Gerrard Street and Wardour Street, and the location was part of the reason for his air of lost abstraction that night, which he might rightly have regarded as a high point of his career. It was a corner Ray had gone out of his way to avoid during rehearsals and in his time in London. It was near here that Celia, his first wife – Celia Ann Finney – had stepped into the road and been hit by a taxi and killed instantly.

He had met Celia when she was appearing in a show with him as a member of the Whitley Bay Girls' Choir. In her late teens, about the age Pauline was now, she had joined a close-harmony 'sisters' act called the Harvey Sisters who went out round the clubs as part of a package with Ray. They sang five or six songs in the first half; Ray did his stand-up act after the interval, and then the Harvey Sisters joined him to sing 'Side by Side' with top-hats and silver-topped canes at the end. They always went down well and had to turn away bookings.

Ray proposed to Celia on Coronation Day and they got married on the same day a year later, in 1954. The wedding was a quiet affair and they were on stage together eight hours later at the Hardwick Hartley Social Club in Stockton. Towards the end of the year one of the other girls in the Harvey Sisters left to get married and, encouraged by Ray, Celia replied to an advertisement to audition for the Stargazers, who were a very successful spin-off act from radio's Mike Sammes Singers. Ray had a job in the North that day, and so Celia travelled to London, which she didn't know and had always felt nervous in, on her own. She had been on her way to the audition at an address in Frith Street when she stepped off the kerb and was hit by the cab.

People didn't mark the site of traffic accidents with flowers in those days. But very many years later, when that was the custom, Ray went with a small bunch of white roses and fixed them to a post on Shaftesbury Avenue close to the place where Celia had died. It was the Silver Jubilee, what would have been their twenty-third anniversary, and the streets were thronged and noisy, and he didn't suppose anybody saw.

The opening night of *Startime* had been a great success and the Blacks' celebration party went on into the early hours and was showing no signs of winding down when Ray agreed to go with Pauline to another place she knew. The Rio was a black café on Westbourne Park Road where a few white trailblazers like Pauline had started to go to eat foo-foo and rice and chicken and other night-snack sober-up food. These white 'night people' had also started to go to the Rio to score. And the first thing Ray noticed after the blur of Caribbean and African faces, which was the most he had ever seen gathered together in one place, was the heavy sweet smell of the drug.

Pauline was clearly no stranger at the Rio and was soon the centre of interest, causing small good-humoured hubbubs to ripple out around her wherever she went in the room. There was a juke-box and African high-life music was playing and Pauline danced a little and said 'hi' to this one and that one wearing a version of the same shabby well-cut suit and moved among the plastic-topped tables giving cigarettes around. In return she was invited to take a generous pinch of 'tea' as they all called it and rolled Ray his first, and just about his last ever, drug cigarette.

Soon Pauline was in the middle of the room improvising the words of a deodorant commercial to a bluebeat tune – 'My armpits are charmpits,' she warbled, revealing her armpits at the climax – and Ray, his throat scorched and feeling strange and slightly nauseous, a sickening pulse in the balls of his feet, the alcohol curdling in his stomach, used that as his opportunity to unobtrusively slip away.

It was a few days later when he visited Pauline at the flat in Bayswater where she lived and again found himself somewhere that was totally outside his usual experience. It was a large porticoed house in a long curving terrace of peeling, grey-stuccoed, down-at-heel houses. An echoing entrance hall with a marble console table, several prams and a round, dilapidated plaster-gilt mirror led to a wide staircase with old and faded lino on the stairs. It was a sort of slum, and yet not really. It was moneyed people living in a self-imposed impoverished way – poverty as a living choice. A flap of paper loaded with plaster hung down from the ceiling and a small cloud of gnats hovered in a once-grand corner.

Pauline occupied a room on the first floor of the house which ran all the way from the front to the back. There was a large bed with an ivory satin cover, a beaten-up armchair and a gas ring on a shelf by the sink. It took a while though for these conventional pieces to establish themselves and come through the murk and the nearly blacked-out chaos of Victorian and Edwardian bric-a-brac and bewildering layers of clutter. A child's penny-farthing bicycle leaned against one wall next to a tailor's dummy with a battered 'Anthony Eden' hat perched on top of it. There was a ceramic phrenologist's head and an old gramophone with a horn and a Deccola radiogram and several packets of Oxydol lined up on a table like something to be looked at and chin-stroked over rather than opened and used for getting grease and stains out of dirty clothes. She used a stack of books instead of a bedside table and had a painted paper parasol hanging upside-down from the ceiling rose where you would expect a lampshade to be.

It was early afternoon but it was obvious Pauline hadn't long been out of bed. Clothes were strewn on the floor and draped across the chair. Records were lying on the floor out of their sleeves. She had borrowed a couple of shillings from Ray for the meter and set about brewing some Heinz alphabet soup on the ring. The meter kept up a regular tick which Pauline drowned out eventually with one of the records that she picked up off the floor, blew on casually and dropped on the Deccola. It was a modern jazz group with a vibraphone in the foreground playing the kind of long-hair, whinging neurot music that never failed to give Ray the willies.

He strolled around, like a visitor in a gallery, which in a sense is what he was. The walls had been covered with hundreds of images from comics and magazines and gone over with coats of semi-clear varnish. Posters advertising films and art exhibitions had been pinned up on top of this along with many pictures of African and West Indian men which Pauline had evidently taken herself. The pictures were black and white, and the men in them were sometimes naked or nearly naked and staring gravely into the camera.

He couldn't see what her interest in him meant. He had heard the word 'loyal' used when he was with Pauline at the Rio. The groups of men milling outside on Westbourne Park Road and the blanked-out windows were meant 'to keep the loyals out'. Loyal meant 'white bread' or 'square' and Ray was in no doubt that a loyal was what he was. That night it had been the American tab-collar shirt and Italian-look Cecil Gee suit he was wearing that had allowed him to 'pass'. A sprightly African with the blocky look of the men in Pauline's pictures and the tribal scars had commented approvingly on his 'natty suiting'. He looked up to date and in tune with the new feeling of youthful modernity and adventure that was supposedly about to sweep the country and had found its emblem in *Startime*'s top of the bill, Tommy Steele.

In fact Ray would be one of the people who walked out on Lenny Bruce when Bruce performed his 'sick' act in London four years later, incensed by his jokes about cancer and snot – he actually blew his nose in his hand and smeared the contents across the club's back wall – and his demented drug addict's meanderings and disgusting diarrhoea of the mouth. He stood four-square with the citizens – the 'loyals' if that's what you wanted to call them – who backed the Home Secretary's decision to ban Bruce from coming back into the country in 1963.

He couldn't see what Pauline's interest in him meant. And then slowly he thought perhaps he started to see. At the north-facing window at the garden end of the room was a wheel-mounted painter's easel and a series of small framed portraits she had done. Some were of people he recognized immediately, others of people he didn't recognize at all. Some were sportsmen – the former world welterweight champion, Randolph Turpin; the world's first four-minute miler, Roger Bannister; the South African boxer turned society hairdresser, Johnny Rust. Many, to Ray's bemusement, were comedians he had worked with and knew well – Max Bygraves, Jewell and Warriss, Norman Wisdom, Tommy Trinder; a group portrait of the Goons. What floored him wasn't the fact that she had chosen to paint them but that she had painted them in an intent and quiet, old-masterly way as though she had divined in them a seriousness nobody else had been able to see.

There was Malcolm Vaughan, a balladeer Ray had appeared in pantomime with the previous season, currently in the hit parade with a tear-jerker called 'Chapel of the Roses'. A teddy-boy in drainpipe trousers, a bootlace tie and four-inch brothel-creeper shoes. Laurence Olivier as Archie Rice in *The Entertainer* with the caption: 'Let me know where you're working tomorrow night and I'll come and see you.' (The paint was still drying on this one.) Freddie Bell and the Bell Boys. Diana Dors.

When he moved to a worktop where drifts of reference material were in the process of being sorted, he was unsurprised by then to come across some pictures of himself. They had been taken for a fashion feature in the previous month's issue of a magazine called *Man About Town*. At the end of the session he had been invited to take two of the items he'd been modelling away with him. One of the things he'd chosen was the canary yellow Shetland sweater he had been wearing on the night he first ran into Pauline and which he had picked out to wear that morning. 'I recognized it,' Pauline, who was now standing beside him, said. 'In Beak Street with Dervla the first time I saw you. Under the street lamp in the dark. I recognized the sweater. I'm a fool for yellow. It's so hard to get that beautiful, rich eggy yellow. That's a very good dye. And then I recognized you.' She cleaned up a last spoonful of soup from the mug and removed the soupy moustache that had formed on her upper lip with her tongue.

A change came over Pauline when she began to tell him about her work; she grew serious, which had the effect of making her seem younger, and yet at the same time the flighty callowness she assumed fell away. The commercial vernacular of consumer culture was her inspiration, she said; trying to give legitimacy to things that had been regarded as illegitimate in an art sense until then. Working at Murray's Cabaret Club and being a showgirl was part of that: she found it interesting being an object, a piece of meat on the market, getting spangled up, being weighed up by men. 'And anyway "nice" middle-class girls are just whores, selling themselves for security like my mother!'

She went over to a full-length mirror and used a handle comb vigorously to tat up and bulk out her hair. She dipped her head and put her fingers over her eyes to protect them from the alcohol in the lacquer spray. She spat into a small dish of mascara, mixed it and applied it to her eyes. 'What's needed is an approach which doesn't depend for its existence on the exclusion of the symbols most people live by,' Pauline said. 'I love the city. One of my collections is postcards of Piccadilly Circus. I've got hundreds. My pleasures are the smell of carbon monoxide and to go out on the street at night. Noise. Clothes. I love waking up to the thunder of traffic. The glossy packaging of food.'

When Ray agreed to sit for her, she got him a collapsible three-step ladder to perch on and played the American cast recording of *Waiting for Godot* as background: *We have time to grow old. The air is full of our cries . . . But habit is a great deadener . . . At me too someone is looking, of me too someone is saying, he is sleeping, he knows nothing, let him sleep on . . . I can't go on! . . . What have I said?*

'Oh, I love this,' Pauline said. 'It's so brilliant to listen to when you're stoned.'

'What's it about?' he said.

'It's about two tramps,' she said. 'It's about the love–hate relationship between two people trying to amuse themselves in their time here by playing jokes and little games. The two of them come together out of necessity and play a game to survive life. That's how I hear it anyway. They grope towards each other, and pull away, and grope towards each other. But the closer they get, the nearer they come, the more impossible it is for them to unite. They're both trapped in the cages of their skin.'

'Sounds about as funny as a cry for help,' Ray said. (He would recall himself saying this exactly thirty years later, in 1987, and this room and this house, the gas fire's impotent sputters, the damp, the meter eating up the pennies, the multitude of faces in the varnished mural staring down, when he was cast in a production of *Waiting for Godot* at the Connaught Theatre, Worthing, with Ernie Wise as the second tramp. Eric Morecambe, who Wise had played feed to for forty years, was three years dead. Ray had slipped down and almost completely off Mrs Thatcher's list of invitees to smart and important events. They were both at a loss, adrift in their lives and careers. It was this perhaps that had prompted the producers to team them up as Vladimir and Estragon. It was certainly their personal circumstances the critics reviewed, not the play. The evening, according to one reviewer, was all about 'the infinite pathos of being an "and"'. A writer in another paper quoted Ray back his own joke about the performer who replies to the question, 'You can't sing, you can't dance, you're not funny – as a matter of fact, you've got no talent at all. Why don't you give up show business?', by answering, 'I can't – I'm a star!' The play closed ten days into what should have been a three-week run.)

Pauline offered Ray the skinny joint she had been smoking while she was drawing, but he shook his head. There was a red glow from the clay elements in the gas fire. It had made her cheek and ear on one side, and the side of one leg, go hot and red.

He gave her two box seats for *Startime* at the Hippodrome before he left and agreed to come back and sit for her again in a few days at the same time.

He had started down the stairs when he heard Pauline shout his name. When he put his head round the door he felt a soft object hit it, and then a second, and a third. Pauline was shriek-ing, really laughing. Lying at his feet were the synthetic cotton-wool 'snowballs' that the tubby bandleader, Billy Cotton, pelted the audience with during the closing credits of his hugely popu-lar televised *Band Show*. Pauline had brought them away when she was part of the audience for a broadcast.

Ray saved one in his pocket, said his goodbyes again, and clicked shut the door.

In 1957 Jackie was twenty-six. Not old, but old enough for a boxer with his active fighting life behind him and an incipient limp to begin looking at the life around him at the fights and in the gym and deciding that these weren't places to be either poor or old. 'Old George'. 'Old Harry'. Sometimes just 'Dad'. There were lots of them. Retired boxers, knackered, chap-fallen, doing the sweeper-up jobs as janitors and in the corners as seconds and cut men, going home to their stale empty flats in their sunny slum squares with their old smelly dogs and their radios that can't be properly tuned in and telly pictures jumpy with snowy green ghosts.

Booba had died in February 1956. It happened suddenly in the night in a high, tiled room with the best care and the most modern amenities her son could make available for her but which to the end Booba complained was like a public-house urinal with these ceramic festoons whose like she had never darkened.

She was buried at Golders Green alongside her husband, and very soon her home in the Buildings had been flushed of all evidence of her existence. None of her children wanted the furniture because it didn't fit into their lives. It was too voluminous and dark and reminded them of what they had come from. They had filled their homes with low, lightweight, streamlined pieces which it didn't take three men to carry. There was a wardrobe dealer at the top of Brick Lane who came with a pony and cart and took all Booba's clothes and belongings, plants, ferns, china, away. A team of workmen from the Council moved in and boarded the fireplaces up, installed mains electricity, painted everywhere with the colour they called 'mushroom', a kind of neutral.

After Booba's death Mr Solomons seemed snappish to Jackie – grouchy, offhand, uneasy. He seemed uncomfortable having him around, as if he was a reminder or a reproach. He started treating him increasingly like the other *shtoonks* cluttering up his office and his life. There were new faces, new intelligences to gather in areas where Jackie had no means or right of ingress. For the first time since Jackie had caught on with the undisputed great-I-am of British boxing, Mr Solomons was being encroached on by a rival promoter, Harry Levene, known as 'Harry the Hoarse' after his gravel voice worn out by incessant shouting, who had started luring away backroom people and boxers from the Solomons camp. Jackie had recently been personally despatched with a message to a defector which read in its entirety: 'Why don't you come back to my place, spit in my face, put your hand on it, and wipe it all over?' That was followed up by a present to the man's wife in the post – a parcel containing four dead rats.

This was the state of things when Nat Sellers at the gym called Jackie over one day and told him he was wanted by the boss on a special job. As soon as he heard the name 'Ray Cruddas', Jackie knew what it was. This was a bone he himself had carried home and dropped at his master's feet right on the carpet.

Ray had discovered a Viennese pâtisserie he liked going to on Marylebone High Street latish every morning. He liked to take his place among the blue-rinse ladies and the dapper old émigrés with their patent hair and their patent-leather shoes and their pale watery eyes fixed on a point in the middle distance and enjoy a leisurely breakfast. They did a lovely poached egg there, it was civility itself and nobody ever bothered him.

He had just arrived back from having breakfast one morning when the phone rang. He recognized the voice of Jolly Jack Solomons who he had done some emceeing for as well as a few charity appearances at Solomons' National Sporting Club at the Café Royal. He had gained the impression that the old shark was quite fond of him. 'Ray, are you sitting down?' Solomons said. 'I think you should be sitting down for what I've got to tell you.

'Does the name "Hart" ring any bells?' Ray sensed him repositioning his cigar in his mouth without using his hands. '"Sugar Hart"? Bad man. Very bad man and dangerous company. *Shvartzer* from Notting Dale, if you know what I'm saying. One of our black brothers. The word going around is that you've been doing the naughty with his gel. Giving this Pauline some *shvantz*.

'Bit of a looker by all accounts. Plenty of what it takes. Works down Murray's Club as a hostess. Has to listen to all those old war heroes telling their stories from the war. Laugh at their jokes. Listen to their horseshit and gunpowder tales about how they singlehandedly did the Gerries, get them to fork out for another bottle of fake champagne. "Real pain for your sham friends, champagne for your real friends." All that. But never does none of the other business, so I'm told. Never takes a punter home, never goes home with a Billy Bunter. Not the type who earns four pound a week and sends six pound home to mother, if you get me. Except it seems you've been seen making house visits to this girl.

'. . . Nah, nah, nah, Ray, lissen. Strictly *unter em tisch*, her big, bad boyfriend is out to do you a mischief. You know I've got one or two naughty lads fighting for me, not above upsetting the law, you follow. Well, one of them's been offered a pony to do you over, hospital job, and he might have bitten but for this Hart saying he'd cough up a monkey to see you finished. A beating's one thing, but offing's another, so the lad came to me, and I've come to you. Are you still there, my son?'

'Is it true?' It was all Ray could think to say. His throat was dry.

'Oh, he's got it in for you, I mean really got it in, no error. Going to slit your eyeballs is what I hear. But hold on, the wheels here grind pretty fast. I've already squared it for one of my boys to babysit you for a while until this blows over. Either that, or until you're laid away in the bottom drawer with lavender. Sorry. I know it's not a joking matter . . . It isn't funny. But this boy I'm putting with you is one of the best. I'd trust him with my own mother. OK? Bell me later. You look out.'

It was half an hour before Ray heard the door. 'Mr Cruddas?' The voice on the intercom was high-pitched like a boy's. 'Jackie from Mr Solomons' office. Said to say the word "Booba" so you'd know.'

Ray was shaken. He was in shock. He was shaking. His finger trembled on the buzzer when he buzzed Jackie in.

By the time he unmortised and unbolted the door he could feel himself coming apart. His body was liquid. His muscles were convulsed. His body was spasming and there was nothing he could do. He was like something stricken by a roadside, lame and fluttering; like a tree when the winds blow and the seasons change, his whole body fluttering and trembling.

Jackie recognized this. He had seen it before. He had seen boxers get like this in dressing-rooms before fights, go to pieces, unmanned with dread and fear and vivid premonitions of having their noses crushed and choking on their own blood. Just lose it. He did then what he had sometimes done in the past. He did what his Ely ancestors had done to settle some wild-eyed, ready-to-bolt pure-bred, when the trick was to stay close to the horse's flailing hoofs and sweating creeping flanks.

He embraced Ray. He encircled him with his arms, put his body close to his body and held on to him tightly, Ray's arms fast to his sides, his legs going, his breathing uneven, calming him in the throes of his fear convulsion, the naked shaking animal.

He often felt he learned everything he was going to know about him in that moment, his weak places and his ambition, and how much uncertainty and how much vigour, and how much generosity and how much spite. It was the way you got all the important information about your opponent in the first clinch. Where his eyes were and how true his legs felt; the smell coming off his skin.

Ray went on shivering, and Jackie went on holding him in the poky hall of his beleaguered new flat. Ray didn't resist. He behaved as if this was a perfectly normal thing for a stranger to do, a Samaritan act like lending your coat to somebody who has just been hit by a car or felled by a bomb, the world calamitously changed; everything unwinding in silence. The sound of Ray's teeth chattering drummed loudly in Jackie's head.

After a while Jackie went into the kitchen, boiled water, found the tea, tipped a good measure of brandy in both cups. The bottom of Ray's cup rattled against the edge of the saucer when he started drinking, but as the alcohol and sugar took effect he started to come back to himself.

'Sorry.'

'No need to apologize. I'm your shadow, for a little while anyway. Till Mr Solomons whistles me home. You OK?'

It was then that Jackie started to give Ray the background on the situation involving this Soledad Hart, always known as 'Sugar', whose interests extended to gambling rackets, strip joints, protection, property, drugs – 'all sorts of nastiness'. Jackie had occasionally come across Hart on his travels – 'not all that big of a man but well assembled, always well turned out, with a massive neck and a razor-blade parting' – and had first heard from the doorman of a club in Kingly Street who also owned an all-night drinker in West London where Hart and the Pauline girl went that the knives were out for Mr Cruddas, who Sugar Hart was making no bones he wanted to see topped.

Ray was supposed to put in an appearance at a ladies' luncheon in Richmond that afternoon, a booking that Jackie persuaded him to keep. He drove him there and drove him back. He drove him to the theatre that evening, escorted him inside, parked the car, and found a place in the bar where he could see everybody coming in, his routine for the next six months.

He slept on the sofa in the living room that night and next morning went out and bought bread, milk, orange juice, eggs. He made wholemeal toast and poached the eggs. 'Nah,' he said when he saw Ray getting ready to go out for lunch with a senior television executive at Isow's, 'you don't want to wear that with that.'

He went through Ray's wardrobe and picked him out a green brocade tie. He examined his feet and shook his head. He went and fetched a pair of expensively turned, pointed, hand-sewn shoes and a pair of subtly patterned brown silk socks.

'And only the one whisky sour, you know they make you talk bollocks!' he called after him when he dropped him in Soho. 'And don't forget you've got a show to do tonight!' Ray hesitated on the pavement for a moment trying to decide if Jackie was being serious, and then they both laughed.

'When did I first realize I was a star? When I got my first death threat.' It was a good line. He'd feed it to the interviewers and the interviewers would laugh and their editors would highlight it in enlarged letters on the page beside a picture of him looking urbane or moody or (less often) a picture of him laughing. He said it on *Harty* and many lower-rated television shows. It comes up in the clippings again and again.

5

All that spring Jackie arrived to collect Ray at the Scran Van with the smell of the cull pyres in his hair and on his clothing, and ash and white soot – 'the dust of death', Mighty rather dramatically called it; 'the Devil's dandruff' (strangely the same name that Jackie's son, Barry, gave to the powder he shoved up his nose) – coating his shoulders. Jackie scrubbed himself red every morning but still the smells seemed to stay on his breath and in his nostrils and he was reminded for the first time in a long time of the Billingsgate fish smell carried by brash Mr Solomons and which would linger about him like a rumour no matter what.

During that spring the scenes in the countryside around Rusty Lane were hellish and other-worldly and reminded the people who lived there, especially at night times, of apocalyptic visions and infernal depictions in dark, dimmed old Bible paintings.

Driving home at night from Bobby's, Jackie would begin to be aware of the putrid smoky smell seeping in through the radiator and around the windows before he entered the area of the thick white smoke-fog made of powdered bone and hide and animal render, and lazy plumes of fat-saturated smoke blowing out to sea. There was a lot of traffic movement at that time of night, and driving along the coast road Jackie would pass army Land-Rovers and large container wagons queuing at the quarry entrance. (Some of the wagons, he knew, contained full loads of ash from the pyres, classified as hazardous waste. It made him think about things he wouldn't choose to think about in the lonely early hours with the heater on and the radio playing and Ellis restless and sneezing behind the dog-guard. It made him think about the human ashes coming from the crematoria at Auschwitz and Birkenau and how they had been put to use as thermal insulation and fertilizer and, most horribly to Jackie, used instead of gravel to cover the paths of the SS villages located near the camps.) The pyres burned for weeks, glowing jewel-like and stinking in the dark, each of the hundreds of pyres feeding its own consistent, blue-orange blooming corona of flame.

People witnessed terrible things in those months, and heard about terrible things, and went about their business every day trying not to breathe in the foul stench from the unburied, putre-fying carcasses, a smell that they locally called 'the honk'. These were sights and smells that were new and distressing not only to the recent townie blow-ins. A new sound filling the blanket silence was the sound of wagons reversing, the monotone *beep-beep-beep* which until that spring of the foot-and-mouth had never been heard in the fields and lanes round there.

On some days there was a strange pink mist flushing the air, caused, as everybody knew although it was never mentioned, by the explosion of the unviscerated bodies. The wife of the farmer at Townfoot Farm where they had had the whole herd slaughtered had a Hindu gentleman come round to free the spirits of the animals in their terms, which she said made her feel less desolate spiritually.

People worried about the carcinogenic compounds being released into the atmosphere by the cheap coal and creosoted railway sleepers brought in to set the pyres, and about the water table being poisoned through seepage. There were theories about the virus travelling as part of a huge haze cloud of man-made pollutants which had recently been spotted drifting in the upper atmosphere from the Asian continent, or blowing in on a massive plume of sand that satellites and research ships had tracked as it swirled out of northern Africa. Jackie had an improvised mask made of a handkerchief soaked in whisky, a tip he had picked up in the suffocating London fogs of the early fifties. And suddenly, too, in a landscape devoid of livestock you could hear the crows.

Jackie tended to bring the shepherds, Telfer and Ellis, in with him most mornings, and they also carried the smells of the mass burns and the heavily disinfected carcass heaps in their coats. Because of the restrictions, he had started driving the short distance to the coast and exercising the dogs in the dunes. Ironically, around that time there were some beautiful mornings, sunny and chill, the air coming in off the sea still salt and unpolluted. It was on one of these mornings that Jackie had come down the dune slacks where several patches of early yellow colt's foot had already taken hold to find the two big dogs playing tug-of-war with what, from a distance, looked like a deflated football with the terrier Stella working up sand and yapping all around them. It was only as he drew nearer that he was able to see that the object they had between them was one of the pieces of half-burnt skin that had started wafting around, and that burned or stamped on to it were the first two digits of a cow's cataloguing or identifying number.

The bad news from Kevin Wilkinson in West Allen about Telfer had been that he had found a tumour in the bladder which in his opinion was inoperable. He wouldn't commit himself to how long he believed the dog had left and said only that quality of life was the important consideration: he would have his up days and his down days, but when the time came when he obviously couldn't struggle on any longer, Jackie would know. The dog was incontinent sometimes, but Jackie was quite happy to clean up after him and even reassure him that it was all right to soil the place where he lay. He had to get up in the night and sit with him sometimes, and often had to support his hind legs after he had helped him into the garden. There was a faith-healer Jackie had heard about who specialized in domestic animals and, although he would have laughed at anybody who had suggested such a thing two months earlier, it had come to the point where it

171

was something he was starting to consider seriously. For some of the older people living in the town the smell of the pyres had a deep nostalgic association. By the time the honk and the charred mist travelled the five miles to the nostrils of Mighty's regulars at the tea van, the death smell and the nasty gagging sweetness had been rinsed out of it, and much of the bitterness had abated. To them it was like a glimpse at the past – a welcome whiff of old industrial times and a last gasp of disappearing worlds. From the country the pyres sent a ghost smell of factory chimneys and booming heavy industries, smarting the eyes and furring the nostrils, like a million kettles left on to burn.

The men who gathered at the Scran Van on those mornings were in noticeably good spirits, less taciturn and more talkative than usual. Some mornings some of the marksmen stopped off for a breakfast on their way through and brought news of other places. They had been called in from as far afield as Northamptonshire and Devon, where they had real-world jobs such as village butchers and publicans. They were happy to talk about the good money they were making and show off their rifles and bolt guns and say again – many of the men said it – that the difficulty with killing these animals was that they were so human-friendly. 'This whole thing has torn the shit out of me, really,' one of the marksmen, an older man, said one morning, and that closed the subject. It blunted it of whatever edge or morbid interest it had held until then and, although the ashy fall-out went on falling more or less continuously, it fell from then on without comment.

Invisibly, a fall-out of fat coated the plants and trees in the Park, and fell faintly on the yellow-green young leaves of the trees in the little grove, cordoned off and isolated now at the eastern end of the Moor.

The cows had been rounded up on the sixth day of foot-and-mouth and herded away, and a tape barrier and 'DO NOT ENTER' signs had gone up around the whole perimeter of the Moor, making it a criminal offence punishable by up to five years in prison to set foot on it. Enclosed and inaccessible, the trees, which Ray could see from his window budding into another season, seemed, even when a breeze ruffled their branches, to make a silence.

It was a situation that had left him feeling miserable and in a yearning, anxious state. He had a skin irritation which he hoped wasn't a recurrence of shingles. He was getting nervous stomach aches at the club. He had started to wake up with nose-bleeds sometimes in the middle of the night.

Ray woke to the sound of honky-tonk piano music being played far away in the basement of the house. Marzena, his wife, liked to listen to this jangly, happy music while she worked. 'Yes! *Happy!*' Marzena sometimes said to Ray, leaning in to press her face against his face where he was slumped low in a chair. 'That great tremendous word.' Then she would give him a kiss.

Winifred Atwell playing 'Roll Out the Barrel' and 'I Can't Give You Anything But Love, Baby'. Joe 'Mr Piano' Henderson or another long-forgotten boxing-glove pianist banging out 'Yes, We Have No Bananas', 'Ma, He's Making Eyes at Me', 'Ain't She Sweet'. On and on and around and around they went, these and other saloon-bar favourites, one tune dissolving into the other with a heart-in-the-belly hiatus of only half a beat, free-associating like thoughts.

'Light music, light heart!' Marzena was aware that this also grated with Ray, but she found it fun occasionally to disgruntle him. 'You don't believe it, and it is your absolute choosing, but there is no rule that all life is emotional grappling.'

'Heart of My Heart'. 'My Old Dutch'. These were the sounds of Marzena's childhood and young womanhood in Zalipie, in the southern border region of Poland near Tarnow. The music she would hear on the second-hand transistor radios laid out on cardboard on the ground among the cooking utensils, anoraks, shoes, suitcases, bleeping space toys and household gimmicks in the open-air market in the gardens opposite the old rusting hulk of the Dunajec Stadium. The backpack she brought with her when she first moved in with Ray came from the Tarnow market. A red plastic handbag. At least one pair of shoes.

Joe 'Mr Piano' or Winnie Atwell played, and the *babushkas*, come down from their little two-room *chatas* in the mountains, wheeled wobbly trolleys around the coldly lit, cinderblock super-market, a barrel-roofed supershed that was the hub of the rural community, lumpy red-faced men always with a cigarette going, the air thick with smoke, everybody smoking like chimneys, fist-fuls of play-money zlotys, pickled cabbage from a barrel, pigeons in wooden pens, five or six to a cage, red radishes, knobby cucumbers, wild green asparagus that the children were sent to look for near the village cemetery, choosing Swedish matches because Polish matches tend not to ignite. Marzena's father had been an underground-cable layer until the trouble with his legs; her mother was a cook at the local ball-bearing factory's 'house of culture'. The pantiled roofs of the Tarnow/Rzeszow tenements. The faceless buildings of functionalist state architecture all along Wieniewska Street, which had been rechristened with every new regime. 'Ta-Ra-Ra-Boom-De-Ay' clanging through the super-market Tannoy. 'When Somebody Thinks You're Wonderful' on the plastic radios and stolen tape-cassette machines. 'Volare'.

This life of Marzena's that she had left behind was symbolized for Ray by the small packet that arrived at Moor Edge Terrace for her from her mother on the second Tuesday of every month. It was addressed in heavy, stubby pencil, tied with cheapest-quality string, and encrusted with many small-denomination stamps. It was Marzena's habit to put the packet from her mother aside until an auspicious moment came to open it. Ray noticed that sometimes she would spend a long time examining the wrinkled outer wrapping and the postmark before she began slowly to pick apart the knots her mother had tied sitting on her bed with the religious paintings arranged above it in Zalipie six days earlier. Once this had been achieved Marzena very quickly scanned the letter and the cuttings from the *Gazeta Wyborcza* which were enclosed and, so far as Ray knew, never looked at them again. 'Home is a feeling, nothing more,' Marzena had said to him on one of the first occasions they went out together. 'Once you leave, you become a stranger. I lost my home and that's for ever.'

Marzena was a sculptor. Her chosen medium was brick – bricks and mortar. Blockish red Accrington brick was her favourite, and she toiled in the dust-laden air of the windowless basement of the house in Moor Edge Terrace making walls: crooked walls, tumble-down walls, plumb walls, walls with insulating materials and reinforcing cable left poking around the edges like sandwich filling, walls with ragged holes knocked through them, walls with private objects, their existence known only to Marzena, secreted in the concrete between the courses.

The music played and she shovelled lime and mixed cement in delicious puddles and, her blond hair tied back from her thin planar face, she split her nails and ignored the dust and briskly broke bricks in half with a tap of the trowel handle and eventually emerged exhausted, face whitened, ears afire. She was absurdly happy. Ray didn't pretend to understand.

Something else he didn't get was why Marzena continued to cross the city on buses several days a week, going out to work as a cleaner. It didn't make sense to Ray: his wife went out to clean for other people, but they paid somebody else to come in and dust and skivvy for them. 'Am cleaner,' Marzena would proudly tell anybody who asked what she did. 'Give me scourer and Flash and dirty kitchen, oven full of caked-up crap, am happy as peeg in sheet.'

Another quirk of Marzena's was that, although she had enough money to buy whatever might catch her eye, she generally preferred to wear other women's cast-offs. It particularly rankled with Ray that the original wearer of many of his own wife's clothes was the wife of his business partner and his principal backer at Bobby's, Ronnie Cornish.

Marzena had been going out to clean for Mrs Cornish for quite a while before she ever met Ray, and she had always found her to be very charming lady, friendly and very nice. The Cornishes lived in a beautiful twenty-four-room, early eighteenth-century house with idyllic views stretching for miles across the surrounding countryside. Completed in 1738, Coldside Hall had a stone-and-stucco, neo-Palladian exterior, mullioned windows and all the rooms were filled with English and American furniture, oriental rugs, silver, paintings, prints, powder horns, antique globes, sea charts, early maps, rare books – and Ronnie's mother's mangle, restored and polished and put on display in the casement window of one of the grand apartments on the *piano nobile*, where the original proprietor had *shmoozed* and entertained tenants, voters, parsons, gentlemen and other local worthies, much as Ronnie was doing more than two hundred and fifty years later: Hope and Ronnie Cornish's lavish parties at the Hall were famous across the North of England, and invitations to them were shamelessly wheedled after and highly prized.

A team of women from the village came in to maintain Coldside Hall. Marzena's tasks were now confined to the Cornishes' apartment in the football-stadium complex, which was mainly kept for business use – entertaining business colleagues, clients, and so on – and which his wife always referred to jokingly as Ronnie's 'bunny hutch' or 'love shack'.

The house facing the Moor where Marzena had lived with Ray for the three years that they had been married was good – it was a pleasant house; comfortable. Many rooms. It was OK. But it was old. The stairs and the old boards at Moor Edge moaned and creaked. The water pipes banged as though somebody was beating them with a hammer. Marzena came across evidence of mice in the kitchen sometimes; mouse droppings on the floor and on the bread board. The doors and windows had shrunk or buckled over the years and let in cold and draught. Wiring was old – big switches that went off with loud click; dusty, fabric-covered flex. All this there was more than plenty of in the old country. Plus Ray was crazy careful about the heating and bills; he liked her to have individual heaters on in whichever room she happened to be, at those times when she was in the house on her own. She would hear him going around feeling the radiators looking for signs that they had been in use, very late at night, after Jackie had dropped him back from the club. Ray wasn't terrible man. Ray was kind man, thoughtful man, apart from this cratchety Puritan streak.

But the apartment the Cornishes owned! It was Mr and Mrs Cornish's apartment in the new multi-million-pound development at the football ground with the high decorative arch and the marble concourse of fountains and the fashionable wine bars and the health clubs where you could see straight in through the plate-glass windows and the uniformed staff with the discrete little TV monitors at the desk who said 'good day' and 'a bit brighter today' and sometimes stepped around the desk to touch the button which called the lift although it was no trouble to do this (it was a pleasure to do this – no static shocks from the friction of any treacherous nylon carpets) yourself – it was this place that Marzena, picturing her mother's incredulity, her constant calling out to Teo, Marzena's father, pressed close up to the baking oven in the next room, would describe in drooling detail in her letters home.

Turning the key and stepping into the apartment in West Stand Tower she immediately felt like glamorous television lady or model in the fashion magazines. She only had to touch a button and blinds came out of the wall and slowly screened off the room's wrap-around floor-to-ceiling windows with a mechanical hum and a jerky motion which (she had to admit) reminded her a little of the crematorium near the city boundary at Tarnow. There were chaises longues and foot-rest armchairs and leather sofas and pony-skin day beds – so many chairs in so many designs and so many finishes she could never decide where to sit. Wafer-thin televisions with surround-sound speakers, and not one but two hi-fi systems that fitted flush against the wall. Designer directional lights and soft indirect lighting. Walls whose colour could be made to change from orange to pale violet to aqua blue at the flick of a switch. The tractional drag of the close carpeting; the deep fleeciness of the towels and robes.

Although she didn't smoke, sometimes during her break times Marzena would pretend to, feet up, with an unlit cigarette in her raised right hand, a coffee which she could sip as if it was a Long Slow Screw Against the Wall cocktail – she always got good laugh from these dirty English names, the English too embarrassed to say them until they are completely drunk – on the table beside her.

She was doing this one day, stretched out on a chair shaped like a bolt of lightning when, looking down, she noticed for the first time some stunted trees trying to grow out of a few inches of muddy canal bank or unculverted stretch of river. Immediately above them was a sub-level car park for the use of the workers in a concrete office block. As she watched, a piece of feathered wild-life waddled out and grubbed around in the muck like a wind-up toy. It was like looking at a piece of petrified, medieval North-umberland still clinging to existence at the very edge of the modern city, and was many worlds away from international executive space. Rain rushed in flurries and slanted against the window with a pinging sound which she knew meant it was close to hail.

The first time Ray encountered Marzena she was shaving his mother. She was a care assistant in the nursing home where his mother was living, and she was bending over her with a disposable razor and a bowl of water, her back to the door, when he blundered in. He was still living in Devon then, and had come straight to the fearsome smells and polished surfaces and chronic overheating of Teresa Beard House ('Quality care for the elderly') from the train.

'It is important to mirror them,' Marzena said that first time when she saw his face. It said her name on a laminated tag on her chest: her Christian name and a Polish surname he couldn't pronounce. 'Do you not think? It is important to be a mirror, and not turn away and pretend what is there is not there. You can't live unless you are seen plain by someone. Seeing others plain is not a bad thing, but a good thing. Betty had a beard and also a very fine moustache, and so we had to shave the beard and moustache away because she's lady not man, didn't we, sweetheart?'

He had brought with him what he usually brought – some fruit, some weekly women's magazines bought in the station – and he put these down in the only space he could find on the top of the cabinet by the bed. He sat down and looked for the first time at the tiny, frail figure propped up on pillows in the small white bed. Her head was so light now it made no impression against the pillow. Her hair was thin and there was some unpleasant crusting around her eyes and around her mouth, which Marzena was gently trying to prise open between her thumb and her forefinger in order to get some pills and a sip of water in. 'Pills to give her a happy head. They give her a happy head,' she said to Ray's mother. 'Don't they, poppet?' And then to Ray: 'You must be Betty's son. Look who's here to see you, Betty. Look who's come all this way to see you. Can you open your eyes today, precious? Look, Betty. It's your son.' And his mother opened her eyes and weakly smiled at Ray, and with her bony, bent fingers (with, for all the nurse's efforts, Ray couldn't help noticing, crescents of dark matter still encrusted under the nails), blew him a silent parched kiss.

Except, *It's not me she's seeing,* he wanted to tell the Polish nurse Marzena, who was looking gratified and delighted in her green-and-white striped tabard uniform. *Not Raymond Cruddas the son she brought up and worked hard for years to feed and clothe and take care of after her bastard husband my swine of a banjolele-playing father turned his back on the both of us and walked away. That's not who she's seeing sitting here. She's seeing the other Ray. The one off the telly. The one with his face in the papers. Well, maybe not in the papers so much any more. But the one who never used to be off the telly and splashed all over the fishwrap papers, in their time. My mother's seeing the Ray most of the other sad old desperate cases in here think they see. I'm not joking, old girls who don't recognize their husbands, who can't tell their sons from Burt Reynolds and answer '1901' when you ask them what year they're in, they all beam when they see me come in the door, like I'm their private friend. You've got to see them. Smiling like Christmas and laughing uproariously before I've even opened my mouth. Giving their cheek to be kissed; squeezing my hand; calling me 'Ray'. People who don't know up from down think I've been in their home, met their family, have good feelings about them and root for their being. They don't know me from a bar of soap, but the point is <u>they think they know me</u>. Because I came into their houses with a smart wig on and a bright smile and a song and made them laugh – they chuck me under the chin and coo and gurgle and really think I give a shit.*

He wanted to tell her all this. But he didn't. Not yet. Not that time. He decided to save it, because he was comfortable with the fact than she knew no more about what had happened in the sixty-five years of his existence before he walked through that door than he did about the kind of experience that the just over forty years (he was guessing) of her first life in Poland had taken in.

In fact in her present circumstances Marzena struck him as much more 'naturalized' and far less of an outsider than himself. She spoke English with a quirky, pronounced Geordie twang that connected her to the area in a basic way that he could no longer claim.

It was a voice that Ray was reassured to hear when he called the home. He started to ask for Marzena by name when he phoned to check on his mother's condition, and on his trips back to the North East to visit his mother they began meeting up for a drink, a walk by the river, a brief unromantic Indian or Italian meal. She told him what had made her want to escape from Poland. He told her why he had chosen to leave the city where history or chance had located her and which she had come now to regard as her home. On one of the first occasions they saw each other on neutral ground, away from Teresa Beard House and its dark promises of 'end-of-life care' and 'planned pain management', he felt compelled to tell her that the weightless husk of a person sprouting hairs on her face and incapable of raising a spoon to her mouth and sometimes gibbering and drooling and smelling sometimes, his mother who she had to bathe and baby-talk and care for every day hadn't always been that way. He told her that she had once been a hard-working, lively woman, saddened by the turn her life had taken, but with a kindly nature and a genuine love of people and a communicable appetite for the world. He told her that she used to have nice hair and nice clothes which she knitted and made herself on an old-fashioned treadle machine. He told her that she hadn't always had to have help in the toilet or be constantly reminded of her name or have holes cut with a razor-blade in her ugly shapeless old lady's shoes.

She just said, 'I know,' and poured wine into his glass and into her own glass, and they went on eating.

Betty had been forty-three when Ray finally made his name with *The Big Show* on the television. The following year, with a showcase season in the West End in the offing, he had decided to make his life in London. Ray bought his mother a bungalow in a quiet suburb before his departure from the North East. There was everything in it Betty had never had before. But she found many of the modern conveniences burdensome and a challenge rather than bringing any lightening or improvement to her life. The first time he paid his mother a visit in her new house, Ray found the fridge empty and switched off. 'Mam,' he called to her, 'there's nothing in this fridge.' 'That's right, pet,' she said. 'I don't eat a lot and, anyway, it's winter, so it's a waste of electricity.'

Betty hadn't really been suited to the quieter rhythms of sub-urban life. Although it was an easy bus ride back to the streets where she grew up whose every scarred stone and dog-marked corner was familiar to her, she had grown to feel isolated and unnecessary – 'a pointless article'. Very few people passed her window on Linden Avenue, and there were rarely any children out in the street. There was no pub and no shop on the corner that she could slip out to if she found herself short of bread or low on sugar or suddenly fancied a slice of ham for her tea. 'I'm neither use nor ornament,' she'd tell Ray when he phoned at the appointed hour, because she was afraid to pick up the heavy ebonite phone squatting reproachfully in the corner unless she was sure who it was. Like many of her pleasant, strait-laced neighbours, she sus-pected, she had come to feel like a footnote to her own life.

A wool shop on Stephenson Street back in the old neighbour-hood had proved to be the answer – a cosy cave with a tinkling bell on the door and a two-bar overhead heater, packed full of knitting wools, patterns, stuffed knitted toys, baby clothes, satin ribbons, 'layettes' (Ray never found out what these were) and a constant through-traffic of pregnant women, women with babies, women with school-age children whom it became Betty's plea-sure to see grow up and return in time as customers with babies and children of their own.

She lived in a two-room flat above the shop, which was next door to the double-fronted draper's where Ray had spent so many hours in the winter when he was three staring at the unflinching family of mannequin models in the rain hats and the raincoats with the mysterious mechanical rain drizzling steadily down on them. By the time she retired, that shop had become a Slots o' Fun with prizes of crystal rose bowls and decanters and reproduction revolving bookstands and trivet tables in the window. The shop on the other side had gone through many changes of use, from Wilson's pork shop, to greasy-spoon, to laundryette, to betting shop, finishing up as a Booze Buster off-licence. The whole row had narrowly escaped being demolished in a road-widening scheme in the late sixties, when there was a lot of money sloshing about for projects of that kind and local politicians were well known to be as bent as corkscrews, getting rich on the skimmings of the municipal-construction game. (It was in those years that Ronnie Cornish, as the main manufacturer of bricks in the area and with a number of key place men on the Council, had begun the business of building up his considerable fortune.) Betty's row had survived until 1985, the last small black stain on a clean field of popular modern redevelopment.

The wool shop established Betty as a figure in the community. As well as providing continuity, she was one of the few people in the area who had a telephone in the early days, and she was happy to take messages and let people use the phone in the shop to make calls. A friend of Betty's called Mrs Sudgeon also started to sit in the shop and tell fortunes. Hannah Sudgeon was blind; the sockets of both her eyes were empty and sealed with stitches, which frightened some of the children. But she claimed to be able to foretell the future by the sound of a person's voice and by the message she received from a point on the arm just below the elbow. She could be found at the shop most days, often with her hands at the level of her low chest and a skein of wool stretched between them and Ray's mother industriously rolling the wool into balls. The two of them would sit together knitting baby clothes, romper suits, bonnets, tiny cardigans, the needles monotonously clicking, and Mrs Sudgeon would repeat her frequently stated, truly frightening belief that death was a force of loneliness only hinted at by the most ravening loneliness we know in life: the soul does not leave the body but lingers with it through every stage of decomposition and neglect, through heat and cold and the long nights.

Since her death, whenever Ray thought of his mother, he thought of her in the shop, with the brown shelves with the chipped underpainting, the cave-like atmosphere, the invitation to 'Join Our Christmas Club', the soft wool toys with their economic three-stitch noses and glass button eyes; the plaster Venus de Milo which stood for years on one of the shelves with a telephone number scribbled hastily in pencil along the back of the relaxed right leg.

An elderly man called Sullivan would come in to Teresa Beard House several days a week and sit at the piano and knock out some of the old songs. On a few occasions when Ray called Marzena at the home to ask after his mother he could hear the old people singing 'Run, Rabbit' or 'When You're Smiling', the words miraculously returned through the addled haze of dementia, touching old cords, Sullivan thumping away. And now he heard the same songs as he was lying in bed some mornings, drifting up from the basement, the soundtrack of Tarnow market, one of those coincidences that are just part of the mysteriously connected random flow that constitutes life.

Over the years Jackie had accumulated a collection of floor plans for most of the chain hotels in the British Isles. On all of them he had marked up the structural walls in Biro or coloured pencil and made a list of the rooms that abutted a cement wall and were also away from the road, and away from the lift and the service lift. Ray was a fanatic about quiet, and it was one of Jackie's responsibilities to see that he got it. Sometimes it meant exchanging rooms with Ray in the middle of the night. There'd be a knock at the door and Ray would be standing there without his wig, in his dressing-gown, looking beat and orphaned: 'Would you change rooms with me?'

'Let's see,' Ray would invariably say, half an hour after they'd checked in somewhere. 'You have the cement wall, but you're close to the road . . . All these cars outside will be starting their engines to check out at 8 a.m. . . . Jesus! All those terrible hours that people get up! I know they'll be waking me. Let's see yours, Jackie.'

Ray was still a light sleeper. He had woken up several times during the night thinking he heard wind gusting through the trees – more noise, with, it seemed to him, an odd desolate note, than he had heard the stand of trees on the Moor ever make before. In fact it was the strips of police caution tape quarantining the trees, snapping and humming in a sustained, unearthly way in the wind.

There was still a wind now. He was aware of it rattling the windows, which were the original windows that had been put in when the house was built. The panes in the bedroom were still the original Victorian panes which, when light reflected on them, seemed still to be in the process of setting. The surface had a volatile look, as if it was sliding and bunching; it had the tallowy droop and inelasticity of ageing skin. When Ray lay in bed watching the light play on the windows sometimes they reminded him of his own skin. He examined the underside of his upper arms now to see if he could spot any sign of growing 'bingo flaps', as he had heard them called at work – a reference, he gathered, to the swaying underarms of the women who waved winning cards in the air at bingo halls to claim the 'house'.

Moor Edge Terrace was built in the 1870s. One of the original owners of number 19 had been a painter and woodcarver called Ralph Hedley, and the house had stayed within the Hedley family for generations. It had come on to the market for the first time only in the 1990s, and as soon as he heard that the Hedley house (as nobody other than himself thought of it) was for sale, Ronnie Cornish had made a pre-emptive offer and scarfed it up.

Ronnie was an unlikely fine-art aficionado. But the peculiar fact was that he knew more about the life and work of Ralph Hedley than anybody living. Ronnie had a number of collections. He had a library of rare atlases by Blaeu, Mercator and Ortelius, and collected Early American natural-history renderings by Audubon, Catesbury and Wilson; John Gould's birds; the illustrations of the voyages and explorations of Cook, Wilkes and La Perousse. He had amassed a strong collection of hand-coloured, sixteenth-century county maps of Cumberland and Westmorland, Durham and Northumberland, and the Border Country, made by Saxton, Speed, Norden and other seminal English mapmakers. But Ronnie's special collecting passion was for the oil paintings – especially the paintings showing the daily lives of working people in the North of England – of Ralph Hedley.

A cheap print of a painting of Hedley's called *The Brickfield*, originally issued as a promotional gimmick with the 1903 Christmas number of the *Weekly Chronicle*, had hung in the lean-to building – part doss-house, part out-house – that Ronnie's father called an office at the original family brickworks under the railway arches at Hetton. The print had faded over the years, and become dirt-ingrained and mildewed; it was chewed away at the corners and patched in a couple of places with tape. But when the old works closed, and the old workers and Kidda, the nag who had been used to haul wagons of clay through the factory, had been put out to pasture, Ronnie resolved that, whatever it took, he would buy Hedley's original *Brickfield* painting as soon as the profits that the new mechanized processes were supposed to generate started flowing in. As it turned out, it didn't take a lot. He got a dealer he knew to put out feelers, and *The Brickfield* was soon tracked down and acquired, along with some preparatory sketches and Hedley drawings in colour pastels. From then on, though, it stopped being so easy. Ronnie wanted more Hedleys – he wanted to be *the* Hedley collector; he wanted the pleasure of absolute possession – but the supply had quickly dried up.

Paintings by Hedley rarely appeared on the art market. Most of his best work had stayed within his own family or the families of the local industrialists and others who had originally commissioned the paintings. Many of the owners were elderly people, and Ronnie was accused on more than one occasion of putting undue pressure on them to sell when they had made it clear they didn't want to sell to him, and even of ambulance-chasing, and he didn't deny it. He wasn't ashamed; he was a collector, with all the paranoid, irrational, sociopathic, controlling tendencies that implied.

Meanwhile, starved of the paintings, Ronnie turned his attention to other areas of Hedley's work. One of the ancillary Cornish businesses was a demolition contractors. And Ronnie, like his competitors in the architectural salvage trade, was not known for his scrupulous observance of listed buildings consequent procedures. If architraves, friezes, pediments, stone cornices, Georgian fireplaces, even doors were there for the taking, then they were taken, regardless of whether a building was in use or abandoned: cherrypicked with permission or without, legitimately or not.

Ralph Hedley had used his house, which was now Ray's house, as a workshop and a showplace for his talents. It had been the place where he was able to refine the skills that were to earn him a reputation for being the most gifted architectural carver in his part of England.

Hedley was heavily in demand during Tyneside's biggest boom in building in the 1880s. Building contractors ordered decorative carving in hotels, banks and shops, and the Hedley workshop provided mantelpieces and wooden moulds for plasterwork in new houses, as well as innumerable brackets, festoons, and balusters, and huge lengths of egg-and-dart moulding.

Excellent examples of his work in all these areas were to be found from cellar to attic at Moor Edge Terrace. For the dining room he had produced a huge sideboard showing scenes from the Northumberland battle, the Chevy Chase. There were decorative balusters rising through the house, scalloped corner niches, and columnettes. He had installed fine wooden panels in the master bedroom, together with a frieze of cornucopias overflowing with fruit, with a ceiling rose of similar design. All of it now gone, stripped out between Ronnie Cornish acquiring the house and Ray and Marzena moving in.

From his bed Ray was able to see where the frieze and the plaster cornices had been removed. The room had been replastered and expertly skimmed, but the marks still showed. In certain lights he could see the scars around the perimeter of the ceiling and near the tops of the walls. Shadow indentations of how the room might have looked in its Victorian heyday were still there. The room itself had been transferred intact and in its entirety to Ronnie's office, or one of his homes.

For the first year or thereabouts that he lived in the house Ray had been unaware of the Hedley connection until a neighbour, a lecturer at the University, conversationally pointed it out.

He didn't suppose he minded the fact that, in effect, he was living in a denuded, scooped-out shell. And he was pragmatic enough to know that, even if he did, there wasn't a lot he could do about it. He was in hock to Ronnie. Ronnie advanced him the money to buy the house. (This was nominal, of course, as Ronnie owned the house.) Ronnie had put up the start money for Bobby's, and Ronnie was swallowing the losses the club was incurring since foot-and-mouth. Ray was paid a salary, plus an incremental (so far notional) share of any profits earned.

Ray owned – he was paying the mortgage on – Jackie's house. Jackie's house was in Ray's name. Jackie was seventy and might have expected to own something, but he owned nothing. Both Ray and Jackie had to jump when Ronnie said jump. They were dependent to an unhealthy degree on Ronnie's whim. When light washed the walls, throwing the scarring into relief, Ray, in his half-awake state, was often reminded of this truth.

He got up, ran the razor over his face and went for his run, following the bucking blue-and-white streamers and the boundary path around the Moor.

He saw the old man some mornings, leaning on the iron gate, mooning after his Daisy and Bessy and Flossie, his Bella and Floradora, his Minehaha and Jill. This morning, though, he wasn't there.

Every Saturday when there was a home game Jackie came and collected Ray and delivered him to United's ground. It was a short trip, in fact only around the corner, but the milling crowd and swelling stream of people made it simpler to get there by car.

He had an arrangement where he stood on his hind legs and read the team sheet out, introduced the manager and did a stint for the corporate crowd in one of the big, bright new clangorous executive entertainment suites on match days. And this was another thing Ray supposed he owed to Ronnie Cornish, Ronnie being a big-noise director.

It was early when they set off. It was a few minutes after twelve, and the game didn't start until three. The programme vendors, 'swag' sellers and portable canteens were just setting up, and the carnival was just getting going. The first hint of onions frying was starting to drift on the air. When there was a game, Mighty put on a blue-gingham uniform and a lace-trimmed blue-gingham apron and waited on in one of the maze of upper-tier bars and restaurants at the ground that were part of the 'hospitality experience'.

On those days when Mighty was earning at the football, the Scran Van was taken over by her daughter, Andrea, and Andrea's young teenage daughter, Kelly. Ray always looked out for their 'HOME COOKEN AND HOMEMADE PIES' sign set up against the Park gates and the big fist with the felt hammer in it which was fixed to the crown of Andrea's cap, and Jackie always gave them a wave and a friendly toot as they were passing. The last time they'd seen Kelly, she had had white strings hanging from the lobes of her ears, and Ray asked her what they signified. 'Just dental floss,' she said. 'I had my ears pierced for ear-rings, and the man told me to keep the piercings open with floss. It might look unusual, but it doesn't hurt.'

There was the usual queue snaking around the souvenir super-store and the notice was in its usual place just inside the atriumed main Reception: 'SMART CASUAL – STRICTLY NO TRAINERS, DENIM OR FOOTBALL SHIRTS'. Ray signed the book (always a difficult moment because the man keeping Reception had a toupé that in cut and colour closely resembled his) and rode the glass-pod lift to Level 4. 'It couldn't look phonier if it had a chin strap,' he had recently heard somebody joke about the steward on Reception's hairpiece, which had given Ray pause for thought about his own. He made a conscious effort to unglue his eyes from the man's dense, unbreathing comb-over as the lift carried him up through the building, and looked south across the old green-patinated buildings made of the hard local stone, and the new multi-coloured chrome-and-plexiglass towers of the shining regenerated city, in the direction of the river.

It was Ray's second season of this Saturday routine, and it never varied: drinks in the Chairman's Suite, lunch, a few jokes from Ray, team changes and parish-pump announcements, the manager's stroking of the faithful, the match, player appearances, more drinks in the Vice Presidents' Suite, drinks in the Directors' Suite, one for the road, home. 'The only place round here that sells more vodka than us on a Saturday is Asda,' the Entertain-ments Director had told Ray, and he believed him. The Business Club level (always welcome news to Ray) was awash with drink.

The first person he saw when he got out of the lift was Thomas Saint, a United hero of the seventies, bald now, middle-aged and thickened, but still known to one and all by his tabloid tag of 'Saint Tommy'. Tommy, in the age-old tradition, had taken his lumps. He was a relic of the legendary drinking days, when players would go off on a Thursday bender and turn up for the match on Saturday still drunk. He had eventually been arrested for exposing himself in a Little Chef car park near Scotch Corner and been sentenced to twelve months' community service. But the North East is a forgiving place, famous for collecting those who have strayed back to its bosom. And now Tommy was rehabilitated, a role model and model citizen, and generally regarded as having a heart as big as a bucket.

He had been given a job as a living exhibit in the club's memorabilia museum and also, drifting through the various hospitality facilities, worked as a presser-of-the-flesh and meeter-and-greeter on match days. And, true to the job description, that was what he did to Ray now – took Ray's hand in his great mit and offered him a hearty greeting: 'How's tricks, me old marrer! Hey, I've got a cracker forya. I was walking along the street the other day and I met a man coming towards me with a sheep under each arm. "Sheering?" I said. "Fuck off," he said. "Find your own."' Ray laughed out of relief at first, and then because he found the joke funny. They shared something for a moment. A throat-clearer on an overcast Saturday morning. A small community of two.

'I was walking along the street the other day,' Ray said, breaking his own rule of never performing for nothing, 'and I met a man who had a pelican on a lead. "Are you taking him to the zoo?" I said. "No," he said. "I took him to the zoo yesterday. We're going to the pictures."' More laughter. Another connection. Saint Tommy seemed set up for the day. The sound of his laughter boomed in the nearly empty corridors. 'Have a good one,' he said, laughing into his fist, the laughter eventually thickening into a dubious-sounding chesty cough.

The club crest in shades of blue repeated itself to infinity in the carpet. Ray glanced into a steamy kitchen and into the window-less cell that was the Press Lounge – dingy chairs, fractured ceiling tiles, burn-pocked tables. All the Function Suites opened on to a view of the pitch and, walking into any of them from the enclosure of the corridor, it was always a shock to be confronted by the canyon of the playing area and the seating tiers and the reckless vertiginous sense of falling away.

As soon as Ray appeared in the doorway of the Chairman's Suite, a waitress stepped forward with a tray of champagne and juices, but he shook his head and walked over to the bar. Although it was new, the Suite had been retro-fitted with the trappings of a previous era and had a smoky, fusty, fifties feel: the walls were covered with pale-blue watered silk and hung with a job lot of action portraits in oil of heroes of the glorious past.

The Chairman's guests were, as per usual, a group of crisp little men 'a-swagger with assets', a phrase Ray had heard or read once and remembered. They were members of the same Lodge, the same Rotary Club, the same Round Table, ego-driven and hard-bargaining, men with cautious, ordered lives. 'Big Steamers' was what Marzena called the football club directors, after a line from a poem of Kipling's that she liked and which she and Ray quoted to each other and often laughed about: 'Where are you going to, all you Big Steamers?' 'How were your Big Old Steamers?' Marzena would sometimes ask Ray when he got home, well watered and very tired, and two shows to do later that night at Bobby's. 'Have they managed to bring back the hanging yet?'

'Yes, but. Success on the pitch is the driver of our business. It's all very well this talk about restructuring the debt. But if you look at profits after player-trading . . . Oh, aye-aye. You know what they say: never turn your back on a full-grown comedian. It might bite.' Ray knew without turning round that the speaker was Maurice. Maurice was a long-standing member of the squirearchy, and old school. He was a sharp-featured, dapper man with white scimitar sideboards and vast aviator-style glasses which were wider than his head. Maurice's glasses had turned cranberry-coloured in the concentrated stadium light.

He was a polyurethane-foam millionaire, also the owner of a telephone-cleaning company, which he had just relinquished control of to his son. It was a relationship that was duplicated several times over in that company of worthies: a number of the middle-aged men having drinks were still having their strings jerked by their fathers, and the combination of resentment and dependency accounted for the underlying atmosphere of tight-lipped rage and truculent aggression at these occasions. Maurice was a recovering alcoholic, but he still had his mineral water out of the pewter tankard engraved with his name. 'I stopped drinking in 1980, but I didn't get sober until 1985.' That was his one joke, his joke for all occasions, which he could hide behind when he found himself in the situation of being among strangers and having to say no to a drink, when the shame of all he did when he was brutally, rampantly off the wagon came flooding back.

Maurice had informed Ray on more than one occasion that his life was governed by two simple acronyms: PMA and OPM – 'positive mental attitude' and 'other people's money'. He was a devotee of the inspirational writings of Norman Vincent Peale and a major local contributor to the coffers of New Labour. Government ministers visiting the North East were given use of the company helicopter.

Maurice tried to engage Ray in conversation about the prospects for the team, which had just struggled clear of the relegation zone with four successive wins, and five games left to play. It was a subject in which neither of them had any burning interest. 'You've got to hand it to them, four wins on the stot . . . Steve did well for us on Wednesday, an' he's probably our fifth-choice centre half. But what we need is a strong, speedy, world-class defender, someone who can actually read the game . . .'

Ray's attention strayed to the pitch, where several men in tracksuits were carrying out the pre-match inspection. They walked with their heads bent, as if they were trying to find something one of them had dropped earlier. Occasionally one of the men tested the ground with a toe of his boot. It was a new pitch which hadn't been played on until today. It had just been laid. It had been brought to the ground by lorry. A week ago it had been lying in a field in Lincolnshire, anonymous, unremarked. Then it had been cut and rolled like carpet and transported here, with police outriders accompanying the extra-long vehicle and reporters and television cameras waiting to record its arrival.

Who would be first to have their ashes scattered on it, something that happened in private once or twice a season, although the club denied it ever happened? Had the integrity of the field been respected, or had the strips been laid in no particular order so that together they grew into a different field? How did uprooted grass go on growing? Ray, drink in hand, was pondering this, and Maurice, who now had been joined by another man, was still chitter-chattering, when a bride and groom emerged from the tunnel and wandered out into the darker greenery of the lower field, and love music started playing over the Tannoy.

The windows in the Chairman's Suite were angled outwards, which heightened the sensation of vertigo. The glass was thick, so any sound that penetrated it was strained and drowned out by the chatter. The music outside was faint – too faint to be identified – but almost anybody would have recognized it as a love song: 'Tonight I celebrate my love for you . . .'

As part of the push to 'grow' revenues, the old home dressing-room had been given a lick of rose-pink paint and had a rose-patterned frieze pasted on at the dado level and been converted into a chapel for civil weddings. These were proving to be extremely popular, and five or six weddings took place on the average Saturday. As part of the package, the bride and groom and their friends and families were allowed to come out on the pitch once the ceremony was completed and pose for pictures. That is, the bride and groom were directed along a strip of carpet which had been extended a few yards on to the pitch while the rest of the wedding party stood on the sidelines, well clear of the hallowed turf, videoing and taking pictures. A video cameraman was employed by the club, and the public address pumped out wedding favourites such as 'Evergreen' and 'This Is My Moment', and the faces of the happy couple were put up on the giant screens, with banner messages from family and workmates streaming along the bottom of the frame, and cartoon graphics of kisses and bursting passion-pink hearts.

As Ray watched, the big screen filled with a close-up of a bride in traditional head-dress and lace-and-satin gown stealing a drag on a cigarette between pictures. The cigarette in her mouth was the size of an I-beam. Her make-up had not been put on with this level of magnification in mind. But when the people with her caught sight of Donna (her name floated in a caption heart), a cheer went up and everybody raised their cameras and pointed them at the bright electric mosaic image on the screen rather than at the flesh-and-blood Donna and Rob, her husband of less than ten minutes, standing arm in arm, deep in the mystery, several yards on to the field of play.

Many of the women had already taken off the cartwheel hats that they had rented for the occasion; some of the men were also in hired or borrowed clothes, occasionally fidgeting with their collars or shifting their shoulders uneasily in jackets that were either too small or too big for them. 'For Donna and Rob,' a streamer message said, travelling from right to left across the screen, 'This day will form a milestone in your lives. You will look back on it with love and happiness, as the start in a new phase of your life together – Love you lots, Mam and Dad.'

'We've Only Just Begun' played on the public address. High in the stands, teams of boys were going along the rows, robotically drying off the seats, apparently oblivious to anything going on anywhere else in the ground.

A waitress came and handed Ray and the other men leather-bound menus. Maurice was going on about it not being the same it not being Wembley for the Cup Final, now that he was going to get his hour in the Royal Box. He was always trying to pump Ray about Maggie Thatcher – 'the Blessed Margaret' – and Ray always tried to steer him clear of that subject. Had Ray ever met the Queen, Maurice wanted to know. 'No,' Ray said, although he had. 'No. I've not had that pleasure.' Another drink arrived for Ray. 'Here's courage,' he said to Maurice, who raised his tankard of now tepid mineral water.

If the magazine write-ups were to be believed, a new spirit of pleasure had replaced the tendency to inwardness and the old suspicious dourness. An article in *Newsweek* had recently christened the city the 'New Orleans of Europe'. The football was routinely lumped in with the happy mood of round-the-clock, leisure-and-pleasure hedonism. It counted as recreation – but for many of the corporate supporters it wasn't. Most of those who assembled in the Marcus Price Suite on Saturdays were working. It was work, everybody either planning a deal, hatching a deal or looking for a deal. More deals got done in an afternoon at the football than in a week at the office. But for many people in the new climate of global-branding exercises and fleeting entertainment experiences, work was their fun; work was their recreation.

Many of the corporate season-ticket holders had cutlery, crockery, wine glasses, napkins imprinted with their names and company logos. The ballpoint pens that one firm of financial analysts handed out to their guests bore the slogan: 'There are few ways in which a man can be more innocently employed than in getting money – Dr Johnson.' Apart from football footage from vintage newsreels and out-takes from contemporary matches, the only other images playing on the screens in the bars on Level 4 were from violent natural-history shows like *Man-eating Tigers* and *When Animals Attack*, or documentaries about malicious weather: *Avalanche!*, *Tornado!*, *When Clouds Turn Nasty*.

The Marcus Price Suite was the biggest of the big corporate blow-out facilities, and it was already humming when Ray got there. The whole of one long wall was glass facing the pitch and it took a while for his eyes to adjust to the glare. He spotted Mighty chatting to a table which was unusual in that most of the people sitting around it were women. Several of them were young, most of them looked as if they had arrived fresh from the hairdresser and nearly all of them were barricaded in behind stiff, rope-handled shopping bags with luxury labels and names. There was a kind of pride in whose wife or/and girlfriend was more spendthrift, bankrupting and shopaholic, and the men liked to amuse each other boasting about the damage being done to their current accounts.

A lot of men wore caps when they went outside to watch the match. Lately some of them had started wearing old-style caps of the kind that people dug out to wear at Bobby's, although, unlike Ray, most of the cap-wearers were too young to remember the time when, sartorially, there was nothing more impressive than a rakish cap worn with a smart blue suit. Traditionally, caps had been part of the hunger for the outdoors after a grinding hard shift – the hunger for the allotment, the pigeon ducket or the open field. So it was ironic that, until the tragedies of the eighties and the realization that most stadiums were death-traps, flat caps had been worn to football grounds, which were sport's version of the cavernous, cheerless factories for whose workers they were built.

Ray's first job of the day was going to be to introduce the five members of the latest pop group to be voted into existence by the viewers of a reality-television show. One of the winners was a local girl, and they were there to do a personal appearance, miming to their record before kick-off. A young man in leather trousers who worked for them in some capacity was sent to find Ray and take him to the private box where the group were being 'mothballed' to meet them briefly before bringing them on.

'You know, it's amazing the immediate public that comes around you, and takes you in, and accepts you, and gives you success, and everything,' one of the boy members was telling an interviewer eagerly when Ray stuck his head around the door. 'Oooo, me nana used to love you! She thought you were dead funny!' the Geordie girl squealed when he stepped forward briefly to shake her hand.

The journalist was a woman from the morning paper who had written nice things about Ray and Bobby's. The tabloids, though, had already bolted with stories about the black boy in the group being gay, and had hinted that two of the girls were sleeping with each other. Here already was the familiar style from success to anguish, without a record being sold. The more they were on television, the more famous they became; the more famous they were, the more a target of criticism they became; the more they were criticized, the more they felt misunderstood; the more misunderstood they felt, the more anguish they carried.

'Without that little television box, you're nobody,' the chancer in the leather trousers whispered to Ray. 'With it, you're a king in our society – a television personality.' It was because of situations like this that Ray liked to have Jackie around him on football days. Their code often came in very useful. 'This chap's tall enough to be a policeman,' Ray might say to Jackie, which meant 'He's a total bloody idiot, get me away from here.' 'I'm just going to check the hamper, Jackie' translated as 'I'll swing for this bastard if I have to listen to any more of his inane horseshit! He better be gone when I get back.'

'There are people that don't particularly *need* to be special. There are those of us that are nuts enough to *have* to be special. And we do everything we can,' Ray said to the group's manager or whoever he was. 'One thing worth remembering: in this business, when one door shuts, they all bloody shut.'

In the restaurants and executive boxes girls were going around collecting completed Lottery slips from the tables and taking them to be processed in the machines. Television was in, and a few famous faces off the box were keeping the day on the boil. 'Delegates' as they were always called in the literature, the club's expensively laminated folders, were raucously repeating snippets and bits of sporting gossip that they'd read in the morning papers, and working hard at convincing themselves and each other that their hard-boiled, transactional, buyer–supplier relationships were a species of friendship.

Through the fug of blue cigar smoke turning lazily in the softening light, Ray noticed Ronnie Cornish sitting nose to nose at a corner table with a younger man with a streaky peroxide haircut. This was Lee Yeardye ('How many E's in Lee Yeardye?' used to be the long-running terrace joke), a journeyman midfielder pushing up into his thirties and fast approaching the end of his career – he hadn't started a game in the first team all season: most of his energies appeared to be going into the wine bar he had opened in town with Ronnie's, and Warren Oliver's, backing.

The last time Ray had seen the pair of them together, Ronnie was holding a cigarette-lighter to Lee Yeardye's nose. Ronnie had bet Yeardye £500 he couldn't take the heat of a cigarette-lighter on his nose for three seconds, but the player had won the bet and earned himself a second £500 for doing it a second time. The two of them were always taking each other on at arm-wrestling or single-arm press-up endurance contests in their lounge suits in hotels and bars. Although Ronnie was giving away thirty years, he was usually able to acquit himself well and at least hold his own.

The cigarette-lighter incident had taken place in Ronnie Cornish's office in a former warehouse building close to the river. He had bought five out of seven buildings on the then derelict Newbridge Quays site in the eighties, and developed the area in stages, aided by a raft of local-government and government regeneration grants.

Newbridge Quays was where he put his Ralph Hedley paintings on show and stored his other Hedley booty. Ray had gone in to see the painting called *The Brickfield*, which had been given pride of place, gilt-framed and illuminated, above the mantelpiece in Ronnie's inner office. Ronnie had been trying to persuade him for a long time to come in and see it, but for various reasons – learning how the interior of his house at Moor Edge Terrace had been covertly stripped out was one of them – Ray hadn't found a way to be able to make it until that night.

It was after seven. Most of the people working in the building had gone home. Ronnie's assistant had stayed long enough to buzz him in and meet him at the lift, and then she had also left for home.

The lighting was intimate. Up-lighters gently played light on the robin's-egg-blue walls. The paintings glowed under their burnished-brass picture lights. Hedley's decorative wood carvings – around the door and bookcases, in the wall panels and the fireplace, around the base of Ronnie's vast, catafalque-like desk – had been lightened using a liming process in which the original dark-wood veneers were preserved unharmed underneath. The building had originally been used to store butter and other groceries, and a large port-hole window high up in a corner wall was surmounted by carved festoons overflowing with flowers, fruit, dead game.

'Are you just winding . . . Are you just joking me? Are you joking me? . . . You've got till nine tomorra morning to come back with a *realistic* and that means not pulling my pisser pissing price . . .' Ronnie eventually finished on the phone. 'Can't trust that cunt further than you can throw a bull by the prick,' he said. And then, as if he was just noticing Ray for the first time: 'Ray! How are you!' He barrelled over to a heavy ball-and-claw table inlaid with embossed leather where rows of bottles were glinting. 'Jackie D. Big one. Am aa right?' He made a performance of tonging ice out of a lidded bucket with a leather stirrups design. 'Booze is constant proof that God likes to see us happy,' Ronnie said. 'I'm not wrong. Am aa not right?'

Ray and Ronnie were more or less the same age. Sixty years earlier they had been at school together. Ronnie was one of the hard lads. Ray wasn't. For two years, between the ages of about nine and eleven, Ronnie had subjected Ray to a sustained reign of terror. It all happened as a result of Ronnie going to clout Ray in the playground lavatory one day and his foot slipping (he was wearing shoes with the yellow-rubber crêpe soles that became slimy in the wet) and Ronnie falling and cracking his head on the urinal trough which happened to be blocked and overflowing, with the consequence that Ronnie's hair and his jacket and trousers were wet through and already rank and smelling by the time he eventually scrambled up.

He lay in wait for Raymond outside the back gate at nights, hung around on the street corner near his house where he could see him, chalked up names, got boys who wanted to be in his gang to trip him up and throw sticks and dirt at him, and persecuted him relentlessly from then on. The time Ray hit a timber that had been thrown in his path and came off his pram-wheel 'bogie' travelling at some speed down a banked back lane and ended up in hospital with a split lip and suffering serious concussion – that had been a typical piece of Ronnie Cornish-inspired devilry.

Fifty-five years passed before they met each other again. Ray's mother was dying, and he was taking whatever jobs came his way in the North East. A bluff, powerful-looking, stare-you-down kind of man, silver-white hair worn in a pudding-basin Beatles fringe, face rawly inflamed, had come up to him at the end of a Rotary Club occasion when he was the after-dinner entertainment, and Ray had instantly recognized him as his former tormentor. He felt he would have recognized the bully in Ronnie Cornish even without the childhood misery he had brought him: he seemed to Ray to carry a sense of all the people who had been sacked, short-changed, bullied, abused, and stood on by him on his climb; his inexorable rise from rich to richer: the shadow of all those who bore him some ill will. Ray believed he saw this in Ronnie's aura.

What Ronnie saw when he looked at Ray was only the milksop mother's boy who somehow – it genuinely perplexed him, and at some deep level disquieted him – had gone on to get his face on the television and his name in the papers and become friends with film stars and singers and married high-maintenance pretty women and hung out with the high and mighty. He didn't see the Raymond Cruddas he had glowered up at from a pool of school-yard piss then. He didn't see somebody who was paying his way by performing on cruise ships now – 'grab-a-granny' trips to the Canaries and around the Greek islands – and accepting twopenny-halfpenny jobs like the Chartered Association of Tax Accountants Annual Dinner and RAF Uphaven Sergeants' Mess and the one he had just performed for Ronnie and his fellow Rotarian Big Steamers. For Ronnie, as for the old folks in Teresa Beard House, Ray still had the old special luminosity. Ronnie was still in thrall to the glamour he thought attached to people of the entertain-ment persuasion. He could still hear the crackle of the magnetic field of fame.

The night of the visit to his office, Ray noticed for the first time the trace shadow of a tattoo which had been lasered off Ronnie's neck. He also saw that he had a concealant, a spot of something flesh-toned borrowed from his wife, on the end of his nose where the broken capillaries were. At the side of his face, where the Botoxer had either missed or left showing for authenticity's sake, were deltas, whole Ordnance Survey maps of red thread-veins, close to the surface and aggravated by the glasses Ronnie didn't have on but which had left indentations in the well-cut silver hair above his ears.

They were standing in front of Ronnie's prize possession, *The Brickfield*, and Ronnie was explaining how the artist had posed the figures to depict the various stages of brick-making in the picture. The process began at the back of the image with digging the clay, and progressed towards the viewer as the clay was tipped from the wheelbarrow on to a bench, worked in the mould and tipped out to dry in the sun. 'Worth a few bob, that, like. Worth a canny bit,' Ronnie said. 'That was his speciality, like. Working people. Manual workers. Industrial craftsmen. Gets them very life-like. To my style of thinking, anyway. Hard honest labour that tires you out and makes you sleep. Clever feller.'

Ronnie was wearing the waistcoat and trousers of a light-grey suit. The waistcoat was cut straight at the waist, and kept riding up over his belly. Expanding metal arm-bands cinched the sleeves of his shirt. On his feet were the tan, elastic-sided Trickers boots which are a favourite with farmers on more formal occasions away from the farm.

He moved Ray on to another Hedley painting on the adjacent wall. *Weary Waiting* showed a bedraggled wife carrying a small baby and accompanied by her young son. All three of them were waiting on the steps of a pub where the husband was visible through a lighted window drinking with his friends. 'Wiv aal been there,' Ronnie said to Ray. 'Aa remember me poor ma waiting with us for oors ootside the Big Lamp until the owld cunt give her the money to get some messages, some bread an' some bits for us bairns to eat.'

But Ray sensed Ronnie hadn't said all he wanted to say about *The Brickfield*, and the pair of them drifted back there, the ice in their glasses clinking. 'See that?' Ronnie said, indicating the workbench covered in elephant-grey mud in the middleground of the painting with his thick, chipped finger. 'When I was a laddie, probably nee more than aboot six, the owld man stood iz on a bench the dead spit of that doon at wor brickworks there an' telt iz to jump. 'E put iz on the bench and said, "Jump and I'll catch you," and I jumped and he took his hands away and I fell on the floor. He picked me up and stroked me hair and said, "Never trust anybody in your life. Not even your own father." He said, "Keep your friends close to you and your enemies even closer." Very Victorian, the owld man. Well, you knew him. Very fucken strict.'

Persian rugs lay around overlapping one another on the floor of the office. There was the heady sweet smell from a bowl of fully mature fleshy pink lilies. The fender in front of the fire was made of the rim of a railway wagon wheel. In front of it was a clippy mat made from pieces of rag cut from old clothes.

Ronnie went over to the table to make more drinks. 'Still a lot of Hedley paintings oot there neebody can trace,' he said. 'That's the choker.' And it was at that point that Lee Yeardye had arrived. Ronnie had evidently been expecting him because he just bellowed, 'Come on up, sonner!' into the entryphone without the preliminary of asking who it was.

With Lee was Warren Oliver, who Ray knew shared ownership of a luxury cruiser called *Petrarch* with Ronnie. They also shared vanity number plates – 2 BE on Ronnie's Bentley, NOT 2B on Warren's Merc – which they said they'd bought as a joke.

The three of them – Ronnie, Lee and Warren – were part of a consortium which had plans for moving into the casino trade at Blackpool. They were bidding to build the 400-bed, £130-million, 2,500-slot-machines Caesar's Forum Resort ('Lavish with gleaming statuary, gorgeous gardens and fabulous fountains!'

according to their prospectus, which Ray had seen), helping turn Blackpool into the Las Vegas of Lancashire – or the 'Lost Wages' as Ronnie, Lee and Warren called it whenever talk turned, as it inevitably did, to this latest licence to print money.

They had recently returned from a flying, 'fact-finding' visit to Las Vegas and were still reliving their adventures. 'Yi cunt yi,' Ronnie said to Lee, 'pissed as a rat, stottin all ower the place the whole fucken time . . . You were that pissed, if a fly had farted you would have fallen ower . . . Forst thing he did when he woke up every mornin', nee geein', was make himself a "Chaos". Southern Comfort and Bailey's. Caalls 'esell a footbaaller. Get a few of them inside yi. Blow your fucken heed off.'

'We had a top chuckle though, didn't we?' Lee said, draining his drink. 'Frickin hilarious. Saw Steve Martin at the what's-its Palace.'

'Dean Martin,' Warren said. 'Fucking toppers.'

'Is he dead now, him?' Lee wanted to know.

'I hope so,' Ronnie said. 'They buried the cunt.'

Lee had arrived carrying an expensive black briefcase with lots of external cargo pockets and silver clasps and straps, and Ronnie had opened it and was delving in one of the pockets. Eventually he produced the wad of Cup Final tickets that Lee had been given the task of black-marketeering on behalf of the other players in the squad. He and Lee had a brief, suddenly serious conversation, and money changed hands. Their business completed, Ronnie reached into the bag, the joker again, and spun a video across the room directly into Ray's lap.

'Fantastic Facials!' it said over several pictures of red-lipped women giving black men blow-jobs. 'Face-blastin' action! Hot gooey loads of sticky cum!' 'What yi after, like?' Ronnie said, coming over and standing next to Ray. 'Whatever yi fancy, Lee can get. He can get yi owt yi like. Cunt's hung like a fucken yak.'

'Ron,' Lee said, lying back with his feet up on Ronnie's desk, 'if you went out with your mate to a party and you got pissed, really pissed, blacking out, and you woke up the next morning sleeping next to your mate, and your arse was really sore, would you tell anybody about it?'

'No,' Ronnie said.

'Do you want to come to a party tomorrow night?'

They laughed. Warren coloured up. Lee passed him the note and Warren took his line of cocaine from the desk. He offered the rolled note to Ray, but Ray shook his head. He indicated his fibrillated heart, opening his jacket and patting the place where his heart was with his hand.

'Fucken puff!' Ronnie said. And then: 'More drinks! Let's get radged! Fucken radgerated! No going back!' He brought the bottle and splashed Jack Daniels in Ray's glass. He helped Warren and Lee to more Rémy, and then some for himself, a good four fingers. He bent briefly over the desk and beat his chest theatrically with both fists when he stood up.

'Group hug!' Ronnie demanded. 'Group hug!' he shouted. And then when they were all standing in the middle of the room with their arms around each other and their heads together: 'Four-way kiss! In a non-gay way!'

When they were separated, Lee reached down and cupped the crotch of Ronnie's trousers. 'Just checking.'

Ray tapped the microphone to confirm it was working. 'Ladies and gentlemen, if I may have your attention, it's that time, once again, when it is my pleasure to introduce the manager of the greatest team in Britain, the lifeblood of the Geordie nation . . .'

The manager bounded on to the stage, took a piece of paper with his prompt notes on it out of his breast pocket, and began to address the faithful. 'As nobody in this room needs reminding, we haven't even been at the races for much of this season. The good news, apart from the twelve points we've picked up from the last four games, is that Paulo's back in light training. Martin's groin strain is responding to treatment . . . deserved the three points . . . one unit together . . . light at the end of the tunnel . . .'

Every platitude. But platitudinous is what it had to be, like putting a watch wrapped in a sock in a basket with a new puppy. Reassuring. Restful. Monotonous. Soothing. 'Everybody's bubbling and lively down there and I feel confident we're going to go out today and do a job for you. I'm expecting one-hundred-and-ten-per-cent commitment from the boys. We've made the final of the Cup. They know that. But they also know that that means nothing unless we go on and drastically improve our position in the League. They know . . .'

Ray couldn't believe it. He beheld their uplifted faces. They were transported; transfixed. The room was filled with the sound of contented purring. He, on the other hand, perhaps because he was on stage behind him rather sitting out in front, wasn't susceptible to the hypnotic powers of Great Mogadon, the manager.

Lunch was still being served to late-comers at the rear of the room, and Ray diverted himself watching the comings and goings of waiting staff and trolleys, the wafting of the service doors, the private jokes, the near-collisions. And as he watched he witnessed one of those slow-motion accidents – when time slows down and everything that happens happens in swimming slow motion.

Mighty had been serving soup to a smartly, even flashily, suited-up man – a 'suit' – when the ladle slipped, and slipped and skittered through the swollen knuckles of her arthritic fingers when she tried to catch it.

Ray waited to see how the man was going to react. The answer was: not sympathetically or with restraint. The answer was: not well.

Kevin Arlen had hit the jackpot with a sandwich factory catering for the take-out lunchtime trade. He was also a city councillor. He sat on a number of key committees crucial to Ronnie's business.

He was on his feet. The thin green soup was distributing itself from the corner of his jacket to his trousers. Mighty, who had grown very pale, was using a cloth to dab at the stains, but Arlen dashed her hand away.

Ray chose this moment to stop looking. By making a quarter-turn he could see behind him out of the window while still appearing to be hanging on every stilling word the manager was saying. The stands had started to fill up now; the logo created from the seat backs was beginning to disappear; but the final wedding of the day was still being processed through.

As he looked, giant eyes seemed to be appraising Ray from the big screen over the pitch. The eyelashes were dotted with football-size pearl decorations, the eyelids metallically striped in the team colours. The appearance of the bride's face on the screen brought a half-hearted ironic cheer. Then whistling and clapping started, and then what to Ray sounded like obscene chants.

The new pitch had been laid in strips. You could still see the unincorporated seams and joins. He felt his head then, worked his fingers along the line where the fake hair met what was left of his own. Then he stopped that when he realized he was doing it in plain view of everyone in the room.

When Ray turned and faced the front again he saw that Mighty had pressed the cleaning rag to her face and that Jackie had introduced himself into the picture. It was a tableau that had attracted the interest of only the nearest tables. The room was still held in the spell of the manager's soothing, sleepytime stories.

The manager was a decent man. Ray believed so anyway. He stepped forward and led the applause when he had completed his flannel.

As soon as he came off the stage, Ray slipped behind a utilities column to gather himself for a few seconds. This was ritual. It was what he always did when he had been up in front of an audience. He'd been doing it since he first stepped on a stage. He allowed himself a deferred blush – the redness that experience had taught him how to hold at bay while he was performing; a purgative flushing of the face. It lasted a few seconds and then was gone. Then he felt fine.

The lunchers were starting to file out to claim their seats and sip the atmosphere. Ray began to make his way back through the crowd, nodding hellos, stopping to shake the odd hand. When he emerged into the now nearly empty rear part of the suite, he saw that Kevin Arlen was sprawled in his chair with the soup stains darkened on his jacket and trousers and an affronted look on his face, clearly pushed there by Jackie.

Mighty was being comforted by another waitress.

Jackie was standing eyeball to eyeball with Ronnie Cornish, whose face Ray could see was very red. 'Bastard back off or I'm going to fucken chin you.' Ray couldn't say he had seen a person snarl until that moment, but Ronnie was snarling. All dog. The wad of neck behind his collar was purple. Jackie's face on the other hand was cold, almost serene. Decreased facial expression – what they call in neurology a 'masked face'; an intermittent tremor of his hands.

It had grown so quiet – all of them there were inside their own pocket of quiet – that you could hear the starched, valet-finish cuffs of Ronnie's shirt make a scraping noise against the leathered backs of his hands.

Ronnie had never made any secret of the fact that he regarded Jackie as a hanger-on. It was a word that had been bandied about more than once in Jackie's hearing since they had been yoked together in business with Cornish. In spite of himself he felt exactly as hurt every time he heard it as he did the first time he heard Ronnie Cornish calling him that.

Jackie's belief was that everybody was hanging on to something, and sometimes it was another person, because all you had in life were other people. Ray wanted him there. He was employed. He had a job. He served a need, even if dickheads like

Cornish – even if Ray, and Jackie himself – didn't exactly understand what that need was.

In their younger years, Jackie had encouraged Ray to get on, to be lucky and stay sharp. He had always offered sound counsel to Ray on who could be trusted, who should be steered clear of, what was a good or bad business scheme. Not counting the times Jackie had had to put his dukes up for Ray. The best way Jackie had come to think of it was that, in one way or another, he helped restore what the world drained out of Ray every day.

Now Jackie wanted Ronnie to call him that word again, standing right where they were. He hoped he would. It would give extra thump to his punch. It would bring added sweetness to the moment when he dropped him.

'I think he only keeps you around to remind him if he forgets to zip up his pants when he comes out of the Gents,' Ronnie said, flyballs of spit spraying in Jackie's face.

'Oh,' Jackie said, 'I think that's much more your department than mine, pal.' And then he remembered. It all came back to him: keep your thought processes clear and your reasoning ability good. Think perceptively and make appropriate decisions. He seemed only to bring his arm back a very short distance when he popped him, a nasty drilling little punch in the short ribs.

As Ronnie hit the deck a deafening roar greeted the teams coming out. Feet stamped on the bare boards overhead and all around the ground, and the noise rumbled and broke like a wave against the back of the house where Marzena was, and where she had her back bent trowelling mortar.

In her cellar studio, Marzena felt the crowd noise rather than heard it; it bellowed out and crashed against the rear wall of the house and rebounded down the long narrow garden. Marzena experienced the noise as a kind of blow-back – a hollow boom. She turned up the volume of the record she had on. It was Richter playing Schumann. Sviatoslav Richter who was enslaved by obsessions. Richter who could recall the name of every person he had ever met and lost sleep when one escaped him. Who was driven nearly mad by a droning melody in his head, which he finally traced back to his childhood love of Rakhmaninov's *Vocalise*. Who played at Stalin's funeral.

She reserved the Richter for match days, and played him only when she was sure she was alone in the house. Sometimes then she would also take out her letters from her mother and the clippings from home and allow herself some moments of lonely melancholy, the oceanic feeling she liked in the bowels of the house, so close to two such disparate sources of noise.

Jackie returned to the ground later that night.

The mother of one of Barry's glue-sniffing or fire-extinguisher-'huffing' little friends from Rusty Lane, probably not even as old as himself, was getting married. And although it meant breaking the conditions of his bail, Barry – 'Jaxon' to them – had volunteered to turn up and be the DJ. Jackie was supposed to collect him and drive him home.

From the street, Jackie could see red and blue disco lights flashing in a window of an upper level of the otherwise darkened West Stand. It was a metallic, multi-masted structure poking up against the sky, changing in colour from yellow-black to pewter with the sodium lights and the clouds and looking weightless and light enough to rise and spin away.

As he waited for the lift Jackie could hear the kind of harsh, industrial, blood-pulse music he had got used to hearing at home rattling down the lift shaft. When he put his hand against the casing of the lift he felt the music reverberating in his arm. He felt the normal hum, and overlaying it was this pounding jack-hammer *thump, thump, thump.*

When the doors opened at Level 3, the noise drew him to where the wedding party was. Turning a corner, the music went up a level and Jackie became aware of an unusual amount of activity in the area of a doorway twenty or thirty yards ahead of him. People, mainly panda-eyed teenagers, were spilling in and out. Beyond the door, a heavy in a satin bomber jacket who he recognized from earlier in the day was talking unanimatedly into a headset.

When Jackie was nearly level with the door, two whippety boys came flying through it. 'Last thing I saw he was just rockin' out to Metallica,' one said to the other.

'Buzzin' off his nut, man. He's been bangin' loads of E's. He's been greedin' them off me,' his friend said, as they hurried back in the direction of the tremendous noise of the electronic clicks and bleeps and mechanical, throbbing music.

When Jackie arrived at the suite where the party was, he found a bewildering complication of colour, noise and movement. Tired groups in the preliminary stages of party fatigue were slumped at the tables and on the couches around the walls. There were a few people dancing. These included the girl Eleanor's three-year-old, OJ. OJ was wearing elephantine jeans and a baggy T-shirt. The two letters of his name had been etched into the back of his cropped haircut and coloured in with orange Day-Glo paint. OJ was dancing with another little boy. Both had silver chains looped low from their belts into one of their pockets. They seemed to be having a good time, but OJ didn't recognize Jackie.

Barry was high up on what he always referred to as the 'scaff', which actually did look like a kind of altar draped in a black scrim. Human voices – baby burblings, airport departure announcements, voices from old sitcoms – would occasionally surface in the sea of sound. Flamenco guitar cut in for a few seconds, Africans chanted, strings soared. Barry was wearing headphones and leaping around like a four-year-old rather than the nearly middle-aged man he was. It eventually dawned on Jackie that batty Barry was trying to get him to look at a large screen where the message

'Hi Dad!' had been flashed up. Jackie saw the message and raised a hand to indicate he had seen, but Barry was signalling to him to turn around and watch the screen again. It seemed he had been awaiting Jackie's arrival and had a surprise all prepared.

Up on the screen fizzled scratchy old home-movie footage of the gaffer Mr Solomons gooning and waggling a torpedo cigar at the camera, white light flooding his big bald face and head and pushed and pushed until it flared and exploded, this one shot, over and over until it became a strobe effect, the potentate alternately emerging from and consumed by strafing light.

The retina images took a few seconds to disappear, and the next thing Jackie knew he found he was looking at himself up there, swarmed over and camouflaged by rapidly blooming and diminishing blobs of colour, his body mottled by what his eyes began to pick out as sheep tumbling and slowly falling from the jaws of a mechanical digger, tumbling and falling and then the overlay became swags of swirling smoke before the waxy globules of lava colour came on again, and underneath it all, all this time, was him when he was the 'Nipper', up in the ring, muscles firm and bunched, limbs greased and lithe, feinting, skipping, film that he didn't know had ever been taken, the Cathedral looming up sometimes, filling out the background, scratches and stains, arbitrary zooms, multiple superimpositions – Jackie as a phantasm, sampled by his son, grist to Barry's mill.

Trying once to find a way to explain 'turntablism' to his father and what he spent his time doing in his room all that time, Barry had said that he thought his task was to find little ghosts in other people's music and set them free.

The curious antiquity of the film of Jackie at Ely was emphasized by the techno soundtrack. He said afterwards it had been like seeing a ghost, or even a corpse, in a way. He said it had been a shock to be reminded that he was going on carrying that dead person inside himself, not once but twice in one day.

6

To improve the lay-out of the gardens and grounds at Coldside Hall, the house where Ronnie Cornish and his wife, Hope, lived and entertained unstintingly, the village had been removed and rebuilt in an Italian style in the early nineteenth century. Hills had been installed, a Gothic folly built, the river rerouted and widened. The landscaped grounds had been walled off and fenced in.

A major trunk road had been driven through the resited village in the sixties and a concrete footbridge erected to enable the people who lived there to move from one part of the village to the other. But first one half of Coldside withered and died, and then the villagers from the other side eventually either died or moved away. On the Sunday that Jackie drove up to collect Ray from a party at the Hall, the pedestrian bridge was in the process of being demolished.

Jackie could see the ribbon of road from the slope that rose up at the back of Ronnie's house. In another month or so the road would be screened by the trees, which also helped to muffle the drone of the traffic. But it wasn't yet May, and the trees were just coming into leaf. It was its proximity to the road that had allowed Ronnie to acquire Coldside Hall at what now looked like a give-away price. If anybody knew that Ronnie had an interest in the company that had won the contract to build the trunk road, it was a point that was never raised at the time.

It was nearly dusk. Car headlights were clicking through the trees. Occasionally the lights of the television crews flared briefly to indicate that there was some activity at the end of the lane leading to the Hall. The police had erected barriers there, and Jackie had had his identity checked turning into the lane and again at the main gate at the head of the drive.

Demonstrators were out in force. They were protesting against the Government's handling of the foot-and-mouth crisis. There was a lot of anger. One woman attached to the department with the main responsibility for managing the culls and carcass disposal claimed she had had acid mine-water aimed at her face and raw meat nailed to the bonnet of her car.

The protesters' chief target was the Deputy Prime Minister, who had travelled to the North East to launch 'UK is OK', a Government-backed, damage-limitation campaign whose aim was to bring back those overseas tourists who had been frightened off after a picture had gone out of the Prime Minister wearing a bright-yellow contamination suit. Entertainers, celebrity athletes and others had been recruited to reassure potential foreign visitors that the English countryside was open for business, and that they didn't either have to bring their own food in with them, or leave their clothes behind to be burned when they left.

There was a stone terrace at the back of the Hall, but it was deserted. A row of windows at the lower service level was brightly lit. The light spilling out of the windows in the rest of the house was pink and softly glowing, with the guests only an indistinct, barely moving shadow under the high ceilings, like syrup in the base of a tall drink.

Below Jackie was a garden with box animals and obelisks. Two men had stopped by a spouting marble fountain for a smoke. Jackie was watching, but he was also aware of being watched. In addition to the dozens of uniformed officers, the grounds were crawling with Special Branch. Each time he felt himself coming into the field of vision of one of these expressionless, civilian-suited men, Jackie instinctively tried to compensate for the unevenness in his stride caused by his bum knee.

Lights came on in a house on the other side of the valley. They came on in different rooms at the same time, a sure indication that they were on a timer and the owners were away. An invitation, if you happened to be a burglar.

The pyres were still burning, lending, in patches, a crimson and orange glow to the sky. A row of winches for lifting carcasses was lined up hidden behind a hedge. Fields patched the valley beyond the road, crossed with power lines and dotted here and there with square, solid-looking buildings, but nothing was moving except the car lights through the darkened trees. The fields were eerily empty.

A gravel path curved down to the house. As he descended the path, Jackie could hear a string quartet playing American show tunes and light classics and the steady burble of conversation. A woman and a man in white chefs' hats had come out of the kitchen to take the air. From somewhere above them came a tinkling theatrical laugh of the kind you would expect at a very bad play.

Jackie's feet crunched on the gravel. He stepped on to the grass. Soon he was able to make out individual faces at the windows, which were framed with heavy swags of curtain. He thought he knew the window where Ronnie's mother's old mangle was on show like the Parthenon marbles, and pictured Ronnie telling the tale to his distinguished guests, while his guests smiled and nodded and looked around for more stimulating conversation or a waiter to freshen their drink.

Suddenly then, out of the blue, Jackie thought of Jimmy and the night very many years ago when they had been the side show at another celebrity mix-and-mingle. Jimmy Li had died, but he had only just died, at the turn of the year. Against the odds, Jimmy had had a long and, so far as Jackie knew, a fulfilled and happy life. He had been taken on by a capable, dedicated Jamaican nurse called Elva, and Jimmy and Elva had lived snug as bugs for the past twenty years on the thirteenth floor of a high-rise in the middle of Birmingham, where Jackie occasionally visited them. Jimmy was crippled, and confined to a wheelchair, but they enjoyed some good times. The veteran Jamaican jazz musician Terrance Wilkins and other friends would sometimes call in for a meal when Ronnie Scott's Club on the nearby canal had closed. Jimmy would rustle up oxtail with red beans, a chicken curry or crab in a black-bean sauce and they would reminisce far into the night.

Jimmy had made it to seventy-nine. Jackie couldn't walk in the small streets off Piccadilly without remembering the night the pair of them had gone into the tiny basement place in a gas-lit arcade to get their tattoos done, in Jimmy's first week in England. Jackie had had 'WORK' and 'PLAY' on his fingers. Jimmy had gone for a baby bird between his left thumb and forefinger whose beak opened and closed as he flexed and unflexed his hand. On the inside of his left wrist he had had a cut dripping with blood. Jackie noticed many years later that the tattoo place had been incorporated into an expensive bar where the gossip-page photographers hung around outside, and he and Jimmy had had a good laugh about that.

In their flat, Jimmy and Elva had a photo-mural of a Caribbean beach covering one wall. On his last visit to see them, Jimmy had accompanied Jackie in his wheelchair to the lift when he left. When he looked out through the tiny scratched window, through a hole in the graffiti, Jackie had seen Jimmy wheeling himself away, his arms still looking strong, back along the landing to where the music and his friends were.

Ronnie Cornish's brother-in-law, Hope's brother, George Veitch, lived in the gate-house at the Hall, where he was employed as a groundsman/gardener. Jackie got on with George, who in his youth had boxed a little and always gave Jackie his due. In the failing light he saw George in his garden tying back runner beans, and reminded Jackie of his father, content in the solitary endeavour. George had grown up in the city, making machine parts for many years. But living out at Coldside had given him a countryman's outlook and a weatherburned country face.

'Hoo's it gannin, Jackie?'

'Not bad, George.'

George was wearing a tweed cap and a new-looking quilted body-warmer that Jackie knew would almost certainly have been passed on from Ronnie. Nearly all George's clothes were Ronnie's cast-offs, altered, cut down, taken in.

'Havven seen yee roond for a canny while,' George said, stopping work to talk. 'Aa naa aal aboot yi stickin' one on his nibs, like.' He gave Jackie a sly look. 'Aa divven naa what it was aboot, an' aa divven want ti naa. Yi naa what thi say: hear everything, say nowt. That's my policy. Aa stay oot on it, me.'

The string quartet at the house stopped playing. Jackie became aware of it only when it stopped. There was just hubbub noise; the sound of somebody tipping ice. 'What do you make of this Fraudley Harrison, then?' Jackie said. Boxing was always a safe gambit, a subject where there was little or no chance of saying anything that could get back, or be taken or interpreted in the wrong way. Ronnie could throw the switch and cut off the oxygen supply to both of them. They knew that. In his own case, Jackie suspected Ronnie already had. 'Worra fuckin' shame,' George said. 'Fuckin' scandal. Cunt couldn't box his way oot of a paper bag if 'e'd pissed on it forst. I feel embarrassed for the lad.'

Across the valley a faint blue mist was coming down, blackish at the edges and luridly streaked with yellow. George had gone back to his beans. 'The stench hasn't been so bad the day, like,' he said. 'Can't hardly tell it from the smell of the cigars.' He looked towards the house. 'Cigars usually means it's Christmas roond here.'

Neither of them said anything for a while. The string quartet started up again, playing what Jackie recognized as a selection from *Carousel* – 'If I Loved You', 'Just My Bill'. Then some pigeons came over. They flew straight over where George and Jackie were standing, then made a sudden turn, all of them turning together, a grey bowed smear against the sky. 'Fleein' excellent,' George said. 'Them younguns is mekkin' the olduns flee.'

They were still standing with their necks craned, watching the pigeons turn and wheel, when the ring-tone on Jackie's mobile was the signal that Ray was ready to leave.

'His master's voice,' George said.

'See you, George.'

'Be seein' you, Jackie. Watch how you go.'

Jackie knew as soon as he saw the way Ray was walking that he had had a skinful. He knew as soon as he spoke that the likelihood was that he had had more than that. 'Bah, I've supped some ale toneet!' Ray only fell into this music-hall Lancashire accent when he was palatic, as they said up there, an expression Jackie liked. 'I love you but I wouldn't tell you,' the other sign of his pissedness, was on the cards. An emergency pit-stop on the way home.

In the event it was Telfer they had to stop for. Telfer was hanging on. He was frequently incontinent, and Jackie had to carry him up and down stairs and physically support him and coax him to eat, but he had good days as well. There had been only a rump of protesters waiting around at Coldside and they had bent their knees to get a look in the car and decide whether the passengers looked to them like people who deserved a boo, but they had found it easy to get away. As soon as they were on the motorway, though, Telfer started making pitiful whining noises and panting and Jackie pulled into the first services stop.

There were two or three trucks in the section reserved for commercial vehicles, but the main car park was nearly empty. Jackie chose a spot close to some picnic tables and a children's roundabout, near to a stand of trees. Ray was asleep in the front, snoring and whinnying, murmuring and crying out sometimes and making disturbed noises in his sleep.

The dogs made straight for the trees. They were a variety of industrial spruce, deep in takeaway cartons and sweet wrappers and old tins. The needles on many of the lower branches had been stripped, as if many people had taken the path Jackie was taking, many times before.

On the other side of the trees was a large industrial estate. The estate occupied the floor of a wide valley and was filled with larger and smaller, part-brick, part-prefabricated sheds. From where Jackie was standing, a gentle slope ran down to a wire-mesh fence, where the dogs were sniffing and running, Telfer seemingly more comfortable since he had been let out of the car.

It was turning cold. Jackie pulled up his collar. He poked a Diet Pepsi can with the toe of his trainer. Then in the gathering darkness he saw a flock of ducks, maybe as many as thirty or forty of them – tufteds, he guessed, from the white undermarkings on their bellies – flying in a V-formation and coming down on what they took to be a lake, but which wasn't a lake at all.

It was the roof of a vast electronics warehouse, flat, translucent, corrugated, several football pitches long and wide and lit from underneath by patches of variously coloured lights. Jackie could see how, from the birds' perspective, flying in from Israel or Lapland, it could look like a welcome expanse of standing water, shining like tinplate, glowing in the declivity, the perfect place to drop into cover.

When they landed, they landed feet first, skidded a short distance, and then either stopped to investigate why the surface underneath them was solid rather than liquid, or kept on running in jerky little waddling steps until they had picked up enough impetus to rise and pitch into the wind and get airborne again. But a few of the ducks had come down close to an edge which, instead of ending in a sheer drop like the others, turned into a steep sloping porticoed roof. The ducks that landed near the sloping roof didn't brake, but slalomed down it and then beat their wings to get them in the air again. And, as he watched, Jackie noticed that many of the ducks, far from being disconcerted by this new experience, were circling round and trying it a second, third, even a fourth time, until the entire flock, or so it seemed to Jackie, was joining in the game of dive-bombing the warehouse roof – washing-machines and refrigerators; televisions, personal stereos, computers, all made in Korea – squawking, and skidding and sliding on their rumps, like something dreamed up at Disney.

After a while Telfer and Ellis decided to join in, excitedly running backwards and forwards along the length of the fence, standing up at the fence watching the ducks, crooning, crazily barking.

Jackie crouched down and put his arms around Telfer, one arm under his chest and the other arm around his hind legs, then straightened up and put him in the car. When he had settled, Jackie smoothed the creases out of an old jumper that had once been Ray's and which had risen to the top of the jumble of layers he had put there to keep the dog comfortable.

Before he started the car, Jackie reached over and straightened Ray's hair, which had gone a bit skew-whiff.

'Jackie,' Ray said.

'I know. You love me but you wouldn't tell me.'

'No, no,' Ray said. 'I just wanted to ask you what day it was. Where are we?'

'Come on.' Jackie released Ray's shirt collar which had got caught under the seat belt. He undid his bow-tie. 'Let's be getting you home.'